DESTINY CAN BITE ME

JON SMITH

BALKON media

DESTINY CAN BITE ME
Published by Balkon Media

Paperback edition ISBN: 978-1-916970-18-2
Also available as an E-book

A CIP catalogue record for this title is available from the British Library.

Cover Illustrations & Design: Balkon Media

ALSO BY JON SMITH

FICTION

The Fifth Horseman

Destiny Can Bite Me (Fang & Loathing #1)

The Stakeout Diaries (Fang & Loathing #2)

Rewrite the Dead (Fang & Loathing #3)

YOUNG ADULT

The Arb

CHILDREN'S FICTION

Toytopia

NON-FICTION

Once Upon A Brand

Founder Mode

The Bloke's Guide To Pregnancy

The Bloke's Guide To Babies

Get Into Bed With Google

Google Adwords That Work

Smarter Business Start-Ups

Start An Online Business

Digital Marketing For Businesses

ONE

If Vincent Lupo's kitchen had ever experienced a golden age, it must have occurred before the invention of penicillin, because by the twenty-first century it had lapsed into a retirement of slow, reeking defeat. The floor's linoleum, patterned with what might once have been cheerful lemons, now puckered and warped in all directions, as if it had survived a minor earthquake and decided to take up interpretive dance. The fridge, a vintage Kelvinator he'd had shipped over from Boston in the 1950s, wheezed like a pensioner in the throes of existential dread, leaking freon and mysterious brown ichor in equal measure. Somewhere, a single bulb flickered behind its nicotine-yellowed glass shade, valiantly illuminating the culinary equivalent of a pre-fungal crime scene.

Vincent navigated the clutter barefoot, toes dodging the moist paper towel blobs he'd weaponised against an outbreak of something greenish in the far corner last week. He wore a T-shirt advertising a heavy metal band that had been uncool since the Cold War, and a pair of sweatpants of indeterminate colour, all his other clothes having succumbed to what he privately referred to as the Laundry Abyss. There were bags under his eyes so profound, if they'd developed zips he could have stored his emotional baggage inside them.

He opened the fridge and immediately recoiled. Not, as one might expect, because of the horror within—Vincent's relationship to horror was that of an old married couple, bored but co-dependent—but because he had expected there to be milk and there wasn't.

"Well, that's a personal betrayal," he muttered, staring into the fridge's depths as if the cartons might re-materialise out of sheer guilt.

Then he noticed the head.

It wasn't the first time Vincent had encountered a severed human head. It wasn't even the first time this century. He had, however, expected them to make more of an effort with the presentation. The head, belonging to a pale man with a semi-regal nose and a hairline in advanced retreat, had been plopped directly onto a square of wax paper, and placed next to a tub of budget margarine. A thick, congealing dribble of blood had begun to seep onto the hummus beneath it, creating a ruddy, marbled effect that even he found a bit on the nose.

Vincent crouched until his eyes were level with the fridge shelf. "Right," he said, in the voice of a man whose brain was holding up a sign reading "Really?" and daring his mouth to argue. The head, for its part, did nothing except stare blindly at the expired olives, looking faintly mortified.

Then the eyes looked over to Vincent.

"The story ends when you bleed it dry," the head whispered.

"Right," Vincent said, waiting for more commentary, or at least a formal introduction, but none was forthcoming. Vincent studied the waxy features for clues. The cheeks, florid and pockmarked, bespoke a fondness for spirits stronger than the ones haunting this kitchen. The lips, blueish but still faintly curved, suggested that the victim had gone out with a sort of half-assed dignity. And then there was the mark on the forehead: a glyph, carved deep, the blood frozen in a spidery network of fractures. Even in the dim fridge-light, Vincent recognised it instantly.

He closed the fridge and leaned his forehead against the battered enamel. "It's going to be one of those weeks."

He filled the kettle, dumped two spoonful's of instant coffee into a mug with a faded cartoon bat, and sat at the rickety table, listening to the fridge wheeze and the slow drip of blood landing, with surgical regularity, into a Tupperware grave. He resisted the urge to Google "meaning of severed head in fridge," but only just.

Mrs Barley, the housekeeper, materialised in the kitchen doorway with the silent menace of an approaching storm front. She wore her hair up in a severe bun that could have survived a nuclear winter, and her dressing gown was ironed to an edge so crisp it could have performed surgery. Vincent had no idea how she managed to live in his flat and still project the air of someone judging it from a safer distance.

She fixed him with the look. Not the one reserved for burnt toast or abandoned mugs, but the deeper one, the one that suggested the universe had personally offended her sense of order. "Vincent," she said, "I appreciate that you have an unconventional palate, but the food hygiene in this establishment is now actively criminal."

Vincent gestured at the fridge. "You'll want to avoid the top shelf until I sort it. Or call the police. Or a priest."

Mrs Barley ignored him and stalked to the fridge. She opened the door, peered in, and made a sound so British in its disapproval that the room temperature dropped three degrees. "You couldn't have left it on the doorstep like a normal lunatic?"

"It was already inside when I woke up," Vincent said. "I think it might be for me."

Mrs Barley looked at him in a way that implied she considered this entirely plausible, if not inevitable. "Did you lock the front door last night?"

"Possibly," Vincent said. "In the sense that I thought about it, then got distracted and poured gin on my cornflakes."

"Vincent. You can't just invite severed body parts in, it sets a precedent. Next thing you know, it's entrails in the slow cooker and you've got the council round."

She reached in, pinched the head by a tuft of thinning hair, and lifted it out with the clinical disdain of a champion flower-arranger appraising a subpar bouquet. The glyph on the forehead gleamed wetly in the cold light.

Mrs Barley raised an eyebrow. "You know this one?"

Vincent hunched over his coffee. "Not personally. But the symbol's from the Carmine Prophecy. The one I co-authored. Ages ago."

She rotated the head so it regarded him, accusingly. "I always said your hobbies would catch up with you."

"Technically, ghostwriting is a vocation, not a hobby."

"Technically, putting your name on an apocalyptic scripture for vampires is a cry for attention."

"It's a perfectly respectable side hustle." He looked at the glyph again. It was impossible to mistake: three intersecting crescents, with a splinter of bone embedded at the axis. Carmine had called it 'the sigil of eventuality'—not that anyone had asked him to get poetic about it, but Carmine was a show-off and could never resist. "They've used the original design. No one's updated it in centuries."

Mrs Barley made a tutting noise. "Copycats are always so lazy." She dropped the head into a ceramic mixing bowl, then began to wipe the fridge shelf with a splash of bleach and a wad of kitchen roll.

"Do you think it's a warning?" Vincent asked, trying for nonchalance and landing somewhere near existential malaise.

"If it is, it's not a very creative one." She didn't look at him. "It's probably just a reminder. You have unfinished business, and you're not getting any younger."

"Neither are they," Vincent pointed out. "They're a head."

"Don't be obtuse. It suits you, but it makes my evening more complicated."

He watched her work, marvelled as always at the efficiency with which she could exorcise the messes he accrued without breaking stride. The new cleaning product she'd sourced from some occult supply catalogue gave off a lavender-and-cinnamon stench that managed to overpower even the formaldehyde aftertaste in the air. She'd probably rid the fridge of spiritual residue by midnight.

Vincent sipped his coffee, considered the humming head in the mixing bowl, and the way Mrs Barley's movements seemed choreographed for crisis. He couldn't remember hiring her. She had appeared in his life the day after the Second Mantic Massacre, moving into the spare room with nothing but a battered suitcase and a promise that she'd "keep things ticking over." He'd been too hungover to argue, and after a week realised she was both impossible to sack and, in her own terrifying way, indispensable.

He also suspected she might be ex-military, but on this point she was cagey.

Mrs Barley finished her cleaning and turned to face him. "We'll need to dispose of this before the bin men get suspicious."

"I was planning to leave it for the vampires. You know, re-gift it."

She folded her arms. "Don't be crass. It's clearly intended to get a reaction. The question is, who sent it?"

Vincent tapped the table, drumming a little rhythm. "Could be anyone. The Carmine crowd had a lot of admirers."

"You mean enemies."

"I mean connoisseurs of creative difference."

Mrs Barley rolled her eyes so hard it was audible. "If you're not going to take this seriously, at least try to act surprised when the next one arrives."

"Do you think there'll be a next one?"

She looked at him, and the unspoken answer hung in the air like the smell of cleaning fluid: obviously.

Vincent opened the fridge again, checked again for milk, and sighed. He'd have to drink it black. "You know, when I started ghostwriting apocalyptic manifestos, I thought it would be all groupies and continental breakfasts. No one ever mentioned the admin."

Mrs Barley set the bowl on the counter, drew a cloth over the head's face, and began slicing a grapefruit with the efficiency of a coroner. "That's because you only read the covers. Shall I fetch you a blood bag for later, or are you fasting again?"

"I'll manage," Vincent said, and pretended the knot in his stomach was caffeine.

He looked once more at the shrouded head, the glyph still bleeding through the fabric, and wondered not for the first time what it would be like to have a life that didn't involve cleaning up after ancient mistakes.

He suspected it would be intolerably dull.

Mrs Barley poured boiling water into the sink, steam blooming up to fog the window. "What will you do?"

"Nothing," Vincent said. "It's almost definitely a prank."

"Almost definitely is not definitely."

He shrugged, and stood. "If they want me, they know where I live. At this rate, they'll turn up in a box from Amazon Prime."

Mrs Barley made a thin, sceptical noise. "Very well. I'll expect a delivery by Friday."

He laughed, and was not sure if it was at the joke, or at how much it wasn't one.

When he left the kitchen, the fridge was empty save for the essentials: tonic water, batteries, half a tub of hummus (now perfectly marbled), and a collection of Tupperware containers that he would never again open without a sense of trepidation.

It was going to be one of those weeks, he thought, as he left the severed head and the prophecy in the kitchen, along with the pungent certainty that the past was nowhere near done with him yet.

Vincent's study—officially designated as the "writing den" in the tenancy agreement and unofficially as "the paper ghetto" by Mrs Barley—had a smell that was hard to pinpoint, but somewhere between burning clutch and the inside of an antique bookshop. It was an odd, loamy sort of comfort, though the comfort was mostly psychological and probably bad for you in large doses. Every surface had lost the battle against his notes and drafts years ago: the desk vanished under a snowdrift of printouts, half-read hardbacks, and the latest proofs from his publisher (who sent him updates under the very mistaken impression that he cared). Post-it notes clustered like yellow lichen across the edge of his monitor, each one bearing a cryptic phrase that was either a plot point, a shopping list, or a threat.

He sat slouched at his battered desk, rolling a ballpoint pen between his fingers and trying to decide whether it was more dignified to finish the next chapter or fling himself out the window. The laptop glared at him with a blank document titled, "FANGS_OF_DESIRE_BOOK_9."

Vincent's agent had once described the Fangs of Desire series as "Twilight for the emotionally literate, but with actual sex." Vincent considered this both an insult and a dare, which was why the main character—a vampire called Lord Sanguinius —was a barely-disguised self-parody and, by all accounts, the most successful literary vampire since Bram Stoker's band of degenerates.

He typed, and deleted, then typed again:

—*Lord Sanguinius gazed out from the shadow-drenched balcony, his heart as empty as the veins of his latest conquest. The city sparkled, indifferent. Below, mortals thrummed with urgent life, while he remained suspended, ageless, alone.*—

He read it over, scowled, and stabbed the delete key until the sentence lay in pieces.

Through the wall, the neighbours appeared to be performing some kind of percussive ritual involving boots and what sounded like a trumpet. Vincent half-wondered if they were communicating with the dead. He opened a new tab and checked his author email, a masochistic ritual he performed at hourly intervals.

You have 3 new reviews for 'Fangs of Desire: Tokyo Drac'.

He read the first one. "Absurd and too smutty, but I read it in a single sitting. Sanguinius is so sad, lol. 3 stars."

The second: "Not enough emotional stakes for a vampire book. Celeste Evermoon is overrated."

Vincent put his head in his hands and groaned. He'd been writing for decades—hell, for centuries, if you counted the pseudonymous tracts and the Carmine Prophecy—but nothing had prepared him for the psychic battery of a Goodreads reader review. "Not enough emotional stakes," he muttered. "Try spending eternity eating nothing but other people's feelings and see how you bloody well like it."

He cracked his knuckles and glared at the screen, as if the cursor was responsible for all his life choices.

He'd known Carmine, of course. The original, the proto-type, the vampire whose name had spawned a cult and a prophecy and, eventually, a series of regrettable graphic novels. They had been friends, rivals, co-authors of doom. The glyph from the fridge was Carmine's design, and Vincent's own hand had traced the first iteration in a London flat not too different from this one, minus the bloodstains. He sometimes wondered if he was destined to spend all eternity cleaning up after that single, catastrophic brainstorm.

There was a noise in the corridor. At first, Vincent ignored it, assuming Mrs Barley had escalated her nightly crusade against the dust colonies. But then the floorboards creaked in a pattern that suggested deliberate footfalls, and a familiar whiff of disinfectant and steely resolve entered the room ahead of its owner.

Mrs Barley swept in with the briskness of a woman who considered door handles superfluous. She carried a mug in one hand (tea, black as the void) and a folded page in the other. "You left this in the kitchen," she said, placing the paper on his keyboard like a citation from the Council of War. "Next time, remember to put the bin out. Or at least don't leave the evidence on the worktop."

Vincent snatched up the paper and scanned it. It was a printout of a message board post—one of the underground forums where supernatural detritus compared notes on haunt-ings, prophecies, and the best deals on human blood. The post read: "Carmine sigil in SE10. Heads up. Literally."

He snorted. "I see the comedy stylings of the undead have not evolved in the last two hundred years."

Mrs Barley perched on the edge of a crate marked "tax receipts 1984-2011" and regarded him with the cool appraisal of a veteran bomb technician. "It's not a joke, Vincent. Heads don't turn up with those glyphs unless someone is making a point."

He rolled his eyes. "The point is probably 'Vincent Lupo is a tragic joke and should reconsider his career path.'"

Mrs Barley ignored the bait. "You were a legend once, you know. Among the right crowd. You had a conscience and a thesaurus, which put you several leagues above the competition."

"Did it? Look where it's got me."

She sipped her tea, watching him over the rim. "There are worse fates than obscurity. You could have been like Carmine. Or worse, like the new breed."

Vincent shivered. The "new breed" was Mrs Barley's euphemism for the latest generation of vampires, all memes and hair gel and no sense of history. "At least they know how to get published," he said.

Mrs Barley's mouth twitched. "Being remembered is over-rated. Trust me."

He drummed his fingers on the desk. "I'd rather be forgotten than become a cautionary tale."

She leaned in. "The glyph means something's coming. Maybe for you, maybe for all of us. Whatever Carmine started, it's unfinished."

Vincent gestured at the heap of unfinished drafts. "Join the club."

She reached out and closed his laptop, gently but with finality. "You need to focus. If they're trying to draw you out, it's because you matter. Don't pretend you don't care."

He tried to protest, but found himself staring at the wall, thinking about the prophecy and the endless circles of doom it had wrought. He didn't want to matter, not in the way Carmine had. Not in the way that led to bodies in fridges and cryptic threats.

He shrugged, picked up his pen, and tossed it from hand to hand. "If someone's trying to kill me, they could at least have the decency to send flowers."

"They wouldn't last in this flat," Mrs Barley said, standing. "I'll make sure the front's secured. In case your secret admirer pays a visit."

She was gone before he could reply, leaving the ghost of her lemon fresh disinfectant and her words hanging in the air.

Vincent opened the laptop again and stared at the blinking cursor. The words wouldn't come. He read through the last paragraph he'd managed before the existential implosion:

—*She clung to him in the moonlight, trembling as he bared his fangs. "Do it," she begged. "I want to feel alive, even if it means dying a little." Sanguinius hesitated. The weight of centuries pressed on his shoulders. Hunger and sorrow, indistinguishable.*—

He deleted the whole thing, then opened the browser and searched for "Carmine Prophecy" out of sheer, masochistic boredom. The results were as dire as ever: fringe blogs, conspiracy sites, links to grainy video "evidence" of Carmine's last moments, and a single, unreadable scan of the original manuscript. His own name appeared in several places, always buried under clickbait or rants about the "vampire Illuminati."

He was about to close the tab when the doorbell rang.

Vincent was unsure whether to ignore it or pretend to be out. He settled for standing up and stretching—every vertebra crackled—and loped to the hallway. The stairs were dim, the only light coming from a window coated with grime and despair.

He opened the door a crack, fully prepared to tell a Jehovah's Witness to sod off, only to find no one there.

He leaned out, scanning the landing. Nothing. Then he looked down.

At his feet was a woman. She looked human, which was already cause for suspicion in this part of town. Her hair was black, knotted with what he thought might be dried blood. She wore a jacket two sizes too big, the sleeves torn and stiff with old gore. She regarded him with one brown eye—the other was swollen shut—and bared her teeth in a gesture that might have been a smile, or possibly a warning.

Vincent was about to speak when she slumped forward, landing squarely on his feet with the boneless grace of someone who'd recently lost a significant amount of blood.

He crouched, checked her pulse. Faint, but there.

"Great," he said. "Just what I needed. Another stray."

Behind him, Mrs Barley appeared, arms folded. "You did lock the door, right?"

"Obviously," Vincent lied.

Mrs Barley sighed, the sound almost affectionate. "Bring her in. I'll get the first aid kit."

Vincent dragged the woman into the hall, leaving a trail of red behind. He glanced up at the landing window and thought, with a kind of resigned irritation, that this was how it always started: with a stranger, a message, and a mess Mrs Barley would have to clean up with bleach.

He managed a half-smile, baring his fangs. "Not enough emotional stakes," he repeated, softly, and set about fixing the new disaster.

TWO

Vincent's sitting room had a kind of dignity, but only in the sense that a condemned man might dress for his own hanging. The furniture—heavy, Victorian, acquired nearly-new for a song from some dead relative's estate—sulked around the perimeter like disapproving ghosts. Ancestral portraits glowered from the walls, all cheekbones and passive aggression, and the bookshelves had long ago surrendered their purpose to teetering piles of dog-eared paperbacks and empty gin bottles. The carpet had once aspired to burgundy, but was now the sullen colour of old wounds.

They pulled off her coat and laid the girl on the sofa, which sighed under her weight as if resenting the extra company. Vincent crouched beside her, frowning at the constellation of injuries already purpling on her arms and jaw. She looked about seventeen, eighteen at a stretch, though the set of her mouth suggested someone who had been forced to grow up in the fast lane and then run repeatedly over by it.

Mrs Barley bustled past, trailing a fug of antiseptic lotion and something sharp—sage, maybe, or the scent of a ritual gone slightly wrong. She dumped an armful of towels onto the coffee table and surveyed the unconscious guest with the chilly impartiality of an A&E nurse at the end of a double shift.

"You got a name, love?" Mrs Barley asked, not really expecting an answer.

The girl made a noise somewhere south of consciousness, then slumped deeper into the cushions. Her knuckles were scraped raw and her hoodie bore the blood-and-dirt insignia of a recent street disagreement. Vincent scanned her pockets with practised discretion and came up empty, save for a library card (name: Ren B), a stick of gum without a wrapper, and a phone so terminally cracked it resembled a spiderweb.

Mrs Barley knelt by the girl's head, pinched her chin between two fingers, and inspected her eyes. "Pupil response normal. No concussion, or nothing you didn't deserve." She said it with a kind of rough sympathy that managed to be both insulting and weirdly reassuring. "Hand me that mug."

Vincent passed her the least-stained vessel within reach. Mrs Barley produced a small flask from the folds of her apron, poured out a shot of glistening emerald liquid, and swirled it into a paste with the handle of a spoon.

"That looks like it would dissolve the paint off a Ford Fiesta," Vincent said, watching with horrified fascination.

Mrs Barley nodded, brisk. "That's the point. Clean wounds, open pathways. It's an old army recipe. Drink this and you can march three days on a broken ankle." She pinched the girl's nose, levered her jaw, and poured the medicine into the gap. The girl's throat worked, swallowing reflexively, and she coughed, rolled, and glared up at Mrs Barley with the baleful eyes of someone who, despite everything, still expected to be mugged.

"Where am I?" the girl croaked, voice sandpapered by pain and surprise.

Vincent gave her his best attempt at avuncular. "You're safe. Don't touch the remote, it resets the universe." He gestured to the room, as if that explained everything.

The girl wiped her mouth with the back of her hand, then sat up so abruptly Vincent nearly lost his nose. "Who the fuck are you?"

Mrs Barley, unfazed, dabbed at the gash on the girl's cheek with a dish towel steeped in the green concoction. "Language," she said. "There's a child present."

"I'm the child," the girl snapped.

Mrs Barley just smiled, thin and satisfied. "Exactly."

Vincent perched on the edge of the coffee table. "I'm Vincent, that's Mrs Barley. You showed up on our doorstep leaking like a sieve. Does that happen often, or is this a special occasion?"

Ren considered this, then shrugged, a movement so defensive it might as well have come with a high-vis vest. "It happens. Not usually with a welcoming committee." She glanced around, taking in the room, the locked window, the crucifix on the wall that had been modified into a bottle opener. Her eyes lingered on the shelf of blood bags in the far corner, then flicked back to Vincent, narrowing.

"Are you a vampire?"

Vincent grinned, showing a hint of fang. "Only on Mondays and bank holidays."

Ren made a sceptical noise. "Great. I get rescued by the Addams Family."

Mrs Barley handed her a glass of water and a biscuit, the latter looking both lethal and home-baked. "You'll live. Unless you'd rather not?"

The girl ignored the question, instead poking at the crusted wound on her arm with clinical detachment. "Did you call an ambulance?"

Mrs Barley shook her head. "Wouldn't do you any good. You're running with a different sort of injury." She dabbed at the blood, and Vincent saw it: underneath the smeared crust, a small tattoo, half-healed and angry-red. Three crescents, interlocked, and at their nexus a line of tiny bone-coloured dots. It was the glyph from the severed head, re-imagined by someone with a steadier hand and less patience.

Vincent reached for her wrist. Ren jerked away, but not quickly enough to stop him seeing the mark. "Where did you get that?"

She snatched her hand back and tucked it beneath her hoodie. "None of your business."

"On the contrary," Vincent said, suddenly very tired, "it's precisely my business. That symbol doesn't appear on random teenagers for fun. It's the sort of thing you find on very old, very dead people. Or worse, on people about to become very dead."

Ren's expression—already trending towards "could bite through reinforced concrete"—closed down completely. "It's just a tattoo. My mate did it. She said it was a protection thing."

Mrs Barley snorted. "Your mate's a liar. Or she has a very dark sense of humour."

Ren glared at Mrs Barley, then at Vincent, and for a

moment the only sound in the room was the clock above the fireplace, keeping time like a prison guard.

Vincent looked again at the mark, this time catching a faint shimmer along its edge. He'd seen that before, in a back room in Krakow, and again in the aftermath of the Carmine massacre. It wasn't ink, not entirely; something else moved beneath the skin, as if the glyph itself was metabolising.

He drew back, wary. "Have you felt... odd? Since you got it?"

Ren shrugged, but there was something brittle in it. "Define odd."

"Anything. Nightmares. Hunger. Rage. The urge to recite poetry backwards."

She rolled her eyes. "I'm seventeen. That's just Tuesday."

Mrs Barley patted her shoulder, almost gentle. "You'll be fine. Just don't poke at it."

Vincent wanted to press, but the look Mrs Barley shot him said "leave it," so he did.

Ren sipped the water and immediately choked. "What's in this?"

"Essence of honesty," Mrs Barley replied. "It's not catching, but you never know."

Ren wiped her mouth and sagged against the sofa, looking all at once younger and more tired than before. Vincent studied her, trying to piece together the logic of her appearance. The glyph, the timing, the old prophecy rattling its chains in his memory. It couldn't be a coincidence. Coincidence had stopped taking his calls centuries ago.

Mrs Barley began packing away the towels and bottles, her movements brisk and final. Vincent caught her eye, saw the question she wasn't saying, and answered it with a tilt of his chin: "Later."

Ren tried to stand, failed, and let herself sink back into the battered upholstery. "Can I go?"

Mrs Barley considered. "In the morning. You need rest. And there's something in the air tonight."

Ren glared. "That's a line from a Phil Collins song."

Mrs Barley's mouth twitched, ever so slightly. "It's a line from life, dear."

A tense, awkward silence descended. Vincent filled it the only way he knew how: with a story. "Did I ever tell you about the time I got a tattoo from the pope's personal assassin?"

Ren looked at him as if daring him to continue.

"It didn't stick," Vincent said. "But I learned three new swear words and the assassin got a free earlobe piercing out of it. Sometimes these things just work out."

Ren closed her eyes, and in a moment was asleep again, jaw set in that same fighting line.

Mrs Barley tucked a blanket around her with professional care. "She's not possessed, you know."

Vincent watched the glyph pulse, a faint but unmistakable light shifting under the skin. "No," he said, voice low. "But something's writing its way in."

Mrs Barley's reply was lost in the creak of the settling building, the ancestral portraits glowering down in silent judgment.

Vincent sat up, suddenly aware of how dark the room had grown, and how the glyph on Ren's wrist seemed brighter by the minute. He wondered if the prophecy was laughing at him from beyond the grave, or if this was just the universe's way of reminding him that unfinished business always, always, came home to roost.

He poured himself a drink, then another, and watched the girl sleep, waiting for the next disaster to knock on the door.

It wouldn't be long.

The girl slept like the dead, but woke the next evening with the same suspicious glare she'd reserved for Vincent the night before. By breakfast—an overcooked egg sandwich and an instant coffee so bitter it could have been harvested from Vincent's own childhood—Ren had recovered enough to loiter at the kitchen table with the twitchy defiance of a feral cat coaxed indoors for the first time.

Mrs Barley presided over the meal with all the warmth of a public executioner, keeping up a running commentary on the weather, the bin collection schedule, and the inferior quality of modern antibiotics. She set a bowl of porridge in front of Ren, who regarded it with undisguised disgust.

"It's organic," Mrs Barley said, which was true, if you defined "organic" as "purchased before the smoking ban and left to develop personality."

Ren prodded the gruel, then looked up at Vincent, who had yet to find the will to sit. "Can I go now?"

Mrs Barley, not missing a beat, said, "Eat first. Then we'll see."

Vincent lingered in the doorway, feeling strangely out of place in his own kitchen. He wanted to interrogate the girl about the glyph—where she got it, what it meant to her, whether it itched in the rain—but something about the set of her jaw told him he'd get nothing except a black eye for his trouble. Besides, he knew the only real answers were upstairs.

So he left Mrs Barley to her domestic siege and climbed the narrow staircase to his study.

The attic was exactly as he'd left it: a low-ceilinged crypt of dusty shelves and unstable stacks, lit by a single bulb and the light of the moon squinting through a crusted window. Vincent inhaled the smell—old paper, dried ink, and a trace of mildew—and felt almost comforted. The clutter was all his, and therefore at least a familiar brand of chaos.

He set to work, rifling through boxes labelled "Junk," "Definitely Not Evidence," and "NO." He bypassed a heap of old receipts and publishers' contracts, and went straight for the cardboard crate at the back—the one with "Carmine" scrawled across the lid in his own careful, hangover-corrected hand.

Inside: annotated proofs, a handful of "special edition" hardbacks (mint condition, never read), and a velvet pouch containing the bone dagger Carmine had once used to cut an ambassador's throat at a New Year's Eve party. The blade still shimmered with a faint oily iridescence, as if it had opinions about being disturbed.

Vincent set the dagger aside and opened the first manuscript. The glyph was there, on the title page: three crescents, the same as the tattoo on Ren's wrist, though this one was rendered in blackest ink and offset by a tidy spiral of Latin text. The lines curled and overlapped in ways that made the eye itch.

He flipped to the back, where Carmine had once scrawled corrections in blood-red biro. In the margin beside a particularly lurid passage, the old bastard had written: *Do not underestimate the appeal of transformation. It is the only thing that matters to them.*

Vincent snorted. Trust Carmine to boil down seven hundred years of existential horror into a sound bite fit for a book jacket.

He dug deeper, through a heap of correspondence that charted the arc of his own moral decline: fan mail from cultists, hate mail from other cultists, increasingly desperate pleas to meet deadlines from his agent. And then he found it—a folder, battered and speckled with what might have been coffee or possibly blood, labelled "Bucharest – original draft."

He opened it, hands trembling just enough to be annoying.

There, on the first page, was the stanza. He remembered writing it, or rather, remembered the aftermath: the sense of cold clarity that had come from a night's worth of absinthe and the vague, urgent need to impress Carmine at all costs.

—In blood it starts, but ink will bind / The living to the past entwined. / When the sign is worn in youth / The vessel wakes and walks in truth.—

It had seemed like word salad at the time, the sort of cryptic, vaguely threatening verse that made prophecies feel authentic while meaning absolutely nothing. But Carmine had loved it, and so it stayed.

Vincent compared the glyph on the manuscript to the memory of Ren's tattoo. They matched perfectly, down to the tick of a line at the top right. No question.

He sat back and let the implications settle, like silt in a muddy river. The girl was a vessel. Whether she knew it or not, something was writing its way in, using her as a page. And given how Carmine had viewed "vessels" in the past, the likely outcome wasn't going to be a celebratory group photo.

There was movement outside in the garden. He peered through the window and spotted Ren in the garden, lit up by the motion-detecting security light, huddled on the back steps in a blanket too thin for the weather, sipping tea with both hands. Mrs Barley stood over her, arms crossed, her silhouette somehow both forbidding and motherly.

He watched as Mrs Barley said something, and Ren laughed. A small laugh, sharp and sudden, and for a moment the wariness left her face.

Vincent shivered. He'd seen this scene before, or something like it—every time a prophecy began to unfold, every time some clever bastard decided the rules didn't apply. It always started with laughter, and it always, always, ended in screaming.

He leafed through the rest of the folder, but found nothing except old bills and a dried flower pressed between the pages. He closed it, set the bone dagger atop the pile, and dusted off his hands.

Downstairs, Mrs Barley's voice drifted up: "Are you coming, or do we need to start without you?"

Vincent glanced back at the manuscript, then at the window and the girl below.

"This is going to end in fire," he muttered, and went down to join them.

THREE

Ren sat on the edge of a sagging wingback chair, clutching a chipped mug of Mrs Barley's black brew. The taste was a mixture of chamomile, and something else that left her tongue feeling gently exfoliated. Her lip, split the night before, had scabbed over nicely, but the rest of her was still on high alert—shoulders knotted, leg jittering, eyes darting between Vincent and the crucifix-slash-bottle-opener mounted above the mantel.

Vincent regarded her from the sofa, body language slouched but fingers drumming a nervous allegro on his knee. He had changed into a shirt that looked crisp from a distance but revealed a constellation of coffee stains up close. Every so often, he'd glance at Ren, then look away with the studied nonchalance of a man ignoring a gas leak in a crowded theatre.

"So," Ren said, breaking a silence that had settled heavy and suspicious, "is this where you tell me I'm the chosen one, or just that I'm dying in a really inventive way?"

Vincent made a show of considering. "Neither. This is the

part where I stonewall and hope you get bored before you ask anything meaningful."

Ren bared her teeth in a smile with all the friendliness of a rusted trap. "Too late. You're up to your bollocks in this. Start talking. What's the symbol all about? Why's it crawling around under my skin? And why do I keep dreaming in bloody rhyme?"

"Dreaming in rhyme is not as rare as people think," Vincent said. "It's a classic symptom of exposure to poorly constructed prophecy. Or public school."

She narrowed her eyes. "And the voices?"

He sighed, picking a flake of something—paint, possibly skin—from the sofa arm. "Voices are standard. You get used to them. Just don't argue out loud in supermarkets, it makes checkout awkward."

Ren stared at him, incredulous. "Are you seriously making jokes? You know I nearly lost a hand to your 'prophecy' yesterday?"

"That's not technically my prophecy," Vincent said. "Just a derivative work. I disclaim all responsibility."

Ren made a noise that suggested she would have thrown the mug at his head if she wasn't still drinking from it. "Then whose mess is it?"

Vincent gave her a sidelong look. "Doesn't matter. He's dead. Or in hiding. Or pretending to be dead in a very public, attention-seeking way. Carmine was never subtle."

Ren squinted, recognition flickering. "Carmine, as in the Carmine Prophecy? That's a real thing? I thought it was just goth bollocks you find in Reddit side chats."

Vincent half-smiled, a gesture that came out more as a

grimace. "Everything's real, eventually. Prophecies just have a better PR team."

The hallway echoed with the sound of practical shoes and thinly-veiled exasperation. Mrs Barley swept into the room bearing a tray of toast and a bottle of cleaning fluid, the latter wielded like a truncheon.

"Drink up," she said, setting the plate in front of Ren. "You'll need your strength. And if you're going to bleed on the carpet again, let me know in advance."

Ren took the toast, but her attention was locked on Mrs Barley. "You know about this prophecy thing, then?"

Mrs Barley wiped a smear off the table with surgical efficiency. "Of course. It's why you're here. You're leaking prophecy."

Ren choked. "Excuse me?"

Mrs Barley shrugged, unfazed. "It happens. Normally we notice before someone gets a tattoo, but what's done is done."

Vincent studied the far wall with sudden interest in the peeling wallpaper. "She's not leaking, exactly. More like... emitting. Broadcasting."

Ren turned on him, fierce. "What the fuck does that mean?"

Vincent raked a hand through his hair, then let it flop back down in defeat. "It means there's something in you that wants out. Prophecy's a bit like a parasite, or a chain email. You get infected, and suddenly it's all omens, weird cravings, and the overwhelming urge to write things down."

Ren thumped her mug on the table. "I'm not a parasite. And I don't want any of this. I was just—" She broke off, the anger wilting, replaced by a tight, contained panic. "I was just trying to get away. They wouldn't let me."

Mrs Barley looked at her with sudden, uncomfortable sympathy. "Who?"

Ren hesitated, then: "Dunno, some sort of cult. I think. I don't know if they called themselves that, but everyone else did. They said I was... the Pen's Vessel." She glared, daring them to laugh, but neither Vincent nor Mrs Barley did.

Vincent's expression didn't change. "Classic. Always with the vessels."

Ren hunched into her hoodie. "They made us copy these books out by hand. Pages and pages. Said it was for the 'transmission.' But every time I wrote, the dreams got worse. And then the glyph showed up."

Mrs Barley knelt in front of her, all the harsh edges softened, just a little. "You ran. That was smart."

Ren nodded, fists tight on her lap. "Yeah. And I nicked one of the books. Figured if I had it, they couldn't finish whatever ritual they were planning."

Vincent cocked his head. "What did you do with the book?"

"Burned it," Ren said. "Or tried to. It bled. Then screamed."

Silence, thick enough to butter, settled on the room. Vincent closed his eyes, pinched the bridge of his nose, and reached for a wine glass left from the night before. He sipped, made a face, then sipped again as if it would get better with perseverance.

"Of course it did," he said, so softly it was almost to himself.

Ren watched him, waiting for the punchline.

Vincent opened his eyes, tired. "Books like that are hard to kill. They usually have contingencies. Fail-safes. Sometimes in the binding, sometimes in the person doing the burning."

Ren's face lost what little colour it had left. "So what, am I going to turn into a book?"

Mrs Barley answered first, voice gentle and uncharacteristically maternal. "No, dear. You're the story. The book is just the carrier."

Ren looked at Vincent for confirmation, but his face was locked in a mask of resignation. "It's not as bad as it sounds," he said, but even he didn't seem convinced.

She leaned forward, voice low and hard. "How do I stop it?"

Vincent swirled the dregs of his wine, watching the sediment spiral. "You don't," he said. "You survive it. If you're lucky, you get to write your own ending."

A silence with the force of a prison sentence closed in, interrupted only by the relentless tick of the clock and the distant sound of crows arguing in the garden.

Ren took a bite of toast, chewing with deliberate aggression. "What happens if I don't?"

Vincent looked her dead in the eye, for the first time since she'd arrived. "Then it finishes writing you. And you're not the main character in that version."

She stared at him, willing him to flinch or look away, but he held her gaze with the tired bravado of a man who'd lost this argument before.

Mrs Barley stood, collected the tray, and gave them both a look that managed to combine exasperation, pride, and the distinct impression that she had already started planning Ren's escape route and Vincent's funeral. "Eat up," she said. "We'll need our strength."

She left the room, and the echoes of her practical resolve hung in the air.

Ren looked down at her hands, the mark on her wrist pulsing faintly with its own logic.

Vincent finished his wine, eyes still fixed on nothing. "It's always the clever ones," he said, to nobody in particular, and then—out of habit or hope—topped up his glass and braced for what came next.

Lunch, as a concept, had never really caught on in Vincent's flat, partly because his lunchtime was midnight, and by that time he was always in the middle of something. Partly because he always considered it an affectation, like meditation or dental hygiene. But Mrs Barley was a zealot for routine, and so, by five past midnight, she had shepherded Vincent and Ren into the kitchen, set a loaf of bread and a jar of something pickled on the table, and issued stern warnings about the consequences of "not finishing what's on your plate, young lady."

The kitchen was less a room and more a holding cell for wayward vegetables and dead appliances. The window, streaked with the run-off of a thousand failed experiments, over-looked the garden—a small rectangle of weeds and feral rosemary, hemmed in by a fence that leaned at a forty-five-degree angle, as if trying to see what was growing on the other side.

Vincent sat with his back to the door, slicing bread with the bone-handled knife that had once been used for ritual sacrifice (and, more often, salami). The knife looked slightly insulted by the banality of its task. Mrs Barley poured tea from a chipped teapot, the brew so dense it barely sloshed in the cup.

Ren perched on the edge of a chair, arms folded, hoodie zipped to her chin. The tattoo on her wrist—three crescents and the chain of bone dots—looked almost like it was bruised on, the skin livid against her knuckles. She watched Vincent, unblinking.

"So," she said, "this prophecy thing. Which is it? Am I going to die, or just lose the plot?"

Vincent buttered his bread with the grave concentration of a man avoiding the topic entirely. "Both are possible," he said. "But let's not get ahead of ourselves. Sometimes these things just... fade away."

Mrs Barley made a sharp, dismissive noise. "Stop bullshitting. If you'd read your own work, you'd know it never fades."

Ren pointed the tip of her bread at Vincent. "See? Even your housekeeper's got your number."

Vincent winced, then set his knife down and leaned back, eyeing the ceiling as if an answer might be written up there, between the cracks. "The Carmine Prophecy wasn't meant to be a real thing," he said. "It was supposed to be satire. I was young, I was drunk, and Carmine thought the world needed a new Revelation for the postmodern era."

"Let me guess," Ren said. "You were the one who wrote it?"

He shrugged. "I ghostwrote it, technically. Carmine just added his name. And a lot of unnecessary blood."

Mrs Barley refilled the cups with a flourish that suggested she could weaponise the liquid at any time. "He's being modest. The prophecy's his baby. Like all men, he regrets it immediately after delivery."

Vincent shot her a look, but Mrs Barley's face was pure granite.

Ren sipped the tea and made a face. "You didn't answer my question."

Vincent met her gaze, and for once his deflection was gone. "It's not about dying. It's about being overwritten. The prophecy is... viral. It wants to be told, and it doesn't care who does the telling."

Mrs Barley nodded. "Like a very enthusiastic fungal infection."

Ren absorbed this. "So it's going to rewrite me into its story."

Vincent nodded, his mouth a tight line. "If you're lucky, you get to keep the bits you like. If not—well, have you ever read fanfiction that was so out-of-character it hurt?"

Ren gave him a flat look. "All fanfiction is out-of-character. That's the point."

Mrs Barley cackled, once. "She's not wrong."

Vincent let out a huff that was equal parts frustration and admiration. "Fine. Yes. You're the page. Something's going to try and write its way in. You resist it, or you steer it. That's the best anyone's managed so far."

Ren looked down at her wrist, then back up. "How do you steer it?"

Vincent shrugged. "Keep moving. Stay unpredictable. Don't let it pin you down. If you stop, if you let the story catch up, it writes you into the script. Happened to the last Vessel. She ended up as a street legend in Budapest, half-woman, half-allegory, entirely insufferable."

Ren blinked, then laughed—short, sharp, defiant. "Is that supposed to scare me?"

"No," Vincent said. "It's supposed to encourage you. The prophecy can't stand irony."

Ren drained her tea, set the mug down with a clatter. "What if I just get the tattoo removed?"

Mrs Barley shook her head. "It's under the skin. You'd have to strip the whole arm."

Ren looked at Vincent, whose face said, *don't even think about it.*

The meal went on in awkward silence, punctuated only by the rhythmic chewing and the occasional squawk from the garden. Outside, the wind was rising, and the fence creaked, as if something larger than a fox was moving around.

Vincent finished his bread and stacked his plate, then began to gather the scraps of paper scattered across the table—old notes, drafts of the Carmine Prophecy, some with corrections in red ink, others with single words scrawled in a hand that looked alarmingly like Ren's.

Mrs Barley leaned in, eyes fixed on Vincent. "You're going to have to tell her the next bit."

Vincent hesitated. "It's not necessary. Not unless—"

"Tell. Her," Mrs Barley said, in the voice that once convinced a demon to apologise for its lack of manners.

Vincent looked at Ren, who had gone very still. "The prophecy is self-replicating," he said, voice soft. "If you're infected, you can pass it on. Sometimes through words, sometimes through blood, sometimes just by being in the wrong place at the wrong time. It wants an audience."

Ren drew her knees up to her chest. "So there's more like me?"

"Probably," Vincent admitted. "But they don't last long. Most burn out, or get swallowed up by the story."

She was quiet a moment, then: "Why me?"

Vincent's answer was a small, bitter laugh. "Why anyone?

You were in the wrong place, you read the wrong book, you ran at the wrong time. The universe doesn't have taste."

Mrs Barley stood, collected the plates, and deposited them in the sink with more force than necessary. "That's enough self-pity for one meal. She needs to know what's coming."

Vincent glanced at the window. The sky had gone black, clouds stacking like wet laundry over the rooftops. In the garden, something moved—just a shadow, but it lingered longer than it should have.

He stood. "Fine. Here's what happens next. The prophecy will escalate. There'll be signs. People you meet will try to push you one way or the other—into telling the story, or stopping it for good. Neither side is particularly nice."

Mrs Barley dried her hands, then came to stand by Ren. "But you're not alone. We can run interference. Buy you time."

Ren looked at them both, and for the first time, some of the fight went out of her. "And if it catches up?"

Vincent smiled, bleak but genuine. "Then at least it'll be a hell of a story."

They cleaned up, Mrs Barley restoring the kitchen to its version of order—bleach, boiling water, the persistent smell of rosemary and loss.

As Vincent went to throw the crumbs out the door, Mrs Barley intercepted him at the threshold. She kept her voice low. "She's not just leaking prophecy. She's a blank page. Something's already started."

Vincent met her eyes. "What do you mean?"

Mrs Barley glanced back at the table, where Ren sat, chin in hands. "Look at her notes. The handwriting's not hers."

Vincent swallowed, realisation and old dread colliding in his chest. "You think it's Carmine?"

Mrs Barley nodded, once. "Or something nastier. Either way, you need to fix it. This time, properly."

Vincent watched Ren, the tattoo burning on her wrist like a deadline. He felt the old, bone-deep certainty of history repeating itself, and wondered which was worse: the prophecy, or his part in it.

FOUR

The knock arrived with the precision of a sniper: three, then two, then three again, so loud and coded it might have been Morse for "open up or I'll keep knocking." All three froze. Vincent's first thought was "bailiffs," followed closely by "prophecy cult," and then, as a distant third, "postman."

Mrs Barley stood, her posture that of a woman about to serve an eviction notice to Death itself. She retrieved a small paring knife from her apron pocket, set her jaw, and stalked to the door. "Talk among yourselves," she muttered, "back in a moment."

Vincent exchanged a glance with Ren. She shrugged, poured more tea, and watched the hallway like a fox eyeing a henhouse full of fireworks.

The hallway was narrow and hostile to visitors. Its sole bulb flickered as Mrs Barley opened the door. "Yes?"

On the threshold stood a woman in her late thirties, hair

cropped close in the manner of someone who found blow-drying a waste of time and patience. She wore a heavy black peacoat over a jumper that appeared hand-knitted but engineered for warmth, and carried a courier satchel slung with the practiced ease of someone prepared to use it as an improvised weapon. Her eyes, a shade too light for comfort, catalogued Mrs Barley in a second before dismissing her as insufficiently threatening.

"Zara Delacourt," the woman said. "I'm expected. Or should be." Her accent was Queen's English, but tuned to the frequency of an inner-city emergency operator: efficient, unbluffable, designed to project over chaos.

Mrs Barley stepped back, the knife still visible but now more of a suggestion than a promise. "Come in, then."

Zara entered the flat like an expert traversing hostile territory. She ignored the mess, and the fact that the ceiling threatened to decapitate anyone over five-nine. She clocked the kitchen and its inhabitants in one glance, then stopped at the threshold, imposing her presence like a librarian with a grudge.

"Lupo," she said to Vincent, with a smile that looked rehearsed in mirrors for situations exactly this awkward.

Vincent tried for a welcoming gesture and landed somewhere near resigned apology. "Zara. I thought you were in Sweden."

"Stockholm was a dead end. I came back." She glanced at Ren, then at the pot of tea, then at Mrs Barley, who had returned to her post at the counter and was now eyeing Zara's bag as if it might be full of live cobras. "Now I see why we always meet at my place."

Vincent grunted. "It's cozy. Easy to keep clean."

"For whom," Mrs Barley eyed Vincent.

"You've met Mrs Barley, my housekeeper." He gestured at Ren. "This is Ren. She's the, er..."

"Vessel," Mrs Barley supplied. "Or the host. We're still working on a job title."

Zara focused on Ren, who responded by pushing her mug away and glaring up. The tension in the room developed an extra edge, like someone had just announced the start of a knife-throwing contest.

Zara addressed Ren directly, voice softening a millimetre. "How's the prophecy?"

Ren snorted, "Still viral. But the side effects are pretty sick, I guess. You the doctor?"

Zara smiled, genuinely this time. "I'm the research department." She unbuttoned her coat, revealing a battered T-shirt with the logo of an obscure science fiction magazine. "I used to do research for Vincent's books, making sure they were historically and geographically accurate. Before he decided to just make it all up."

Vincent's mouth twisted. "Some of us have to pay rent. My readers don't care anyway, as long as there's a third-act breakup and a happy-ever-after."

Zara ignored him and turned back to Mrs Barley. "You have anything stronger than tea? I walked from the station."

"Wouldn't recommend the gin," Mrs Barley said. "We use it as paint thinner."

"I'll risk it," Zara replied, and Mrs Barley, after a moment's calculation, fetched a bottle and three glasses, setting them on the table with a thunk.

Zara sat, uninvited, and surveyed the kitchen like a forensic investigator at the scene of a multi-fatality. She poured herself a shot, knocked it back, then exhaled, as if purging the air of the previous tenants' ghosts.

"Let's get to it," she said, rolling her glass between her palms. "There's a new cult. Breakaway from the Carmine crowd, but nastier. Calling themselves the Carmine Apostolate."

Vincent paled, or at least shifted into a new shade of grey. "Apostolate? That's not even a real word."

"It is now," Zara replied. "They've started distributing tracts in Soho, and someone tagged the National Portrait Gallery with your sigil." She pulled a crumpled flyer from her bag and tossed it on the table. The paper was glossy, the logo a triple crescent with a splash of red through the centre. Beneath, in heavy serif, it read: *THE PEN'S VESSEL HAS AWAKENED. ALL HISTORY BENDS TO HER SCRIPT.*

Ren read it, deadpan. "Catchy. Bit dramatic, though."

Zara arched an eyebrow. "That's not the dramatic part." She leaned in, dropping her voice. "Bookshop in Bloomsbury—specialises in apocrypha and rare prophecies. Burned to the ground last night. No survivors, but plenty of charred bones with your mark on them, Lupo."

Vincent tried for bravado and produced only inertia. "Probably an insurance scam."

Zara took another shot, this time pouring one for Ren, who drank it without flinching. "I don't do insurance. I do data. These people are serious, and they've already started hunting for your 'Vessel.'" She jerked her chin at Ren, whose posture had gone from wary to combative in under a minute.

Ren picked up the flyer and turned it over, like it might have a secret message on the back. "I still don't understand why it chose me?"

Zara shrugged. "Because you're here. Because someone had to be. Prophecy's a pervert for coincidence."

Mrs Barley finished her own drink, not bothering to hide her scowl. "We can handle a few thugs with a branding iron. What's the real risk?"

Zara slid a small plastic evidence bag across the table. Inside was a fragment of charred bone, or maybe wood, etched with a glyph that made Vincent's stomach ice over. "They've weaponised the text. Started embedding it in physical anchors. Last I heard, they were trying to resurrect the old rituals from the Bucharest archives."

Vincent, more out of habit than hope, asked, "Is Carmine himself involved?"

Zara shook her head. "Still presumed dead. But you know how it is—prophecy cults recycle leaders like popes." She eyed Ren, then Vincent. "I'm not here for the nostalgia. I'm here to make sure this doesn't go viral again."

Ren drummed her fingers on the table. "What do you need from me?"

Zara regarded her with the analytical detachment of a scientist dissecting a rare frog. "Just do exactly what you'd do anyway. Stay alive. Stay unpredictable. If you get any more dreams, document them. We'll compare notes. And if you see anyone in a red cassock, run the other way."

Ren looked at Vincent. "Red cassocks? Seriously?"

Vincent gave her a bleak smile. "Don't judge. Everyone has a kink."

The conversation splintered, like all the best ones do. Mrs Barley fussed around the kitchen, muttering about "academic types" and the superiority of a good mop to any occult theory. Zara and Ren bantered in tight, elliptical spirals, both clearly enjoying the intellectual fencing. Vincent watched, detached, as the world he'd spent years evading reconstituted itself around him, piece by piece.

He tried to imagine running, just packing up and fleeing the prophecy and its weird, recursive pull. But he didn't move. He just poured himself another drink, listened to the static hum of the fridge, and waited for the next disaster to announce itself.

It was only a matter of time.

The night drew on, the kitchen gradually refilling with the stale hope of a normal life. But the air was different now. Charged, as if the prophecy was listening in, waiting for its chance to jump hosts.

Zara, in a rare moment of stillness, fixed Vincent with a look. "You know you're the anchor, right?"

He feigned ignorance. "For what?"

"For all of it. The prophecy, the cult, the girl, the story. You were always the anchor. The rest of us just orbit."

Vincent gave her a brittle smile. "No one likes a fixed point, Zara."

She shrugged, finished her drink, and stood. "Doesn't matter. When the page turns, you're still there. Might as well make it interesting."

She left the kitchen, Mrs Barley trailing after, and Vincent heard the two of them conferring in low, rapid voices. Ren, still at the table, traced the outline of the triple crescent on the flyer.

Her lips moved silently, like she was practicing the shape of her own signature.

After a long minute, she looked up. "How will I know whether I'm thinking my own thoughts or what the prophecy wants me to think?"

Vincent thought about the evidence, the dreams, the mark on her wrist. "I think you're the author. The rest is just editing."

Ren considered this, then nodded. "Could be worse."

And, in a tone so dry it could have been powdered, she added, "At least I get good material."

Vincent almost laughed. Almost.

Zara re-entered the kitchen and took a seat. She did it with her trademark combination of intellectual impatience and social tone-deafness—one eyebrow cocked, both hands clasped on the table as if preparing to deliver a TED Talk on the inevitability of their collective doom.

"You kept the Archive, right?" she said, eyes fixed on Vincent.

Vincent grimaced, as if anticipating dental work. "You mean the one I promised to torch twelve years ago?"

Zara shrugged. "You and I both know sentimentality trumps self-preservation."

Ren perked up. "What's the Archive?"

"It's where Vincent keeps all the things he'd rather forget but can't bear to actually bin," Zara said. "Early drafts, annotated maps, failed blood spells, the odd cursed fountain pen. Everything from the Carmine days."

Ren nodded, eyes glinting with the prospect of a proper horror story. "I want to see it."

Vincent looked to Mrs Barley for backup, but she just grinned and gestured to the ceiling. "Don't keep a lady waiting."

He sighed, rolling his shoulders like a condemned man limbering up for the scaffold. "Fine. But you're vacuuming after."

The climb to the study was the stuff of health and safety nightmares. The staircase had two working lights, neither of them on the same circuit, and the runner carpet tried to assassinate them at each step. The air on the landing was even thicker than in the kitchen, marinated in decades of second-hand smoke and existential malaise.

Vincent led the way, pushed open the door, and revealed the den of literary iniquity.

Zara took it all in with a professional cool. "You haven't redecorated since Victoria was on the throne."

"Didn't want to risk disrupting the chi," Vincent muttered, heading for the bookcase behind the desk. He reached for the third shelf from the bottom, fingers slipping over the dust-coated volumes, and pulled a battered copy of E. L. James' *Fifty Shades of Grey* until it clicked. With a creak and a sigh, the shelf swung forward, revealing a cavity hollowed out from the ancient plaster.

Inside: a shoebox, a stack of manila envelopes, and a jar labelled "for emergencies—do not open." The box was duct-taped shut, covered with warnings in at least five alphabets.

Ren peered over his shoulder. "That's it? Looks like a time capsule for an under-funded primary school."

Vincent set the box on the desk and began peeling away the layers of tape. "If you're going to sneer, do it after the haunting."

He popped the lid and immediately recoiled. The air inside shimmered, as if the box had been holding its breath for decades and just exhaled a mass of bad ideas.

He fished out the first artifact: a sheaf of yellowed papers, each page covered in blood-red script that writhed and bled onto his fingertips.

Zara made an approving noise. "The original Carmine draft."

"Unedited," Vincent said. "Wrote it in a fever. Carmine wanted it raw." He flicked through a few pages; the glyphs on the margins pulsed, faintly luminescent. Ren leaned in, close enough for the ink to scent her hair.

Next, he withdrew a quill pen, its point still wet. The feather twitched in his grip, then stilled. "Don't let this touch your skin," Vincent said, "unless you want to hallucinate in Latin for the next week."

Ren grinned. "Noted."

He set the quill down—carefully—and reached for the envelopes. The top one was addressed to "The Unwilling Recipient" in Vincent's own hand, though he'd never written it. He opened it and out slid a single page, the handwriting instantly familiar.

It read: *It begins again. Try not to cock it up this time.*

No signature, no date, just the one line, written in a hand that was Vincent's but, he would swear on his own grave, not written by him.

He handed the note to Zara, who read it, then turned it over as if expecting a punchline.

"This isn't prophecy," she said, tone darkening. "This is narrative recursion."

Ren frowned. "English, please?"

Zara set the letter on the desk. "It's not a message predicting the future. It's a message from the future. Or from the next loop. The next iteration. Someone—maybe you, maybe Carmine, maybe the prophecy itself—is resetting the script. Improving the draft."

Ren absorbed this, chewing her lip. "So I'm not just in the story. I'm the story being rewritten."

Vincent poured himself a glass of red from the bottle hidden behind a pile of shapeshifter dark romance novels. He drank, then refilled. "Brilliant," he said, his voice a one-man Greek chorus of disappointment. "All these years, and I'm still getting marked up by an editor."

Mrs Barley, who'd materialised in the doorway like the world's most judgmental Valkyrie, watched the proceedings with arms folded. "Did you find what you were after?" she asked Zara.

Zara pocketed the note, her expression grave. "Yes. And I don't like what it means."

Vincent, feeling the beginnings of a headache settle in behind his eyes, slumped into his desk chair. "Does it mean we're all doomed?"

Zara considered. "It means we're all characters. And the author's getting impatient."

The study fell silent, except for the fridge downstairs, which kicked on and stayed on, its drone suddenly so loud it might have been reciting incantations of its own.

Ren stood by the window, tracing the Pen's Vessel tattoo on her wrist. The skin there looked raw, as if the label had been branded rather than inked. She pressed her thumb over the mark, testing the pressure.

"What if I just walk away?" Ren asked, not turning from the glass. "Get on a train, change my name, don't look back?"

Vincent gave a laugh so hollow it threatened to collapse the building. "Stories don't let you walk away. Not if you're the main plot."

Ren was silent, shoulders set. Then, with a quick and violent motion, she turned away from the window. "So what now?"

Vincent finished his wine. "Now we wait for the next chapter. Or the next visitor. Or the next disaster."

Zara nodded, already making for the door. "I'll call my contacts. Maybe see if the recursion can be mapped. If it's rewriting itself, there'll be a pattern. There always is."

Mrs Barley watched them file out, then lingered until the others were gone. She closed the study door and leaned in, voice low.

"You need to stop treating this like it's your fault," she said to Vincent.

Vincent stared at his hands, ink-stained and trembling slightly. "What if it is?"

Mrs Barley shook her head. "Doesn't matter. The story's bigger than you. Always was."

Vincent looked up, and for once, his smile was almost sincere. "Still hurts, though."

Mrs Barley patted his arm. "You're allowed to hurt. You're not allowed to give up."

She left, closing the door behind her. Vincent stayed where he was, surrounded by ghosts and failed drafts, the weight of the next move pressing in on all sides.

He glanced at the note on the desk—*Try not to cock it up this time*—and wondered what version of himself had written it. And whether, this time, he might actually take his own advice.

Downstairs, the fridge droned on, and the story waited for its cue.

FIVE

Ren came to with a gasp, the sort that sucked the rest of the room into her lungs before she could even open her eyes. It was a familiar species of awakening: clawing, urgent, the tail-end of a nightmare clinging to her ribs like a burr. The unfamiliar part was the smell.

She was in Vincent's spare bedroom, or what passed for one —a converted box room, its dimensions optimistically measured in half-metres, crammed with goth paraphernalia and Vincent's attempts at oil painting. The walls were the sort of black that absorbed light and possibly tax fraud. The bedding was a massacre of mismatched throws, each one more synthetic and static-prone than the last. The air tasted of mildew and that uniquely haunted dust which only accumulates on book spines and unwashed dreams.

Ren was cocooned in at least three blankets and a sheet that had welded itself to her face with dried sweat. She tried to shift, but her head pounded in protest, a dull ache radiating out from her nose. She touched her upper lip and her fingers came away wet, slick, and—she peered through the gloom—black.

"Oh, what the actual fuck," she croaked.

It wasn't blood. Or if it was, it had been filtered through an oil refinery and come out the other side as pure, uncut nightmare. It beaded on her fingertip, thick as printer's ink, and when she smeared it on the bedsheet, it left a slick stain that seemed to glisten and steam in the chill. The effect was, if nothing else, on-brand.

A piece of paper stuck to her cheek. She peeled it off, half-expecting it to be a Post-it note with one of Vincent's motivational messages ("You're not dead yet! Try harder!") but instead it was a torn scrap, the edges charred and the handwriting unfamiliar. The message was terse:

The girl will fall in line, or she will fall apart.

Ren squinted at it, willing her eyes to work. The words didn't just sit on the page; they crawled, shivering at the edges, as if resisting being read. She folded it once, then twice, and tucked it into the pocket of her hoodie where it joined a fossil record of previous disasters.

Vincent materialised in the doorway, his silhouette framed by the smudged orange glow of a hallway bulb that had never recovered from the Thatcher years. He wore a dressing gown that might have been burgundy once, and his hair was in the kind of disarray that suggested he'd lost a fight with both the pillow and the concept of personal dignity.

He eyed her, then the black trails seeping from her nose, and then the bedsheet, which now looked like it had been involved in a high-profile printer suicide.

"Morning," he said, voice sandpapered by old cigarettes and

older regret. "Did you sleep, or just haunt the mattress all night?"

Ren tried to sit up. "Define sleep."

"If you dreamt of drowning in your own thoughts, then yes. Welcome to the family curse." He advanced into the room and perched on the edge of a rickety desk, the sole concession to 'furniture' apart from the bed. "You bled all over the pillow," he added, not unsympathetically.

She dabbed at her face again. "It's not blood."

He squinted, then nodded, as if this was a clinical distinction worth observing. "Ink? Prophetic residue? Or just a really ambitious sinus infection?"

Ren considered. The taste in her mouth was metallic and unfamiliar, but not entirely unpleasant. "Could be any. Or all. Or whatever happens when you OD on supernatural metaphors."

Vincent sipped from his mug, made a face at the bitterness, then sipped again. "Mrs Barley's brewing some sort of curative," he said. "She wouldn't let me near the stove. Apparently, I 'contaminate the air with sarcasm.'"

Ren managed a half-laugh, which turned into a cough, which turned into a second, smaller nosebleed. She mopped at it with the back of her hand, smearing the ink across her cheek like warpaint. "I had a dream," she said. "Except it wasn't a dream. It was—" She hesitated, trying to find a word that didn't sound like a symptom. "Scripted. I was moving but not in charge. You know that thing where you watch yourself from above?"

Vincent nodded, eyes gone hollow for a moment. "Third-person omniscient. It's a classic side effect. A lot of writers get it.

Usually before they flame out."

Ren's voice dropped. "Do you ever get it?"

He stared at the mug, as if hoping for an answer at the bottom. "Not anymore. Sleep's a luxury product, these days. And the dreams—" He trailed off, shrugged, then tried again. "If I do, I get the editor's cut, not the author's."

Ren's hands trembled, just a little, and she tucked them under the blankets so he wouldn't see. "I think something's changing. In me. Or around me." She took a breath that rattled in her chest. "It's like I can feel the prophecy shifting. Like it's waiting for me to—" She shook her head, lost for the right verb.

Vincent's posture softened, the sarcasm draining away to reveal the crumpled empathy underneath. "It wants you to finish the story," he said. "That's the problem with prophecies. They're never happy with where they are. Always got one eye on the next chapter."

Ren thought of the scrap of paper, the crawling handwriting, the warning she didn't need because her own body had made it clear enough. "Is it safe? For me to stay here?"

Vincent considered, then pointed to the walls. "This room's warded six ways from Sunday. If a prophecy tries to off you here, it'll have to sign a tenancy agreement and pay a hefty security deposit first." He grinned, but it didn't reach his eyes.

She didn't ask what the other five ways were, or what happened to previous tenants. Instead, she focused on the smallest thing she could manage. "Do you have another pillow?"

He stood, and for a moment the dressing gown gave him the air of a haunted rector. "I'll nick one from Mrs Barley. She won't notice, unless it's the one with the lavender sachet."

He started to go, then paused in the doorway. "Hey, Ren?"

She looked up, expecting another bad joke.

Vincent's face was raw for a second. "You're not falling apart. You're just being remixed."

She couldn't tell if that was meant to be comforting. But it helped, in the way that knowing your diagnosis sometimes does, even if the cure is a very long way off.

He left, and the hallway swallowed him.

Ren sank back into the bed. The blankets were too much, but she let them pin her there, just for now. The black ink from her nose had left a small constellation on the pillowcase, each spot like a little planetary system of failed endings.

She wiped her face again, this time smearing a deliberate streak from cheekbone to jaw. In the gloom, it made her look like she was halfway through becoming someone else.

She thought of the phrase: *The girl will fall in line, or she will fall apart.*

She wondered, not for the first time, if those were really different options.

She lay awake, listening to the house settle and the fridge hum, until Mrs Barley came in an hour later with a mug of tea and a fresh pillow. By then, she had already decided not to tell anyone about the other thing she'd found on waking: the way her pulse now ticked in syllables, not beats. The way, if she listened close, she could hear the story thinking.

She pressed her thumb into the black ink, felt it warm beneath the skin, and closed her eyes.

Ren counted twelve cracks in the kitchen ceiling before she'd finished her first piece of toast, and by the time she'd forced down the second, she'd also catalogued the six new bruises on her arms and the five ways Mrs Barley's herbal tea tasted like punishment. The kitchen was cold, uncharitable, and if it had ever known sunlight, it had long since burned the memory out of its own walls. The back door was cracked for "ventilation," but the only thing making its way inside was the noise of next door's toddlers resisting bath time, and a weather front best described as 'enthusiastic mildew.'

Vincent stood at the counter, glassy-eyed, sipping at a medical bag of synthetic blood as if it were a gin and tonic. The straw protruded at an angle that suggested he'd given up on appearances, but not quite on life. He'd changed out of the haunted rector dressing gown, but the T-shirt he wore (World's Okayest Dad, ironically acquired) and the tracksuit bottoms weren't fooling anyone.

Mrs Barley was nowhere to be seen. Ren suspected she was either out back interrogating the compost bin or making an offering to the local Neighbourhood Watch, whose passive-aggressive notes ("Please refrain from burning bone in your garden, some of us have allergies.") arrived with the frequency and fury of biblical plagues.

Vincent broke the silence first. "You look like you died in your sleep and didn't get the memo."

Ren shrugged, then wiped her nose with the back of her hand. No ink this time, just the faintest smear of dried black under her left nostril. "You're not looking so embalmed yourself."

He grinned, an expression with all the warmth of a refrigerated mortuary drawer. "It's too early in the evening for compliments. Especially from a woman who nearly haemorrhaged a printing press all over my spare bed."

Ren turned her wrist over, checking the mark. The triple crescent had faded to a faint bruise, but something new had appeared on the inside of her forearm, just below the elbow crease: a slim, stylised quill, its ink point buried deep in the vein. The skin shimmered where the symbol met flesh, and every so often it pulsed, as if remembering to exist. She touched it, expecting it to feel raised or hot, but it was just skin—her skin, or something pretending.

Vincent, catching the movement, frowned. "That wasn't there yesterday."

Ren rolled up her sleeve, exposing the mark fully. "Neither were the bruises, but I don't see you worrying about those."

He abandoned his blood bag, loped over, and inspected her arm. He didn't touch it—he never touched, unless he was drunk, or there was a wound to poke—but the scrutiny was intense enough to leave its own pressure. "That's not the Vessel sigil," he said, voice almost reverent. "It's a variant."

Ren tried to keep the quiver out of her voice. "So what does it do? Does it, like, overwrite my genome, or just make me crap out poetry at a thousand words per day?"

Vincent's lips twitched at that, but the smile died on arrival. "It's an Editor's Mark." He said it quietly, as if even the words could summon something. "It's what you use when a prophecy's gotten out of hand and needs to be forcibly... redirected."

Ren stared at him, not bothering to hide her scepticism. "So someone's trying to rewrite the rewrite?"

Vincent hesitated. "Or reformat. Or footnote you out of existence."

Ren wanted to laugh, but the look on Vincent's face drained the joke. She poked at the mark, willing it to make sense, or at least to hurt. It didn't.

The back door clattered, and Mrs Barley entered, hands full of feral rosemary and an air of controlled violence. "You're glowing," she said to Ren, voice flat as the table. "Not metaphorically, unfortunately. There's a visible light signature."

Ren blinked. "Are you saying I'm radioactive?"

"Worse," Mrs Barley said. "You're trending."

Vincent rubbed his temples. "This is escalating."

Mrs Barley dropped the rosemary in the sink, washed her hands with surgical thoroughness, and fetched her phone from an apron pocket. She typed with two fingers, each keystroke a death knell. "I'm messaging Zara. She'll know what this is."

Ren watched the mark. It really did glow, faintly, in the kitchen's sickly halogen. She twisted her arm, hoping to catch it in a flattering light, but it just made the bones under her skin stand out. She finished her toast, the act of chewing the only thing anchoring her to the moment.

Vincent's phone buzzed. He glanced at it, then at Mrs Barley. "How did you get her to reply that fast?"

Mrs Barley shrugged. "Told her it was urgent and you were being unhelpful."

Vincent shot a look at Ren, as if to say "See what I put up with?" but she was busy re-evaluating her life choices.

The doorbell rang. This time, no one bothered with the preamble. Zara let herself in, striding through the hall like a debt collector on commission. She wore the same peacoat as yesterday, but now it was buttoned over what might have been pyjamas, and her hair was damp from a rapid, aggressive shower.

She scanned the kitchen, clocked the glowing sigil, and immediately started unpacking from her bag: a jeweller's loupe, a glass slide, a pipette. "Don't move," she told Ren, not unkindly, and took her arm in a surprisingly gentle grip.

Ren flinched. "You're not going to take blood, are you?"

Zara shook her head. "Not unless the mark's parasitic. Then I'll cauterise and apologise later." She bent close, examining the sigil from all angles, her own breath fogging in the chill. "It's beautiful," she said, matter-of-fact. "Not Carmine. This is newer, more iterative. You're an early-access beta version."

Vincent hovered behind her, equal parts curious and horrified. "Editor's Mark, right?"

Zara grunted. "Of a kind. But it's not standard. Someone's customising the payload." She looked up at Ren, eyes sharp. "Whoever did this, they're not interested in just using you as a page. They're trying to hack the prophecy at the source."

Mrs Barley made a noise halfway between disgust and admiration. "So what's it do?"

Zara considered, then poked the mark with a capped pen. "If I had to guess? It's a remote access tool. You're now officially networked to whoever's writing the edits."

Ren processed that. "So someone can rewrite me from a distance."

"Yes," Zara said, and even she sounded impressed. "But you're not overwritten yet. You're still mostly you."

"Mostly," Ren echoed, and this time she laughed, bleak and sharp. "Maybe I'm finally becoming interesting."

Zara capped her pen, eyes not leaving Ren's. "No. Just narratively convenient."

Vincent slumped back into the chair, as if the truth had weight and he was copping the brunt of it. "This isn't just a repeat," he said. "It's a mutation. The prophecy is adapting."

Mrs Barley fetched drinks for all, coffee for Zara and herself, a blood-bag for Vincent, water for Ren. The gesture was so domestic it bordered on parody.

Zara blew on her coffee, waiting for the next disaster. "We'll need to contain it. Or at least sandbox her until we know what the mark's doing."

Ren looked at her arm again. The quill was brighter, the pulses closer together. She felt it now, in her head and her hands and somewhere just behind her eyes: a low, insistent thrum, like a voice just out of range, waiting to tell her what to do.

She hid her hands in her lap. "Should I be worried?"

Zara shrugged, sipped her coffee. "If it were me, I'd start panicking. But you're handling it. That's a positive sign."

Vincent looked at her, a long stare. "You don't have to be stoic. This is... unprecedented."

Ren shrugged, but she gripped the mug tighter. "It's fine," she lied, and tried not to wonder what the next version of herself would look like.

They'd all run out of clever things to say at least an hour ago.

Ren sat hunched at the edge of the sofa, one sleeve shoved up, thumb digging at the skin just below her elbow. The mark quivered like it had its own pulse. It threw off heat, and at every other interval, a subtle throb sent an aftershock through her skull and straight into her teeth.

Across the table, Zara flipped through her notes with the air of someone trying to piece together a murder using only crayons and bendy straws. The pages, most stained and a few singed, made a brittle, nervous shuffling. Occasionally she'd pause, mutter a string of polysyllabic invective, then scratch a new calculation in the margins. Her hair, always aggressively straight, now kinked at the temples from sweat and static.

Mrs Barley commandeered the armchair, umbrella balanced like a petulant lapdog. She'd spent the last several minutes muttering under her breath, sometimes in English, sometimes in a Latin so antique it made the flat feel medieval by association. Her hands performed slow, secretive gestures, and every so often she'd flick a glance at Ren's arm and then cross herself, just in case.

Vincent, who'd claimed the kitchen stool and most of the remaining wine, regarded the gathering with the fond exhaustion of a zookeeper on the wrong side of the bars. He tried to pour himself a glass, missed, and poured it directly into his mouth instead. He winced as the alcohol hit a canker, and then said, through the hiss, "Anyone else feel like they just kissed an electrical socket?"

No one replied. The flat vibrated with silence, the only noise the low, petulant hum of the fridge and the gentle tick of the wall clock in the hall.

Ren scrubbed at the mark again. It was no longer just pain; it was a vector, a tiny engine burning under the skin. Every pulse set her heart off-beat, syncing her blood pressure to some external source she had not consented to. It would have been poetic if it wasn't so fucking irritating.

She finally snapped, "Is this going to get worse, or am I just lucky?"

Zara didn't look up. "Probably both," she said, pencil dancing on the edge of the page. "If you're feeling drawn toward an inciting incident, that's the sigil doing its job."

Vincent's eyebrow ratcheted up. "Pain with a side of plot? Marvellous. How long before she starts levitating or barking in Latin?"

Mrs Barley's eyes narrowed. "You should be so lucky. The last person I saw with a mark like that ended up prophesying the Corn Laws in Aramaic, then drowned himself in a bird bath."

Ren grunted, partly out of respect, partly to cover the fact that her teeth were now vibrating. She pressed two fingers to the pulse on her wrist. The beat was steady, but every third or fourth tap landed out of time, as if her body was trying to Morse code a distress signal.

"I think it's syncing," she said, and regretted the word instantly.

Zara looked up, alert for the first time since the last crisis. "Describe it."

Ren chewed her lip, surprised to find she still had one. "It's like... I'm a metronome. Or a bloody pacemaker. I can feel it locking in. Sometimes it's ahead, sometimes it's behind. But it's getting closer."

Barley's umbrella twitched. "Something wants you on schedule. For what?"

Zara paged backwards through her notes, index finger trailing a line of ink. "The sigil was designed to establish a persistent narrative connection. If you're syncing, it means the other end is broadcasting. Which means..."

Ren finished it for her. "Someone's using me as a beacon."

"You know, when they said the undead would walk among us," Vincent said, "I thought we'd get more perks. Maybe a dental plan."

He caught Ren's eye, and for a moment the air went elastic. He tried a smile, failed, then ran a hand through hair that was two days overdue for shampoo and several centuries overdue for an epiphany.

"Well," he said, "do we wait for the apocalypse to knock, or do we go knocking ourselves?"

Mrs Barley was already standing. She snapped her umbrella shut and slung her bag over one shoulder. "No one with half a brain waits for trouble to finish its tea. Let's go."

Zara gathered her papers and stood, but not before taking a careful photograph of Ren's arm. She leaned in close, lips pursed. "The pattern's changing. It's not just a mark now, it's writing. Look—" she pointed, "—there are letters forming. A language."

Ren squinted at the skin, now a bruise of shifting blue. The characters pulsed, warping with every beat. She couldn't read it, but she didn't have to. The meaning came through like a punchline after a cruel joke.

"Alleyway," she said. "Scene change."

Vincent made a noise halfway between a laugh and a groan. "The script wants us to go bin-diving. Brilliant."

Ren stood, stretching out the cramp in her calf. The moment she put weight on her leg, the pull intensified. It was no longer just in her arm—it ran down her spine and into the soles of her feet. Every step she took, the flat's floorboards echoed back, louder than they should.

She grabbed her jacket, zipped it up. "I swear, if this drags me to a Starbucks, I'm defecting."

They left the flat in the kind of order that only comes after disaster, Ren leading, the rest forming a loose and jittery phalanx behind. They took the stairs two at a time, the sound of their footsteps drumming a warning down the stairwell.

Outside, London was a humid smear of street lights, drizzle and damp. Rain had started to fall in earnest, the droplets fine enough to be mistaken for dust, but persistent enough to soak a jumper in minutes. The neon from the off-license next door ran in rivulets down the brickwork, pooling in the cracks of the pavement.

Ren paused under the awning, and for a moment, the city's noise dialled down to a whisper. She could still feel the mark ticking under her skin, but now there was a direction to it—a tug toward the east, down the side street lined with bins and broken promises.

She turned, caught Vincent's gaze. "Are we doing this?"

Vincent nodded, his hands already in his pockets, shoulders hunched like he was trying to deflect the rain with posture alone.

Mrs Barley was already halfway down the street, umbrella up, parting the mist like a prow. Zara jogged to keep up, one hand clutching her notes, the other shielding her phone from the weather.

The walk was short, but each step wound the tension tighter. The city's usual soundtrack—sirens, shouts, the distant bark of a dog—faded until all that remained was the scuff of their boots and the relentless tick of Ren's arm.

Vincent hung back, scanning the sightlines. "Anyone else feel like we're walking into a trap?"

Mrs Barley didn't slow. "It's not a trap if you know it's coming. It's a party."

Ren snorted, then stepped forward. As she approached a cafe, the sigil's pulse became almost unbearable, every beat matched by a spike of heat and a faint, whispering echo in her left ear. She tried to ignore it, but it began to articulate, to form words—not her own, but written somewhere deeper.

She stopped at the door and looked back. "It's... speaking. The mark. It says—"

Zara stepped close, eyes shining. "What?"

Ren closed her eyes, focused. The words weren't in English, or any language she recognised, but the meaning was precise, surgical.

"'Round the back. End the story.'"

Vincent groaned. "Always with the metaphors."

Mrs Barley stepped past, umbrella tip tapping the threshold. "Not a metaphor if it kills you," she said, and led them on.

SIX

The alley behind the café was exactly the sort of place you'd expect to find a body: part damp bin-park, part pop-up latrine, all of it lacquered in an oily sheen of neglect. Above the scene, the neon sign of Occult Café flickered its promise—COFFEE | CHAI | CRYSTALS—strobing blue and sickly pink against the stonework. Rain, having given up any pretext of cleansing, sluiced down the gutters in long, greasy streams, pooling around the corpse with a diligence most municipal services could only envy.

Ren reached the mouth of the alley first. She clocked the huddled heap of what might have been laundry, then realised what it was, then immediately wished she hadn't. She turned her face to the wall, spat once, and drew the hood of her jacket low over her eyes, as if darkness could shield her from whatever had gone on in this backstreet theatre.

Zara followed, trenching through the ankle-deep gutter with the pragmatic stride of a woman who'd worn heels to a boggy field. Her phone torch cut a bar of white across the scene, illuminating the tableau in slices: the splayed hands, the head pitched at an angle calculated for maximum audience impact, the spill of blackish blood which had already started to congeal into something closer to tar than anything human.

Vincent trailed a careful three steps behind, arms folded across his chest as if bracing for a pop quiz on his own worst memories. He watched as Zara crouched beside the body, snapping on a pair of nitrile gloves with a crackle that sounded almost cheerful in context.

"You alright?" Vincent asked Ren, though his attention never left the corpse.

"Lovely night for a constitutional," Ren said, her words muffled by sleeve and street noise. She risked a glance back at the body, then dry-heaved with the daintiness of someone who'd learned young to keep her stomach's secrets. "God, the smell."

Zara, squatting over the victim, exhaled through her nose and said, "You get used to it. Eventually." She pressed two fingers to the dead man's neck—not out of hope, but for the formality—and then with a series of brisk, oddly gentle movements, began to catalogue the scene. "White male, late twenties. No wallet, no phone, no keys. No dignity, either, but you can't have everything."

Vincent edged closer. The body was posed, he saw now, with the grotesque exactitude of a deranged theatre director: right leg extended, left arm draped, fingers just so. The jaw had been forced open, and a rolled scrap of paper had been wedged between the teeth. The whole tableau was so artificial, so deliberately performative, that Vincent's first, traitorous thought was, "It's a joke."

His second thought was, "It's my joke."

Zara shot him a look. "Well? This ring any bells?"

Vincent swallowed, then reached in, plucked the scroll from the corpse's mouth, and unrolled it. He recognised the font immediately, as well as the words:

You cannot drink from the cup of immortality and not expect it to poison you, darling. That's why the clever ones stick to whiskey.

He read it twice, then let out a long, low groan. "I cut this line. From *Bloodlust & Biceps*. It was supposed to be a metaphor, not a... punchline."

Zara gave a dry little laugh. "Sounds like a must-read. Well, seems like someone's not a fan of the editing."

Ren straightened up, wiped her mouth with the back of her sleeve, and peered at the note. "Is that the one with the blood orgy in Chapter Three?"

Vincent shrugged. "They all have a blood orgy in Chapter Three. It's about building a brand. Giving readers what they want..." But no one was listening to him.

Zara gloved a hand through the dead man's hair, angling the head to examine the scalp. "No trauma to the skull," she muttered. "But look here." She pulled the collar aside, exposing a line of shallow incisions, each precisely two centimetres apart, starting just beneath the jaw and running down into the shirt.

"Patterned," Zara said. "Not random. Some kind of signature?"

Vincent stooped, squinting through the neon haze. "Could be a ritual. Or just someone trying to send a message."

"Or both," said Zara, snapping a quick photo. She moved

the victim's hand—carefully, as if not to disturb an exhibit—and revealed a second scrap, folded tight in the palm.

Ren, who had at last mastered her gag reflex, said, "Can you not just... email a threat these days? Or graffiti it on a wall in a public toilet like a normal psycho?"

"Handwriting has more intimacy," Vincent said, a bitter edge to his voice. "Like getting a Valentine from a stalker. Or a handwritten rejection slip from a publisher."

He took the second scrap, unfolded it, and winced. This one was even worse:

My darling, you always were better at fiction than reality. Now see how the pen tastes when you're not holding it.

Vincent read it aloud, and Zara snorted. "That's definitely addressed to you."

Ren shivered. "This is messed up. Even for your circle."

Zara finished her forensic sweep, cataloguing every angle with a phone camera and a little notebook that already bulged with the unfiled sins of the last two months. "No ID," she said, "but the prints are probably gone anyway. See?"

She held up the victim's right hand. The fingerprints had been sanded down, the skin raw and pink and bloodied. Even in the streetlight, the effect was obvious—whoever had done this wanted the man untraceable, anonymous, a cipher built for Vincent's attention.

"They made him into a character," Vincent said, softly. "A blank protagonist."

"A dead protagonist," Zara corrected. "There's a difference."

The late-night café's back door, half-open, admitted the steady hiss and gurgle of an espresso machine, the noise cutting through the alley like a dentist's drill. It added to the surrealism:

high-grade homicide, artisanal caffeine, and the vague sense that someone in the café was about to step out for a fag and find their night irrevocably ruined.

Ren edged around the puddle, crouched beside Vincent, and squinted at the wounds on the neck. "They look like... ellipses?" she said, voice uncertain. "Like... you know. Dot dot dot."

Vincent peered closer. "Or an ellipsis with a full stop. Like an unfinished sentence." He wanted to laugh at the absurdity, but his stomach was too busy trying to coil around itself.

Zara, whose patience for literary symbolism was matched only by her contempt for unsolved murder, snapped a final photo and stood. "We'll need to move the body. Last thing we want is the police getting involved at this stage."

Ren's eyes widened. "You mean we're just taking him with us?"

"Not him," Zara said. "The story. We take the story, and we write the ending ourselves."

Vincent stared at her, then at the corpse, then at the notes still clutched in his fist. He tried to imagine the kind of person who would stage a murder based on the deleted lines from his old manuscripts, and failed. Or, more accurately, he succeeded, but the person he pictured was himself, twenty years younger and twice as angry.

He folded the scraps, pocketed them, and stood. The rain had started to turn to sleet, each droplet reflecting the neon in miniature.

"Anything else?" Vincent asked, voice barely above the espresso hiss.

Zara peeled off her gloves and binned them in a plastic bag, which she knotted with military efficiency. "One more thing," she said, pulling a third slip of paper from the victim's jacket. She held it up for him to read:

"Chapter Seven. Don't cut this one, darling."

Vincent didn't smile. He just stared at the paper, feeling the weight of the world's most elaborate editorial note land squarely on his chest.

Ren clapped him on the back, hard enough to jolt him from the moment. "Look on the bright side," she said. "At least you have a fan club."

Vincent thought of the corpse, the ellipses, the raw fingerprints. "Yeah," he said. "They're killing for the material."

Zara gave a small, practical shrug. "We hide him in the bin. It's not foolproof—someone could still find him—but it buys us time. Come on."

Vincent grunted, bent, and hefted the corpse like a sack of wet books. The body slumped in his arms, oddly light and horrible. He carried him to one of the alley's metal bins; Mrs Barley, who had been keeping watch near the door, stepped forward and tipped the lid open like she'd done it a thousand times before—though usually with filing cabinets.

"Safe passage, then," she said, voice low and absurdly earnest as she peered into the bin. "Don't let the other side turn you into an editor." She gave the corpse a little nod that might have been a blessing or a reprimand, then let Vincent lower the man into the refuse with an efficient shove.

They closed the lid, and moved off into the street. Mrs Barley placed a sympathetic arm on Ren's shoulder. " I'd like to tell you that will the first and last corpse you'll see."

"But it's not likely, is it?" Ren asked, chewing her bottom lip.

"No." Mrs Barley said and pointed her umbrella in the direction of home.

Vincent found Mrs Barley sat at her usual post, the table's Formica surface cleared of everything except a wire basket of bills and a single, ceremonial-looking pencil sharpener. Mrs Barley worked the pencil with the patient menace of an old-school executioner, pausing now and again to eye the point before returning it to the blade. She wore her apron over a thick cardigan, and her hair was done up so severely that Vincent wondered if she'd resorted to glue.

"Expecting trouble?" Vincent asked, glancing at the gathering of weaponised pencils now arrayed like a tiny phalanx beside her tea mug.

Mrs Barley didn't look up. "It's been a week for it. Besides, a sharp pencil's better than a blunt stake, unless you're after splinters." She finished with a flourish and set the latest addition to her arsenal into a ceramic mug labelled "World's Greatest Housekeeper (According to the Dead)."

Vincent grunted and aimed for the fridge, rummaging for anything with an alcohol percentage north of "breakfast juice." He poured a finger of gin into a mug—Mrs Barley's, by mistake, but it seemed appropriate—and slugged it back. He was halfway to a second when he noticed the envelope: thick, creamy, spattered with what looked suspiciously like arterial spray, and resting dead centre on the pile of post.

He nudged the envelope with the tip of the mug. "Fan mail, or a summons?"

Mrs Barley shrugged. "No return address. Arrived special delivery while you were sleeping. Courier didn't even want a signature." She pushed it towards him with two fingers, as if it might bite.

Vincent examined the front. In neat, typewritten block capitals: VINCENT LUPO, ESQ. No street, no city, just his name, as if the universe needed nothing else to find him. He weighed it in his hand, then slid a thumb under the flap and opened it, careful not to rip the contents.

Inside: a single sheet, crisp and perfectly white, the text set in a font so austere it bordered on theological. He read it aloud, because that's what you did with threats, prophecies, or very good jokes.

"LUPO THE LIGHTLESS,

YOUR DIVINE DICTION ENRAPTURES ME.

I WILL SEE THE STORY THROUGH TO ITS PROPER END.

CHAPTER SEVEN BEGINS WITH ANOTHER DEATH.

ARE YOU READY TO WRITE IT PROPERLY THIS TIME?"

Vincent stared at the page, then at Mrs Barley, then back at the page. His fangs itched, a dull ache behind the gums, but he kept his mouth shut and instead poured himself the rest of the gin.

Mrs Barley took the letter, scanned it, and let out a low,

unimpressed hum. "So polite, these maniacs. Always with the formal salutation. Never a please or thank you, though."

"Must be an American," Vincent muttered, but the joke landed with a thud.

From the living room, Ren's voice cut across the tension: "You've got the worst groupies." She padded into the kitchen, hair still wet from her shower, and peered at the letter upside-down. "They don't even mention me."

"Give it time," Mrs Barley said, already sifting through the rest of the post with a movement so practised it bordered on ritual. "You've only just gone viral, dear."

Ren perched on the edge of the counter, helping herself to a handful of dry cereal from the open box by the sink. She looked at Vincent with an expression halfway between amusement and concern. "So what's the plan, genius?"

Vincent considered, then held the letter up to the light. There was nothing on the back, no watermark, no hidden message. Just the promise of more death and, presumably, more critique.

He slumped into a chair. "Assume the next body will turn up with red ink corrections and a suggested reading list."

Mrs Barley sharpened another pencil, the shavings falling in a tight spiral onto the table. "Or," she said, "we could get ahead of the editor. Make them come to us."

Vincent eyed her. "You're suggesting a trap."

She nodded, once, the bun on her head bobbing in approval. "It's what I'd do, if I were the author of a mess like this."

"Where?" Ren asked.

"The Occult Bookshop," Mrs Barley said. "The home of all the best stories."

Ren grinned, teeth bright in the dim. "I'm in. Can I pick the bait?"

Mrs Barley's eyes twinkled. "Of course, dear. Just don't get any on the carpet."

Vincent folded the letter, careful and deliberate, then tucked it into the breast pocket of his shirt. He looked at his hands, ink-stained and shaking slightly, then at the two women in his kitchen, plotting a counterattack with the same calm they might use for a shopping list.

Outside, the rain hammered at the window, as if trying to get inside. The flat felt impossibly small, all of them crammed together under one roof, waiting for the next chapter to drop.

But for the moment, they were ready.

Vincent raised his mug in mock salute. "To Chapter Seven, then."

Mrs Barley clinked her own tea cup against his. "May it be less bloody than the last."

Ren chewed her cereal, then shrugged. "Doubt it."

Vincent didn't disagree. He just sipped his drink, and waited for the story to catch up with them.

SEVEN

The bookshop had a smell, and not the one you'd expect. Sure, there was the obligatory musk of dead trees and wishful thinking, but over that floated something pungent and sharp, the olfactory equivalent of a broken tooth. They'd let themselves in through the back door at four a.m., tired and grumpy, at the end of a night that had already been too long for any of their nerves.

The place belonged to a man named only in legend, a dealer in forbidden paperbacks and overpriced limited editions, but tonight it belonged to Zara. She moved through the aisles with the confidence of someone who'd read every single reference book in the occult section and found them all wanting. Vincent suspected she preferred the shop in its empty, echoing form—less about the customers, more about the stories they left behind in the margins.

Rain hammered the shopfront, sleeting in sideways to batter the glass. The street outside was a crime scene of neon, every sign down the row jostling to out-shout the next, but inside, the only light was from a battered "Special Offer" lamp on the counter and a flickering florescent tube above the rare-books alcove. The effect was *chiaroscuro* by way of car boot sale.

Ren had her feet up on a stack of discount crystal healing hardbacks, the chair balanced on two legs, daring gravity to make something of it. Vincent, for his part, perched at the edge of a wheeled stool with the tension of a man expecting the fire alarm to go off at any second.

Zara called the meeting to order with the click of a lighter, igniting not a cigarette but a small clove-scented candle on the counter. "We don't have long," she said, eyes flicking to the doorway, where the security shutter hung like the blade of a slow-motion guillotine. "If anyone's tracking us, they'll check here first."

Ren snorted. "You really think the psycho is going to come after us in a bookshop? Not exactly a high-value target."

Zara arched an eyebrow. "You'd be surprised. Most of the worst ones start in libraries."

Vincent rolled his eyes, then immediately regretted it as they caught on the migraine pulse of the strip-light overhead. "Can we get to the point? If I don't get back soon, Mrs Barley will bleach the sheets out of spite."

Zara set down her satchel and began extracting its contents: a sheaf of printouts, a thumb drive, and a pair of reading glasses that looked engineered for peering into other dimensions. "We've had two more incidents," she said, voice dropping into the rhythm of bad news. "Both in the last forty-eight hours. Both with Carmine glyphs, and both—" She flipped a printout, exposing a police crime scene photo, "—staged to look like scenes from your books."

Vincent stared at the photo, then at Zara. "I only published four in that series."

"Unpublished, then," Zara said. "Fanfic. Deleted scenes. Drafts you never finished."

Ren's chair landed back onto all four legs. "Wait. How would anyone even get those?"

Zara didn't answer, just fixed Vincent with a look that said: *You know.*

Vincent's mouth went dry. "You think it's—what, some bloody collector? Or just someone with too much time and an internet connection?"

"I think," Zara said, "that they're using your work as a script bible, a blueprint. The question is how much of it you actually remember, and how much you're willing to dig up."

Ren cracked her knuckles. "I say we smoke out every last scrap. Digital, physical, the whole graveyard. If this psycho is scripting from Vincent's Greatest Hits, we find the setlist before they do."

Vincent recoiled. "You want me to exhume first drafts? Some of those are dangerous. Not to mention embarrassing."

Ren grinned, wolfish. "Not as embarrassing as a corpse with your prologue tattooed on it."

Zara slid a spiral-bound notebook across the counter. "I've started collating. Everything with the glyph. Everything with Carmine's mark. But you're the only one who knows what's missing."

Vincent eyed the notebook as if it might bite. He remembered the glyph, of course—three crescents, joined at the centre, like a third-rate triquetra—and the endless nights in his old, damp flat, scribbling on anything that would hold ink. Some of those manuscripts hadn't seen daylight in centuries. Some had been eaten by rats, others by fire. But he'd never really believed in the permanence of deletion.

He picked up the notebook, hands unsteady. "If I do this, it could get... recursive. The prophecy—"

"Is just a story," Ren interrupted. "You said so yourself. Stories can be rewritten."

Zara's eyes flickered in the candlelight. "That's what I'm afraid of."

A gust of wind rattled the door, hard enough to make the shelves shudder. They all flinched, even Ren, who covered with a cough. Vincent set his jaw, flicked through the first pages of the notebook.

"It's all here," he said. "The glyphs, the rituals, even the bloody footnotes. But whoever's doing this—"

Zara interrupted, "—has access to your process. Not just the product."

Ren cut in, "So we use that. We get ahead of the edits."

Vincent shook his head. "Prophecies aren't meant to be self-fulfilling. They're cautionary tales. If you try to hack the ending, you just wind up in a loop."

Zara closed her eyes, briefly, as if remembering a headache she'd once loaned out to a friend. "Prophecy doesn't require belief, only narrative momentum. If our killer thinks he's fulfilling the prophecy, it doesn't matter whether you believe in it or not. The story goes where it's pushed."

Ren stabbed at the notebook. "So we push back. What's the worst that happens—someone edits us out of reality?"

Zara and Vincent exchanged a look. They both knew,

without saying, that the worst had already happened. More than once.

The lamp on the counter and the overhead fluorescent tube fizzed, then died, plunging the shop into a dim blue haze from the neon outside. For a moment, Vincent felt the pressure of a hundred thousand books, all breathing together, waiting for him to make a move.

He closed the notebook. "Fine. We do it your way. But if anything I find in those drafts tries to eat someone's face, I'm absolving myself of all legal, moral and metaphysical responsibility."

Ren saluted with an invisible pint. "Deal."

Zara replaced her glasses, pinched the bridge of her nose, and said, "We start tomorrow at sunset. Vincent, you'll need to make a list of everything you've ever written with Carmine's name on it. Even the unfinished ones. Especially those."

Vincent's face crumpled at the prospect. "Some of them aren't even coherent. There's one that's just a shopping list crossed with an erotic haiku."

Ren cackled. "No wonder I can't find your stuff in Waterstones."

The wind battered the windows again, and somewhere down the road, thunder rolled, low and disapproving.

Zara packed away the photos and flash drive and helped herself to two leather-bound grimoires from behind the counter. "I'll keep digging. Ren, you do recon on the digital front. Vincent... brace yourself."

He gathered up the notebook and the remains of his dignity. "When you find me weeping over a dot-matrix printout in a bathtub, remember: this was not my idea."

Ren followed him out, but not before grabbing a battered paperback from the discount stack. "Research," she claimed, pocketing it.

Zara lingered behind, scanning the shop as if counting the shadows. She caught her own reflection in the front glass—pale, slightly blurred by the neon's stutter—and frowned, just a little, at the shape of things to come.

Outside, the rain had begun to turn to sleet, each drop a cold nudge towards the next disaster. The three figures huddled at the doorway, already plotting their retreat.

Behind them, the bookshop waited. Its shelves leaned in, straining to hear the next draft, the next story, the next chapter in a prophecy that refused to die.

The night was long, and the storm showed no sign of stopping.

But at least, for once, they had a plan.

Vincent spent the final hour before sunrise pacing the flat with all the grace of a caged hyena. Each lap took him from the window—where the city's sodium haze blurred the outlines of everything worth seeing—to the fridge, then back again, always skirting the spot where Ren had gone feral in her sleep.

She was curled in the corner of the sofa, knees up, arms folded tight, hoodie yanked down to swallow her face. The effect was cartoonish, like someone's first attempt at human origami, but the dead give-away was the one foot poking out, toes twitching whenever she hit a particularly energetic patch of dreaming.

The rest of the flat was silent, save for the persistent hum of the fridge and the metronomic tick of Mrs Barley's hallway clock—she'd "borrowed" it from a vicar, the story went, though Vincent suspected it had more to do with an unsolved poisoning incident in Surrey. Either way, the clock kept time as if time was something you could keep, and each tick felt like a countdown to something he was absolutely going to regret.

He'd left the light off, relying on the fridge for illumination. Every time he opened the door, the blue-white wash made him look less alive, the bones in his hands showing through the skin like a warning. He stood in front of the open fridge for minutes at a stretch, the cold seeping into him, trying to convince himself that he wasn't hungry, just thirsty for answers.

On the counter: a notebook, pristine and untouched, the kind that dared you to make a mark on it. Vincent had positioned it where he could see it from anywhere in the kitchen, as both challenge and threat. His fingers ached to pick up a pen, but he knew better. After everything Zara had said, after the evidence and the corpses and the creeping suspicion that his own drafts were walking the streets, the only thing scarier than writing was not writing.

He made another circuit of the flat. The floorboards kept their secrets, creaking just enough to let the building know you were alive. As he passed Ren, she muttered something, a fragment of nursery rhyme, then rolled over and punched a cushion with the commitment of a boxer. The hoodie was too big for her, but she wore it as a shield against everything, including herself.

He returned to the fridge and opened it again. Inside: the

usual chaos. A blood bag, labelled "Premium AB Negative" in a font designed to suggest medical authority; a half-empty bottle of gin; three containers of leftovers, all indistinguishable in the dark; and a single, sad carrot, blackening at the tip.

He stared at the blood bag for a long moment. The hunger was back, sharp and insistent, and he knew that if he didn't deal with it now, it would come for him in his sleep. He took the bag, twisted off the cap, and raised it to his lips. The taste should have been comfortingly metallic, the flavour of life-in-waiting, but instead it was—

Memory. Cold, slick, like licking a postage stamp soaked in tears.

Fear, sour and electric, crawling under his tongue like ants.

Ink, black and ancient, staining his mouth with every swallow.

He gagged, coughed, and spat a thick clot of it into the sink. It splattered and stuck, refusing to be washed away even when he blasted the tap at full force. The taste lingered, coating his mouth and throat with a bitterness that felt almost alive.

He looked at the bag in his hand, heart thumping in a way it hadn't since the last time he'd been properly afraid. The cap was still sealed. Untouched.

He set the bag down and examined his own hands, searching for an answer in the webwork of veins and scars. He was sure he'd opened it. He could still feel the slick residue on his teeth, the way it had clawed at his throat. But the seal was intact.

A chill ran up his spine, the kind that starts as a reasonable shiver and ends with you sleeping with the lights on for a week.

On the outside of the fridge door, written in a patch of

condensation that had appeared near the handle, a message had appeared. It hadn't been there before. He was certain.

YOU DRINK WHAT YOU SPILL.

Vincent's fangs throbbed, a reminder of his own bad wiring. He backed away, hands shaking, then turned, slow and deliberate, to check the rest of the flat.

Ren was still asleep, mouth open, a tiny line of drool darkening the sleeve of the hoodie. She muttered something again, softer this time, the words strung together in a rhyme so perfect it hurt.

"In the story's heart the ink runs cold,

the letters breed, the lines unfold.

Speak your secrets, spill your blood,

and drown your monsters in the flood."

The words hung in the air, fragile as a spiderweb. Vincent wanted to laugh, or cry, or drink something that would burn the memory away.

Instead, he stood in the dark, counting the seconds between each tick of the clock, and waited for the next page to turn.

EIGHT

The university had a way of hiding its most dangerous assets in plain sight, but sometimes it doubled down by hiding them in plain, unsupervised basements. Zara's archive existed in a kind of spatial and administrative limbo beneath the theology building—through a door marked "Sub-Basement 2A: Storage," down a flight of steps so uneven they might've been poured as a prank, and into a corridor that could charitably be described as "load-bearing mildew."

Vincent, who'd seen the inside of more archives than he cared to catalogue, still felt a shudder as he trailed Ren through the gloom. The air was heavy with a scent equal parts old paper, leather, and the nervous sweat of research assistants who'd never come back up. Their progress was measured by the clatter of Ren's boots, the steady scrape of Zara's key-ring against her knuckles, and the way Vincent's own nerves sang at the sight of certain sealed boxes along the wall.

Zara led them by the glow of a battered headlamp, which

threw spidery shadows ahead of their footsteps. She ignored the warning signs ("Do Not Open Without Gloves," "Beware: Psychoactive Texts," "Returns Only in Triplicate") and pressed on to the far end, where a pair of iron gates guarded the actual archive.

It took three keys and a muttered codeword to disengage the lock ("Golgotha," intoned like a curse), and then they were inside: a room the size of a minor cathedral, lined floor to ceiling with shelves in every state of collapse. Books spilled from the stacks, scrolls dangled from hooks, and entire cabinets bulged with folders so dense they warped their own drawer fronts. At the centre, a library table supported an architectural model of chaos—more reading lamps than necessary, more coffee stains than strictly plausible.

"Welcome to my kingdom," Zara said, her voice reverberating off the stone. "Watch your step. And your metaphors."

Ren made a show of surveying the space, then gestured at a set of what looked like zip-tied Bibles suspended from the ceiling. "Is that a safety measure, or just the latest trend in ecclesiastical bondage?"

Zara didn't answer; she was already elbow-deep in a crate labelled "Carmine/Lupo, pre-2000," muttering as she sorted through folders and wax-sealed bundles. Ren, left to her own devices, set off on a self-guided tour, poking at odd artefacts and reading the spines aloud with a voice pitched somewhere between stand-up and eulogy.

Vincent lingered at the threshold, resisting the urge to bolt. He recognised too many titles, and each one felt like the ghost of an old mistake. He kept his hands in his coat pockets and tried to look casual, but even the ambient temperature seemed to drop a notch whenever he got near a particular shelf.

"So which one of these is going to infect my brain and turn me into a cultist?" Ren called, holding up a copy of *"Eschatology: A Beginner's Guide for the Overly Invested."*

Vincent didn't dignify it with an answer. Instead, he drifted closer to Zara, whose search had devolved into a kind of archaeological dig—layers of dust, then folders, then entire strata of annotated drafts. She didn't seem to need light, or food, or encouragement; the hunt was its own reward.

"What exactly are we hoping to find?" Vincent asked, keeping his voice down in case any of his past works decided to crawl out and file a lawsuit.

Zara didn't look up. "Original Carmine scripts. Pre-edit. If the killer is following your drafts, we need to know which versions are in circulation."

Ren edged up, carrying a slim volume whose cover had been blacked out with marker, save for the embossed title: *"Sonnets of the Night Market."* She raised an eyebrow. "Is this yours?"

Vincent groaned. "Don't open it. It's really not me at my best."

Naturally, Ren opened it and read the first page. "'To the reader: if you are not yet cursed, keep reading.' Wow, you were really committed to the whole tortured immortal aesthetic, weren't you?"

Vincent gritted his teeth. "It was the nineties. Everyone was tortured."

Zara shot them both a look over her shoulder. "You two can flirt later. I've found something." She hauled out a binder thick with plastic sleeves, each containing what looked like the shredded remains of a novel, plus marginalia in at least four languages.

She flipped it open and Vincent blanched at the sight of his old handwriting: slanted, self-important, as if the pen was trying to outpace the hand. "I thought I'd destroyed the early drafts," he muttered.

"Never trust a university with a shredder," Zara replied. "Besides, there's a market for literary necromancy."

Ren made a gagging noise. "You mean people pay for this stuff?"

"Collectors, mostly. And the odd archivist who's convinced the end of the world is embedded in a marginal note about wine varietals." Zara paged ahead, stopping at a sheet where the ink had bled through, forming a Rorschach of despair. "Here's the bit I was looking for."

She read aloud, her voice flattening into the deadpan of the truly horrified: *When the third sign is invoked, the vessel will take shape, its contours defined by the memory of blood and the refusal of history to stay dead.*

Vincent made a face. "It sounded better when I was drunk."

Ren snorted. "That's also how most tattoos happen."

Zara continued, flipping to a marked page. "The killer isn't just copying the prophecy. He's mixing versions. This paragraph is from the Bucharest copy. This line—*the head will bear the mark, as will the hands*—that's only in the private manuscript."

Vincent frowned. "Which private manuscript?"

Zara looked at him, expression sour. "The one you wrote and never published. The one with the... alternative ending."

There was a silence as Vincent recalled, with increasing

dread, what "alternative ending" meant in this context. "I burned that," he insisted.

Zara tapped the page. "Apparently not well enough. Because there's one more scene the killer hasn't enacted yet. The one at the masquerade."

Ren, who had perched herself on the edge of the table, swung her legs and said, "Let me guess. Enter stage left, there's a party, everyone's in masks, someone loses their head, literally."

Zara nodded, once. "And the head is displayed, public, for all to see. It's the grand finale."

Vincent closed his eyes. He remembered the scene now, in nauseating detail—written in a fever, edited in self-disgust, and (he'd thought) consigned to the flames. It had never occurred to him that anyone would want to make it real.

Ren leafed through the volume. "You even wrote stage directions for the murder. That's bleak, mate."

"It's not a script," Vincent said, more to himself than to anyone else. "It was just... a thought experiment."

Zara shut the binder with finality. "It's a script now. And if the killer is following it, we have maybe forty-eight hours before the next body."

Ren snapped her fingers, as if suddenly inspired. "We should crash the party. Or whatever it is. Get there first."

Vincent's stomach twisted. "Do you know how many masquerades are happening in London this weekend? Or even just in Soho?"

"Doesn't matter," Ren said, "we only need the weirdest one."

Zara agreed, but her eyes were on Vincent, searching for

something. "You sure you don't remember who you sent those drafts to? No collectors, no old flames?"

Vincent hesitated, and for a moment his face betrayed something raw. "There was one. In Shoreditch. Went by 'The Editor.'"

Ren howled. "Oh my god. You dated someone called *The Editor*? That's a level of masochism even I haven't aspired to."

Vincent groaned. "I didn't date them. It was a... transaction."

"Of course it was," Ren said, grinning.

"She didn't leak it or make copies. Of that, I'm sure."

Vincent looked around the archive, at the rows of forbidden knowledge, and felt the past converging on him like a noose. For a moment, he wished he really was just an ordinary garden-variety of vampire, with all the convenient memory loss that implied.

Ren closed the sonnet book, then tossed it at Vincent. He caught it on reflex, then scowled at the inscription on the flyleaf —his own, in a hand that looked much steadier than he remembered: *To all the readers who never asked to be haunted. —V.L.*

She grinned. "Guess we're haunted now, boss."

Zara switched off her headlamp, the darkness closing in with a neat sense of timing. "Let's go," she said, and the echo of her voice lingered in the cavernous space. "We've got a party to crash. And a script to rewrite."

They filed out, the iron gates locking behind them, and left the archive to its sullen, breathing stacks. Above, the world was waiting, and the story was already a chapter ahead.

Rooftops were the only place in the city where Vincent felt like a person, rather than a memo from the universe's department of bad decisions. The wind, knifing up from the river, cut the night into shards and drove the mist sideways, so the air above the archive was a freezing soup of fog, smog, and occasional bats with more ambition than sense.

Vincent shouldered the roof access door shut, letting its slam echo behind him. Ren was already halfway across the gravel, silhouetted against a skyline equal parts gothic spires and buildings named after mobile phone providers. She wore her battered hoodie like a suit of armour, staring into the city with an intensity that managed to look both predatory and bored.

He fumbled a cigarette out of its crumpled pack, then realised the lighter was in his left pocket—naturally, the one he couldn't reach without doing an undignified dance. Ren watched, silent, as he finally got it lit. The tremor in his fingers wasn't from the cold, but the wind did a convincing job of covering for him.

He took a drag, let it out, and watched his own smoke and breath tangle in the air. "You know," he said, "in another life I'd have been up here plotting world domination. Or at least a dramatic suicide."

Ren cocked her head, considering. "Still time for both, if you multitask."

He laughed, brief and surprised. "You're the optimist in this relationship, then?"

She smirked, but it was softer than her usual sneer. "Please.

If I was optimistic, I'd have quit as soon as this thing appeared on my wrist. Or at least after we found a corpse in the street."

Vincent flicked ash over the parapet. "You get used to it. The existential stuff, not the body count."

They stood in silence for a while, watching the lights blur through the mist. Somewhere below, a siren wailed, then cut off mid-scream, leaving only the city's low, perpetual hum.

Ren broke the quiet. "So. Is this where we do the touchy-feely bonding thing, or is it more of a group sulk?"

"Why not both?" Vincent said.

She shrugged, then reached into her messenger bag and produced a thermos, which she uncapped and passed over. He accepted out of habit, not expectation, and sniffed the contents: coffee, cheap, and black enough to qualify as evidence in a custody battle.

"Thanks," he said, and meant it. He took a gulp, the bitterness a welcome counterpoint to the cigarette. "You know, when I turned, I thought I'd lose my taste for this stuff."

Ren glanced at him sidelong. "You didn't?"

Vincent shook his head. "Everything changes, but not in the way you think. You keep the old hungers. Just add new ones on top."

She nodded, like this was the most reasonable thing anyone had ever said. "So you're hungry all the time."

He considered the city, the coffee, the roiling in his own gut. "Yeah. Some days I'm hungry enough to eat the sun."

Ren rolled up her sleeve, exposing the inside of her wrist. The Pen's Vessel tattoo gleamed faintly even in the gloom. She extended her arm toward him, not in jest, not in dare, but with the matter-of-factness of a friend offering a plaster.

Vincent flinched—not from the blood, but from the offer itself. He shook his head, retreating a step. "That's—no. I'm not that desperate."

She held her wrist out for another second, then shrugged, unoffended, and zipped the sleeve back down. "Suit yourself. But if you start moping about your tragic hunger, I will force-feed you my own O-negative."

He grinned, sheepish. "You'd do it, too."

Ren dug around in her bag again, this time producing a bottle of cold-pressed beetroot juice. She tossed it to him, and he caught it, surprised by the weight. "It's a compromise," she said. "Not blood, but it stains everything and tastes like earth. If you don't want it, I'll trade you for the coffee."

He unscrewed the lid, sipped, and winced. "That is vile."

She cackled. "See? Now you're too busy suffering to be hungry."

They settled onto the roof, side by side on the crumbling concrete lip. The city's noise faded into a kind of underwater hush, the lights below them smearing into blue and orange ghosts. Vincent stubbed out his cigarette and stood in silence, feeling the presence of the girl beside him—a strange, human gravity that anchored him better than any mystical ward.

It was Ren who broke the spell, her voice lower than before. "Do you think, if you were still human, you'd have written any of it differently?"

He didn't answer at first. The question was too big, or maybe just too obvious. Instead, he stared into the mist and let the city fill the silence.

When he finally turned to look at her, there was a smile on his face that had nothing to do with the cigarette or the hunger or the noise below. "Probably not," he said, "but I might have remembered to use a pen name."

She laughed, and it was the kind of sound that lingered, even after the fog closed in and the world below became just shapes and guesses.

They stayed up there, watching the lights, until the cold seeped all the way through and the coffee was gone. When they finally went back downstairs, it was as two people who understood exactly what it meant to be haunted—and why you kept going, anyway.

The city kept breathing. The story kept writing itself. And, for the moment, that was enough.

NINE

The rain came at the window with a persistence that made Vincent wonder if the sky was filing a complaint. He lay in bed, face to the wall, listening to the arrhythmic drumline of the weather and the lower, angrier counterpoint of something being violently blended in the kitchen. There was a certain symmetry to it: nature's outrage, and Mrs Barley's, both scheduled for the same hour.

He peeled himself out of bed and padded down the hallway, feet cold on the wood. The kitchen glared with cheap, overhead light. Mrs Barley stood at the counter in what she described as her "formal confrontation outfit"—a navy skirt suit, high-collared blouse, and a set of pearls that could probably throttle a bear. She looked like she was about to chair a war crimes tribunal, not clean the flat.

The blender roared, then cut off. Mrs Barley poured the contents—lurid, viscous, red—into a row of sherry glasses, all the while ignoring the existence of cups more appropriate for breakfast. She caught Vincent's eye, then deliberately poured a fourth, lining them up on the table.

Ren sprawled upside-down on the sofa, head dangling just above the sticky carpet. She was eating toast from the crust inward, crumbs trickling into the hood of her sweatshirt. Her face bore a constellation of sleep creases and the kind of expression only achievable by someone who clearly hadn't suffered much adjusting to Vincent's 'up all night, sleep all day' lifestyle.

"Evening," Ren said, toast muffling the word to 'evnffng.'

Mrs Barley ignored her and fixed Vincent with a look that suggested this was an intervention, or possibly an exorcism. "Sit," she commanded.

Vincent sat. Mrs Barley slid him a glass. He sniffed the rim: tomatoes, celery salt, something sharp and bloody that wasn't any sort of vegetable he'd ever met. "Is this a breakfast or a warning?"

"Both," Mrs Barley said. She slid into the seat opposite, skirt settling with the gravity of a meteor impact. "We have a problem."

Ren made a see-saw motion with her hand. "Is it a 'laundry in the sink' problem or a 'world-ending vampire conspiracy' problem?"

Mrs Barley didn't answer. Instead, she produced a slip of glossy paper from her sleeve, unfolded it with surgical precision, and placed it in the centre of the table.

Vincent reached for it. The flyer was professionally printed, black and silver with a splash of arterial red. At the top, in a font that threatened litigation, it read: THE VELVET VEIN CORDIALLY INVITES YOU TO...

His eyes dropped to the subheading: A NIGHT OF

MASQUE, BLOOD, AND DECADENCE—RECRE-ATING THE FINAL CHAPTER OF *THE CRIMSON ARRANGEMENT.*

He read it again. Then a third time, in case the weather or the blender had scrambled his comprehension. "That's not... they can't..."

Ren rolled upright, interested. "Is that your play?"

Vincent hesitated, then, with the tone of someone confessing to double murder: "Yes."

Mrs Barley's smile was thin as a razor. "Seems your fanbase has evolved. They're now putting on immersive dinner theatre based on your unpublished tragedies."

Vincent pushed the flyer away, as if it might explode. "I burned all copies of *The Crimson Arrangement.*"

Mrs Barley rapped the table. "Clearly not well enough. It's tomorrow night, eleven o'clock, The Velvet Vein." She let the name hang there, a curse or benediction. "You'll be attending."

He almost laughed, but Mrs Barley's face was a brick wall. "I am not attending a vampire cabaret based on my own failed play."

Ren shrugged. "I'd go. Sounds fun."

Vincent gestured at Ren, toast and all. "Why are you siding with her?"

"I'm not," Ren said. "I just think it'd be awesome. Also, if you're the author, you get free drinks."

Mrs Barley nodded, a rare moment of team unity. "And it's the only way to find out who's behind this. They're moving from fanfiction to performance art. Next stop is re-enacting the final scene."

Vincent closed his eyes. He remembered the final scene. It

involved three murders, a simulated blood orgy, and the on-stage decapitation of a character suspiciously named V. Lupo. "No," he said. "Absolutely not."

Mrs Barley steepled her fingers, like a praying mantis about to devour her mate. "If you won't do it for your own legacy, do it for the safety of the flat. Or for the Vessel," she added, with a glance at Ren.

Ren made a show of checking her pulse. "I'm fine. Unless there's another prophecy I haven't heard about."

Mrs Barley ignored her. "We'll need costumes. Masks. Possibly forged invitations." She ticked off the requirements on her fingers, each one a nail in Vincent's coffin. "I'll handle the logistics.

Vincent watched the plan spiral out of his control, as per usual. "I have nothing to wear," he said, desperate.

Mrs Barley smiled with something like pity. "You'll wear a mask, Vincent. That's the point."

He glanced down at the flyer, then back at the sherry glasses. He picked one up, raised it to eye level. The red liquid was thick, clinging to the sides in slow motion. "I thought this was a Bloody Mary."

Mrs Barley shook her head. "It's not for drinking. It's for show."

He put the glass down, hands trembling. Ren, now upright and wide awake, finished her toast and licked her fingers clean. "If we're going to a vampire party," she said, "I call dibs on the most dangerous mask."

Mrs Barley looked at Vincent, daring him to refuse. He thought about the tomorrow night: the music, the strangers, the likelihood of being murdered on stage for the entertainment of immortal perverts. He looked at Ren, who was bouncing with excitement, then at Mrs Barley, who was as immovable as fate.

"Fine," he said. "But I'm not applauding if they get my death scene wrong."

Mrs Barley tapped the flyer. "Good lad. Now drink. You'll need your strength."

Vincent examined the glass, then the room, and tried to remember the last time he'd been to a party that hadn't ended in screaming. He sipped the red liquid. It tasted like beetroot, with a finish of dread.

Ren grinned. "This is going to be brilliant."

Vincent doubted it, but he kept drinking anyway.

The storm came back for round two as evening bled into night, rattling the window panes of Vincent's study with the indignation of a council inspector denied entry. The view from his desk was a war zone of lightning and satellite dishes, every flash revealing a little more of the city's pockmarked optimism. Inside, the atmosphere was no less volatile: the books had begun rearranging themselves again, shifting on the shelves with the passive-aggressive energy of cohabiting ghosts.

Vincent sat at his desk, or rather, hunched behind it, as if to shield himself from the onslaught of his own work. The day's correspondence lay spread out before him—an impossible to-do list of edits, warnings, and polite threats from Zara. The blood bag at his elbow sweated condensation, its label beading up in the chill, but he made a point of ignoring it. His hands, however, had not got the memo. They trembled with the ferocity of opium withdrawal, or perhaps something more esoteric, as he typed, deleted, and retyped the same sentence over and over.

He was so focused on the deliberate act of not feeding that he didn't hear Ren until she was standing in the doorway, a silhouette framed in the blue light from the landing. She wore the same hoodie as always, but now with the sleeves rolled up, revealing the new mark on her forearm: still raw, still glowing faintly in the gloom.

"You're avoiding your lunch," she said.

Vincent looked up, startled. "I'm working."

Ren snorted. "You're not even logged in." She crossed the room, grabbed the blood bag, and held it at eye level like an uncooperative pet. "Drink it, or I'll pour it down your throat."

He tried for a laugh, but the effort caught in his chest. "That's not how it works."

Ren regarded him, her expression equal parts disdain and worry. "You're a vampire, not a martyr. If you waste away, we don't get to the third act."

Vincent looked away, focusing on the city lights blurred by rain. "Sometimes I think the hunger is the only thing that keeps me real."

She perched on the edge of the desk, swinging her feet like a bored child. "That's the shittest excuse I've heard all week, and I spent last Saturday talking to a man who eats light bulbs for fun."

He closed his eyes. "It's not that simple."

Ren leaned in, voice low. "Sure it is. You're scared that if you act like a monster, you'll become one."

He flinched, but didn't deny it.

Ren's tone softened, just a hair. "You think not feeding makes you more human? All it does is make you less of everything. Hungry, tired, useless. Eventually you'll be too weak to even sulk properly."

He opened his mouth to protest, then snapped it shut. She had a point. He hated that she had a point.

Ren set the blood bag down in front of him, her hand lingering on it for a moment. "Look, I get it. Nobody wants to admit they need anything. But right now, we need you upright and not hallucinating about poetry."

He forced a laugh. "That bad?"

She smirked. "You tried to recite Ozymandias in your sleep last night. It was embarrassing for all of us."

He rubbed his temples. "Fine. I'll drink it. Later."

Ren stood, stretching until her spine crackled. "Whatever. Just don't make me do this again."

He watched her go, the room quieter for her absence but not exactly peaceful. The blood bag sat there, accusing. He picked it up, turning it over in his hands.

He didn't want to feed. Feeding, even from a medical bag, reminded him of all the things he'd lost in seven centuries of hungry years. Self-control. Dignity. A pulse.

But Ren was right. He was no good to anyone like this. He was no good to himself, either.

He popped the cap and drank, the taste metallic and thick, almost enough to drown out the background noise of self-loathing.

When he'd finished, he wiped his mouth with the back of his hand and stared at the wall for a long time.

His phone buzzed. It was a message from Ren: "Try not to brood yourself into a coma. Come down when you're ready."

He smiled, bleak but genuine.

He opened a new message and typed out a single word: "Dinner? Tomorrow evening?"

His finger hovered over the send button. He imagined The Editor, wherever she was, receiving it. He imagined her rolling her eyes, then replying with a time and a location, both unnecessarily precise.

He hit send. The little arrow blinked, then disappeared.

Vincent slumped back in his chair, listening to the storm batter the window and the books mutter among themselves. For the first time in days, the hunger was just background noise.

He let himself drift, the city lights flickering in the wet, and waited to see what would happen next.

TEN

The Editor lived in a flat so white it hurt to look at directly, a flat that actively rejected the accumulation of personality. Vincent hesitated on the threshold, feeling grubby by comparison, as if he were about to graffiti an operating theatre. The lights inside were LED, set to the colour temperature of an autopsy, and the only artwork was a vintage Anatomy of Melancholy print framed with surgical precision above the desk. Bookshelves lined the walls—Ladderax, of course, because The Editor believed in the modular rearrangement of both knowledge and furniture—but unlike the towers of entropy in his own home, her shelves were composed, alphabetised, cross-referenced, and, he suspected, dusted weekly.

She opened the door with the wary courtesy of someone who'd been expecting debt collectors, not old colleagues. She wore a long navy cardigan that functioned as both lab coat and social barrier, and she'd pulled her hair back so severely it gave her an academic facelift. The faint scent of wet dog hung in the entryway, warring with whatever air purification system she'd recently installed. He recognised the model: it was marketed to the immunocompromised and the extremely paranoid.

"You're late," she said, then stepped aside to let him in. She didn't bother with greetings, handshakes, or the small talk about rain that had infected the rest of London.

Vincent shrugged out of his coat and hung it on the hook she indicated with a single, queenly gesture. He risked a glance at the interior: white cube shelving, white table, white floors, the only break in the snowfield a sprawl of colour-coded files on the kitchen worktop. In the living room, a single grey sofa clung to the centre of the space like a sandbar in a sterile ocean.

"Sorry," he said, although he wasn't, not really.

"Fine. Sit."

He sat. The sofa was so unsullied it squeaked, a noise that sounded like a violation. Vincent fidgeted, then stilled himself, hands steepled in his lap like a schoolboy caught between a test and a reprimand.

She swept past, the cardigan trailing behind her in a synthetic flag of intent, and returned with two items: a plain glass of water and a brand-new, still-in-the-pack box of tissues. She set the glass on the low table in front of him, then opened the tissue box with the efficiency of a surgeon unwrapping a scalpel.

"Do you want to discuss the terms?" she asked, settling into a chair opposite.

"Terms?"

She regarded him with the kind of dispassionate amusement that made him feel instantly unqualified to share the room. "You asked for a feeding. I'm assuming you've not lost your sense of boundaries since the last time."

Vincent felt the blood creep up his ears. "I—yes. Of course. Standard protocol. Minimum, er, volume. No permanent marks. You can set the limits."

She inclined her head, then peeled a tissue off the top and dabbed at an imaginary spot on her wrist. "The left arm, then. And only until I say stop."

He nodded, suddenly very aware of the way his own tongue pressed against the fangs, as if eager for its cue. He kept his hands on his knees, white-knuckled, and stared at the glass of water as if it might develop a taste for metaphors.

They sat in silence for a long, appraising moment.

He broke first. "You really don't do small talk, do you."

The Editor's gaze sharpened, a scalpel paring away the conversational fat. "We both know why you're here. The preamble is wasted effort."

"I could pretend to care about your latest research grant," Vincent offered, "but I'd just embarrass myself with a bad joke about peer review."

She rolled her eyes, but it was an old, familiar motion, an intellectual tic from the era when they'd fought over the same academic scraps. "The project's been postponed. Funding was cut." She flexed her wrist, presenting it to him with a professional air. "Budget constraints, you understand."

"Chronic," he said, and meant it.

She watched him for another half-breath, then reached into her pocket and produced a compact bottle of isopropyl alcohol, a cotton pad, and a plaster. She cleaned her own skin with ruthless efficiency, then gestured for him to proceed.

Vincent shifted closer, trying to ignore the way the light made his own hands look jaundiced and foreign. "You could at least try to make this less clinical," he muttered.

The Editor's eyebrow twitched. "You prefer ritual? Incense, mood lighting, a little soft jazz?"

"Never jazz," Vincent said, and they almost smiled together.

But the moment was all business. He took her arm, felt the pulse through the thin layer of skin, and shivered. She held herself perfectly still, eyes fixed on the white wall behind him. For a second he felt like an intruder, a parasite, but the hunger was awake now, angry and elegant, and it guided him with a steadiness his nerves couldn't match.

He bit.

The initial puncture was almost nothing, a pinprick, but as the blood welled up, slow and precise, he felt the shock of warmth spread from his lips to the tips of his fingers. The Editor exhaled—an audible, controlled release—and her other hand tightened on the armrest, knuckles whitening.

Vincent drank in shallow pulls, determined not to lose control, not to let the animal under his skin drive the moment. He kept one eye on her face, watched her breathe through the rush, and was absurdly conscious of the timer on the wall ticking down the seconds.

After precisely thirty seconds, The Editor raised a hand. "Enough."

He stopped instantly, but the aftertaste lingered—metallic, spiked with something that felt like memory. He pressed the tissue to the puncture, dabbed away the excess, and applied the plaster with trembling fingers.

She reclaimed her arm, inspected his work, then flexed her

wrist. "Still meticulous," she said. "You've lost none of your precision."

He slumped back, embarrassed by the flush in his cheeks and the ache in his stomach, both hunger and its relief a kind of humiliation. "I do my best. Didn't want to get a bad Trustpilot review."

She snorted. "You're still not funny."

"I'm hilarious in certain circles," he said, but his voice was softer.

They sat like that for a minute, the air humming with unspoken things. The Editor took the glass of water, sipped, and then set it down with unnecessary force. She eyed him, assessing.

"So what's the emergency? You don't usually come begging unless the world is ending."

He considered lying, but the post-feeding honesty always loosened his tongue. "It's the missing manuscript. The one you warned me about."

Her lips tightened, but she didn't look surprised. "You found it?"

"Worse," he said. "It's out."

The Editor leaned forward, expression hardening. "Who has it?"

He shook his head. "Not sure. But there's a fan club. Cult, maybe. It's recursive, the prophecy. Or maybe it's just a bloody script, being followed by the line."

She tapped the plaster on her wrist, a gesture halfway between irritation and nostalgia. "You never should have written it."

"You edited it," Vincent shot back, and regretted the pettiness immediately.

She let it slide. "We can't change the past, Vincent. All we can do is manage the damage."

They sat, old wounds breathing in the silence.

He gathered himself, feeling the new energy seep into his bones. "I'll be careful," he said, then, "thank you."

The Editor nodded, once, and stood. She gathered the medical detritus into a neat pile, then deposited it in a bin under the sink.

As Vincent pulled on his coat, she hovered by the door. "You're still writing guilt like it's a genre," she said.

He looked at her, really looked, for the first time since entering the flat. "And you're still editing people mid-sentence."

They both smiled, brittle, and she opened the door for him. He paused in the threshold, half-expecting a goodbye, a warning, a request for updates.

Instead, she simply said: "Don't come back unless you really need to."

He nodded, stepped out, and let the corridor swallow him.

The air outside was fresher, less disinfected, and he gulped it down, trying to replace the gnawing feeling in his chest with the reality of what he'd just done. He felt better, in the most literal, biological sense. But the hunger had only ever been a symptom, never the cure.

He walked, hands deep in his pockets, through the wet glow of streetlights, trying not to imagine all the things he'd left behind in that white, antiseptic world.

What he wanted, more than anything, was to retreat to his

study and work on his latest novel, but he had a masquerade to attend.

It wasn't even nine p.m. and Vincent's home already looked like the kind of haunted dressing room you only got at end-stage theatre companies or certain bars in Vauxhall. Every item of clothing he'd ever acquired in his seven centuries (the last two in charity shops) had been excavated from storage and flung across the flat, creating a topography of discarded cravats, velvet jackets, and tattered band t-shirts. The detritus was so complete it had overrun into the kitchen, where Ren sat on the counter, legs swinging, constructing a mask from strips of red silk and a glue gun that should, by rights, have been classified as a weapon.

Mrs Barley occupied the one remaining chair, polishing a pair of ancient combat boots and flicking through a catalogue of vintage opera capes, as if she were auditioning for the role of "death warmed over." She wore her hair pinned back, severe as ever, but the effect was undercut by the wine-dark velvet draped over her lap.

Ren eyed the boots, then the cape. "Is that from the Blitz or just a statement piece?"

Mrs Barley gave her a look. "I was there for the Blitz, dear. The statement is that I survived it."

Ren snorted, then resumed her own craft. The silk was probably stolen—Vincent didn't recognise it from any previous costume, and the way Ren cut it implied total disregard for provenance or resale value. She was a bit slapdash with her cutting, so the left eye was slightly larger than the right, which gave it a permanent expression of surprise.

Vincent, meanwhile, was mired in a battle with his own wardrobe. The best he could do was a charcoal suit (two sizes too small, but "vintage" if you squinted) and a cravat so funereal it could have officiated its own memorial. He regarded his reflection in the hall mirror, hoping for "Byronic," but landing squarely on "disinherited undertaker." The feeding at The Editor's had left him juiced and jittery, his skin electric, his thoughts refusing to settle into any of their familiar, comfortingly depressive grooves.

Mrs Barley caught him staring. "You're fidgeting."

He tugged at the cravat. "The fabric itches."

"Of course it does," she said, "it's supposed to make you uncomfortable. It's called dressing up. Now sit down, before you pull a seam."

He sat, obedient as a boarding school dog, and watched as Mrs Barley laced up the boots. He couldn't shake the image of The Editor's flat—its antiseptic clarity, the way her presence had filled every cubic metre, the hunger that was now sated but not satisfied. The memory kept getting snagged on the way The Editor had avoided mentioning the manuscript further, even though it was the only thing either of them wanted to discuss.

Ren cut in, "You look like you're about to get married to a crypt."

Vincent gave her the smallest of grins. "You look like you just burgled one."

She bared her teeth, delighted.

Mrs Barley finished tying her boots and swung the cape over her shoulders with a flourish. "Right. Review the plan, please. No improvisation. No heroics. We are strictly there to observe, collect information, and not get murdered by self-identifying vampires."

Ren was already ignoring the last part. "If we're spotted, do we run, or do we set something on fire?"

"Run first," Mrs Barley said, "then set fire if running doesn't work."

Vincent glanced at the wall clock. "We should go. The Velvet Vein starts locking the doors after midnight. And I'd rather not be the afterparty."

Mrs Barley rose, checked the contents of her bag—compact mirror, keys, three cloves of garlic ("just in case," she said, with a meaningful look at Vincent)—then led the way to the hall. The hallway mirror caught most of them as they filed past: Mrs Barley as a booted revenant, Ren a flash of red-and-black chaos, and Vincent, had he had a reflection, bringing up the rear with all the enthusiasm of a condemned man on a parade float.

Outside, the city was already shifting into its nocturnal gear. The street glistened with fresh rain, and the air had the spicy, back-alley aroma of wet brick and fried food. Ren bounced down the steps ahead of them, pulling her mask into place, and Mrs Barley kept a wary eye on the silent cars idling at the curb. Vincent's nerves twitched at every passing shape, the rush of new blood making every shadow feel like a loaded metaphor.

"Stop walking like you're about to be assassinated," Ren said over her shoulder.

Vincent said, "Statistically, if it hasn't happened yet, I'm overdue."

Mrs Barley snorted, a rare show of solidarity. "At least try to look like you belong."

He tried. He really did. But the cravat was choking, and the suit itched, and every step towards the Velvet Vein felt like a walk deeper into the belly of a monster he'd birthed himself. He couldn't tell if the emotional static was hunger, guilt, or just the anticipation of another disaster. Thankfully the venue was only a mile away.

As they turned the corner onto the club's street—a side road lit by neon and the occasional burst of flickering candlelight— Ren paused and waited for the others to catch up.

She eyed Vincent. "You okay?"

He wanted to say something clever, or at least something dismissive. But the best he could manage was, "Let's just get it over with."

Mrs Barley clapped him on the back, with a force that threatened to dislocate his shoulder. "That's the spirit, lad. Now let's go make a spectacle and find out what we can."

And they did: three unlikely friends in borrowed finery, marching towards the Velvet Vein with the grim resolve of people who absolutely knew better, but couldn't help themselves.

ELEVEN

The Velvet Vein did not advertise. It didn't have to. Its reputation grew in the way of urban rot—inevitable, uncontainable, and quietly devastating to anyone with standards. You either received an invitation, or you didn't. The front, an abandoned speakeasy wedged between an artisanal vape shop and a pawnbroker that never opened, had a door with no bell and a window so grimy it doubled as a black mirror. If you knew where to knock, you were already inside.

Vincent led their advance, a trinity of barely-coordinated awkwardness: Ren in her red silk mask and "war-crime chic," Mrs Barley armoured in the sartorial equivalent of the Geneva Convention, and himself in the funeral cravat that still threatened to asphyxiate him. The bouncer, a juggernaut in a brocade waistcoat, eyed their trio, then nodded with a flick of respect that said he'd seen stranger ensembles tonight and regretted none of them.

They descended a switchback staircase that seemed to go on forever, the walls lined with old taxidermy and glass cases of preserved flowers—each arrangement carefully curated to be both menacing and expensive. The bass vibrated through the stone, a pulse you felt first in the soles of your feet, then in your fillings. The door at the bottom opened onto the main club, and the effect was less "vampire den" than "hell's own Eurovision afterparty."

It was packed: the old guard in bespoke suits and backless evening dresses, their masks subtle as bank logos; the nouveau-riche in neon and latex, faces hidden by elaborate plague-doctor beaks and mirrored visors. The air carried the perfume of spiced blood, unfiltered cigarettes, and the collective effort of several centuries' worth of fashion disasters. Every table held a candle, every candle was black, and every surface shimmered with the kind of residue that could never be fully explained, only endured.

Vincent adjusted his mask (a classic black domino—low effort, high plausible deniability) and surveyed the crowd. The faces behind the masks might have been anyone: distant cousins, ex-lovers, creditors, the occasional historian. He let his gaze pass over them with the studied boredom of a nightclub regular, but inside he kept a running catalogue of who'd be likely to try and kill him, and who'd merely be offended by his presence.

Mrs Barley peeled off immediately, her trajectory taking her around the perimeter with the focus of a crime-scene technician. She ran her finger along the bar, inspected the candle sconces, and paused at intervals to squint at the wallpaper as if reading invisible script. Every so often she would snap a picture on her phone, then tuck it away as if embarrassed to be seen using modern technology.

Ren was less methodical, more kinetic. She shouldered into the crowd, appropriated a champagne flute from a passing tray, and found her way to a low cluster of new vampires who looked as if they'd wandered in from a Camden goth night. They were locked in argument about whether it was more authentic to "feed local" or go on blood holidays to the continent. Ren, whose own feeding preferences started and ended at "preferably not mine," injected herself into the debate with an eye-rolling candour that immediately made her the focus of the group.

Vincent drifted, using the bar as his anchor. The bartender, a beautiful androgynous figure in a Venetian half-mask, greeted him by name, which did nothing to help the paranoia. "Lupo," they said. "You're back on the reds?"

"Trying to be social," Vincent replied, gesturing for a glass of whatever passed for the house special.

The bartender poured something thick and crimson, garnished with a twist of citrus. "On the house. You look like you could use it."

Vincent scanned the room, lowering his voice. "Anything strange tonight?"

The bartender smiled, a sliver of teeth. "Define strange. It's Thursday."

Vincent accepted this with a nod. He sipped. The drink tasted of iron and heartbreak, with a top note of cold storage. He let it linger on his tongue as he watched Mrs Barley circle a set of velvet drapes and Ren goad her table-mates into a competition to see who could recite the most embarrassing urban legend about vampire progenitors.

The club's main room was built in concentric levels, with the dance floor in the pit and the booths stacked in rising terraces like some bloodless amphitheatre. Above, a balcony lined with balustrades overlooked the action, and Vincent could just make out a handful of figures moving with the careless confidence of people who owned the place, or at least paid the cleaning bill.

A few faces, even behind the masks, resolved into memory. There was the Marquis, whose parties in the 1950s had ended more often in police raids than applause; there was Lady D, her mask an intricate mesh of chainmail, whose taste in blood cocktails was only surpassed by her taste in other people's husbands. But none of them seemed to notice Vincent, or if they did, their faces betrayed nothing but ennui.

He was starting to relax—just a touch—when a presence at his side set every warning system back to full volume.

A man in a costume that had been vintage since before Vincent was born (the first time), mask black, mouth set in a subtle smirk, leaned in close enough to be intimate but not threatening.

"Didn't think I'd see you here again," the man murmured, the words precise, the accent unplaceable. "I heard you'd gone out of fashion."

Vincent smiled, letting the mask do half the work. "I'm a classic. Sometimes they come back."

The man laughed, soft and genuine. "Not if you're the writer. Writers are always the first to go."

They exchanged a brief, charged silence. Vincent let the

conversation hang, not wishing to commit to a memory or a recognition.

The man's eyes glinted behind the mask. "If you're looking for trouble, you're a few centuries too late." He tipped his glass—something pale and bubbling—and melted away into the crowd, as if he'd only stopped by to remind Vincent of his own obsolescence.

Vincent exhaled, then realised he'd been holding his breath.

The crowd on the floor shifted, opening up as a new DJ took the stand, spinning what sounded like Boney M on absinthe. Vincent watched the dancers, their movements alternating between lithe and predatory, and wondered if there was any genuine pleasure in it, or if everyone here was just going through the motions until someone called "last orders."

On the perimeter, Mrs Barley completed her circuit and drifted back toward Vincent. Her eyes, sharp behind a pair of tortoiseshell spectacles (worn over her mask, in an apparent act of aggression against both fashion and physics), scanned him from head to toe. "No sign of Carmine's old crew," she said, voice pitched low. "But I found three active wards on the wine cellar door, and someone's using bone ash as a table condiment."

"Club's really improved its hygiene," Vincent quipped.

She ignored the sarcasm. "You see anyone from the prophecy set?"

Vincent shook his head. "Just the usual suspects. One person might have been in the Bucharest crowd, but I don't know his name."

Mrs Barley considered this, then fished a notepad from her purse and scribbled something. "Ren's found friends," she observed, with a jerk of her chin toward the dance pit.

Vincent followed her gaze. Ren was still holding court, mask skewed off-centre, and was clearly in the process of winning a dare. The group of young vampires had shifted from bitching about bloodlines to arguing about whether sun lamps actually worked as a form of recreational self-harm. Vincent was glad to see her smile, even if it was the smile of a cat upending the birdcage.

He turned back to Mrs Barley. "Should we mingle, or maintain plausible deniability?"

She arched a brow. "She's tougher than she looks, she'll be alright."

He drained his glass, then set off for the upper levels. The club's second floor was less crowded, the air cooler, the lighting dim enough that you could pretend to be anyone you wanted. Here, the masks were more elaborate—feathers, sequins, even one that looked like it had been constructed from real teeth—and the conversations were conducted in low, suspicious whispers.

Vincent found a vantage point at the rail, surveying the club below. He caught a glimpse of Ren weaving through the crowd, trailing laughter and half-spilled drinks. Mrs Barley had stationed herself by a collection of old paintings, examining the frames with the interest of someone looking for secret compartments.

The moment of calm didn't last.

A hand closed around Vincent's wrist, cold and hard, and pulled him back from the rail.

He spun, ready to snarl, but the figure who'd grabbed him was only a fraction his own size—a young woman in a mask of porcelain and gold, eyes wide with what might have been fear or devotion.

"You're him," she whispered. "You're the one who wrote it."

Vincent felt a chill, colder than the club air, run through his gut. "Wrote what?"

She laughed, brittle. "The story. The script. You're the reason we're all here."

Vincent tried to extricate his hand, but she held on. "If this is a fan thing, I'm not signing any more—"

She shook her head, slow and deliberate. "It's not fandom, Lupo. It's legacy." Her hand dropped, and she vanished into the stairwell, footsteps swallowed by the bass.

Vincent watched her go, then checked his wrist. There, in perfect script, she'd traced a symbol with her fingernail: three crescents, joined at the centre. The mark of the Carmine Prophecy.

He shivered, and for the first time in months, it wasn't an affectation.

He returned to the bar, still rubbing the spot on his wrist, and ordered another drink. The bartender raised an eyebrow but said nothing.

The club had started to blur at the edges, the crowd denser, the music louder, the air thick with the sense that something important was about to happen and nobody wanted to be the first to acknowledge it.

Vincent glanced at Ren—now deep in conversation with her new cult, faces animated and masks upended on foreheads—and at Mrs Barley, who was in heated debate with a man in a bishop's mitre and a tuxedo. He felt very much alone, very much the outsider, which was both familiar and entirely unwelcome.

He drifted, mind elsewhere, and nearly missed the man in the vintage suit as he brushed past for the second time.

This time, the stranger paused, leaned close, and whispered directly into Vincent's ear:

"The story ends when you bleed it dry."

Vincent froze. The words hit him like a hammer to the sternum: the phrase, exact, from the severed head in his fridge. The signature line of a script he'd cut centuries ago.

He turned, but the man was already gone, lost in the tide of bodies. Vincent felt the glass trembling in his hand, blood—synthetic or otherwise—buzzing in his veins.

He stood there, surrounded by masks and monsters, and realised, with the certainty of a man reading his own obituary, that someone in this room knew exactly who he was.

And worse: they knew what he'd written.

Ren watched from the edge of the dance pit as Vincent went pale at the bar. He'd been a study in nervous energy since they first met, but right now he had the look of a man who'd found his own face on a missing persons poster." She let him sweat for another minute, then made her move.

She intercepted him at the foot of the stairs, grabbing his elbow with a grip that made her intentions clear. "Upstairs. Now."

Vincent blinked, the mask doing little to hide the confusion.

"Can this wait? I'm about to have a panic attack in the genteel sense—internally, and with wine."

Ren rolled her eyes. "You wrote this, didn't you?"

He didn't respond, just let her steer him up the narrow stairs, past a snogging couple in feathered tiger masks and a woman whispering something feral into her date's ear. At the landing, Ren ducked into a private alcove—once a cigar lounge, now the world's smallest panic room—and shut the door with the authority of a woman about to conduct an interrogation.

Vincent looked for a chair, found only a battered love seat, and perched at the farthest edge, knees together, hands steepled in surrender. "Do I get a phone call, or do you just break my fingers until I talk?"

Ren dropped into the seat opposite, eyes sharp above the mask. "You're not funny. Not right now."

He raised his hands. "Fine. I'm listening."

She set her bag on the table and fished out a zine: battered, stained, its edges furred by travel. "I picked this up in Prague last year when I first got interested in... the occult and stuff. Didn't mean anything then. Now—" She flipped it open, thumbed through until she found the page. She read:

"The mark will pass through blood and ink,
the vessel unmarked,
the author unsaved;
when the heart fails to refuse the story,
let the tongue be cut for the greater script."

She slapped the zine on the table, hard. "That's you, Vincent. That's your style. You practically sign it."

Vincent stared at the page, recognising not just his phrasing but his actual, literal handwriting. "It's just a bad translation," he said, voice hollow. "I only ever meant it as a metaphor."

Ren leaned in, close enough that he caught the salt of her sweat, the cheap resin of the mask. "Do you want to be in it? The prophecy, I mean. Did you always want to be the main character?"

Vincent flinched, but the question needed answering. He reached for the zine, fingers hovering just above the paper. "No," he said, but it landed limp.

Ren didn't let up. "Then why am I in it? Why does it talk about a vessel unmarked? Why does every version I find match up with what's happening to me?"

Vincent felt the edges of the room closing in. "I don't know. Maybe you're a better protagonist. Maybe the universe got bored and started revising the cast."

"Bullshit," Ren snapped. "You put me here. You knew exactly what would happen."

Vincent found his voice only by picturing Mrs Barley's disappointment if he let the conversation end here. "I never wanted this. For you, or for anyone. I was trying to stop it getting out. That's why I hid the drafts. Why I—"

She cut him off. "But you didn't. You just left it hanging out there, waiting for someone like me to trip over it."

He closed his eyes. "If it helps, I hate myself more than you could ever manage."

Ren studied him, the anger slowly losing out to a kind of grim, sibling empathy. "It doesn't help. But at least you're not lying about it."

She took the zine back, tucking it into her bag. "So what now? We just keep running until the story's bored of us?"

Vincent tried to laugh, but it turned into a cough. "I think that's the plot."

A knock at the alcove door. Vincent jolted; Ren didn't even twitch.

Mrs Barley opened the door with the businesslike briskness of a health inspector who's already failed the premises. "You two," she said. "Now."

They followed her out, Vincent grateful for the distraction, Ren looking like she'd been denied the last word.

Mrs Barley led them to the far end of the balcony, where a massive oil painting hung crooked on the wall. She pointed behind it, careful not to touch the frame. "Look."

Vincent craned over her shoulder. Scratched into the plaster, still wet and glistening in the club's dim light, was the Carmine sigil: three crescents, joined at the centre, encircled by a scrawl of text in a language Vincent barely remembered but instantly recognised as his own. The smell of acrylic hung in the air, cheap and fresh.

Ren reached out, but Mrs Barley stopped her with a sharp, "Don't touch." She produced a torch from her bag and shone it on the glyph. The light caught the edges, picked out red droplets flecking the wall.

Mrs Barley's voice was grim. "Whoever's doing this is here tonight. Watching."

Vincent swallowed. "It's a warning."

"No," Mrs Barley corrected. "It's an invitation."

They stood in silence, the noise from the dance floor suddenly muffled and far away, as if the story had hit pause while they caught up. Ren glanced at Vincent, eyes wide but steady. He wanted to say something—anything—but his mind was full of all the things he'd written, all the endings he'd tried to erase and now couldn't.

Mrs Barley stepped back, tucking the torch away. "We don't run. Not this time."

Ren nodded, and even Vincent found himself agreeing.

The three of them stood before the mark, united by accident and design, as the rest of the club spun on in its oblivious, bloody rhythm.

And, in the quiet that followed, Vincent finally understood: they weren't reading the script anymore.

They were inside it.

TWELVE

Vincent woke to the smell of bleach, a smell so pure and insistent it felt like the air was giving him a nasal enema. For a second he lay there, eyes squeezed tight, hoping that if he just ignored the smell hard enough it would resolve into the more familiar stench of burnt toast or, ideally, nothing at all. But the universe, as always, failed to read the memo.

The flat echoed with the sound of Mrs Barley taking something out on the kitchen. The rhythm was unmistakable: not the half-hearted dabbing of normal cleaning, but the sort of scrubbing that was an act of war. Vincent checked the clock (ten past seven, which was either heroic or criminal depending on how you felt about early evening), considered hiding under the covers, then groaned and swung his legs out of bed. The carpet was cold, gritty with the confetti of past disasters.

He found Mrs Barley hunched in front of the fridge, her whole body squared for combat. She wore a starched navy apron over a tartan housecoat, the apron's pocket bristling with cleaning implements—spray bottle, sponge, a wooden spoon that had never once been used for food. Her hair was up in its usual silver scaffolding, but several pins had come loose in the heat of the moment.

Vincent cleared his throat. "I take it we've had a biohazard incident?"

Mrs Barley didn't look up, just attacked a spot on the fridge door as if it might sprout legs and run for Parliament. "You could say that."

"Do I want details?"

She wrung out the cloth, knuckles white. "Check for yourself."

She jerked her chin at the fridge. The gesture was so curt it nearly counted as physical assault.

Vincent opened the door, bracing for something that would set the tone for his entire week. Instead, he found the usual parade of leftovers and crime-scene yoghurt, but nestled between his personal stash of AB Negative, (for special occasions—weddings, bar mitzvahs, Liverpool winning the league etc.) and a suspiciously large jar of gherkins, sat a sheet of paper so thick it could have doubled as a riot shield.

He plucked it out, careful not to touch the wet edge. The page was heavy, expensive, the kind of paper that made you feel guilty for not writing something significant. The text, which covered both sides in a slashing, angular hand, was the colour of old rust and unmistakably not ink.

Vincent's pulse spiked, then settled into a dull, familiar irritation.

He scanned the top lines, mouthing the words to himself.

"'*The cup spills, but not for thirst. The vein runs but not for hunger. Let the chorus sharpen their teeth, for the end comes not with the whisper, but with the wail.'"* He glanced down at the bottom margin, where three glyphs had been stamped so hard the paper buckled. "Nice. Subtle."

Mrs Barley made a noise like she was strangling a hedgehog. "So?"

Vincent closed the fridge, holding the page at arm's length as if it might be radioactive.

Vincent looked at the edge of the paper, then at his fingers. They'd picked up a faint smear of brownish-red, tacky and unpleasant. "Right. Well. At least they're using decent stock."

Mrs Barley's eyes narrowed, sharpening her features to an edge not even industrial bleach could blunt. "You've been writing those... poems again."

"Cult poems," she continued, voice clipped as a guillotine. "The ones you said you'd stopped after the Bishop incident."

Vincent let the accusation hover for a beat. "This isn't mine."

Mrs Barley looked like she'd been served a bowl of cold vomit. "It's in your handwriting."

Vincent stared at the script, then flicked his gaze up at her. "It's an imitation. Flattering, if you ignore the obvious psychological instability."

Mrs Barley snorted. "You'd know."

Vincent ignored the dig, studying the sheet with the forensic gloom of a man reading his own bad reviews. The text was dense, written in alternating blocks of English and what might have been Latin but had mutated somewhere in the margins. At intervals, marginal notes slithered into the gaps, written in a looping script that tried and failed to look like his own.

He read another line aloud, voice gone brittle. "'*The scribe's hunger outlives the body. The story feeds, even as the ink curdles.*'"

Mrs Barley wiped her hands on a tea towel that had once been white and now bore the stains of a hundred unsolved mysteries. "What does it mean?"

Vincent set the page on the counter, pressing his fingertips into the paper until they almost broke through. "It's a performance piece. Or a prophecy. Or both. But it's not mine."

Mrs Barley perched on the edge of a chair, folding her arms like a judge at a war crimes tribunal. "If it's not yours, why did it end up in our fridge?"

Vincent wished he could say "coincidence," but the word caught in his throat. "Someone wants me to see it. Wants us to see it." He tapped the corner of the page, where the Carmine triple crescent gleamed faintly. "They're sending a message."

Mrs Barley's face didn't move, but her eyes flicked to the hallway, the back door, the windows—assessing exits, as always.

"You going to tell the others?"

Vincent shrugged, then regretted it. "They'll know soon enough. Ren can't walk past a fridge without getting existential."

Mrs Barley snorted. "So, what do we do? Wait for the next delivery?"

He glanced at the clock, realising he'd been up for less than ten minutes and already the night was demanding answers. "We keep the page. Maybe Zara can analyse it. Or, at the very least, we wait for the inevitable sequel."

Mrs Barley grunted, then returned to scrubbing the fridge with even more intent. "If this stains the door, you're replacing the whole thing."

"I'll add it to the list."

He started to leave, but Mrs Barley's voice stopped him at the threshold.

"Vincent," she said, so quietly it could have been a warning or a prayer. "Don't start writing them again. Please."

He hesitated, then nodded once.

"Wasn't planning on it," he said, but the words tasted like a lie.

Ren arrived to the kitchen in mid-argument, though for once her opponent appeared to be the cup of coffee clenched in her right hand. She jabbed it against her teeth with each syllable, as if daring the mug to contradict her, while her left worked the phone at a speed that would have impressed the average bookie. Her hair was at maximum caffeine elevation, curls quivering with the static charge of someone who'd started the day with Red Bull and a point to prove.

She stopped in the doorway, one eyebrow cocked. "Am I interrupting a murder, or is this just spring cleaning?"

Mrs Barley, still engaged in her one-woman war against the fridge, replied without looking up. "Ask him." She thumbed at Vincent, who was hunched over the kitchen table with the thick parchment spread in front of him, expression somewhere between forensic analyst and dog that's just been shown a magic trick.

Ren advanced, coffee held out like a police badge. "That better not be another—" She stopped, eyes narrowing. "Is that written in... blood?"

Vincent, for lack of a better tactic, pushed the sheet her way. "Congratulations. You're the new reader in residence."

Ren set down her cup, wiped her hands on her jeans, and bent over the document. The muscles in her jaw tightened with each line. "It's not just a poem," she said, voice gone thin and flat. She traced a finger along the left margin, careful not to touch the sticky edge. "This is a script for a play. There are cues —stage directions—'exit, pursued by hunger.' Some of it's in code, or—"

"It's Old Slavonic, but with more sarcasm. From *The Crimson Masque*. Last great effort before the Order banned me from live theatre. They read it as prophecy, or at least as a how-to manual."

Ren read on, lips moving silently, then looked up. "This is the penultimate scene. The one before the massacre." She jabbed at a line. "But these are new. I don't remember you telling me about any of this."

"Because I didn't," Vincent said. "It's new. Somebody's made alterations. Freely, and with no sense of genre consistency."

Mrs Barley, now rinsing her hands with the savagery of Lady Macbeth, snapped a tea towel at a spot on the worktop and said, "So, they're improvising. Lovely."

Ren squinted at the page again, now with the care of

someone searching for land mines. "Who's the extra character? 'The Phantom Author?' That's not you?"

Vincent shook his head. "I always wrote myself out by Act Three. The rest was meant to be a warning, not an audition."

Ren's phone chimed. She ignored it. "So we've got a killer with access to your back catalogue, a taste for symbolism, and a strong opinion on the importance of rehearsal. Anything else?"

Vincent took the sheet, flipped it over. "They left a note." He pointed to the margin, where a single word, block-capped and still tacky, had been scrawled in a different hand.

SOON.

Ren, coffee back in hand, lifted her cup in mock salute. "To progress."

Vincent allowed himself a half-smile, then set the sheet down with exaggerated care. "It's not progress. It's escalation."

They sat in silence, all three, watching the script as if it might perform itself. The fridge, its battle over, resumed humming in the background—a drone that was suddenly louder than before, as if even the appliances had clocked what was coming.

Vincent stared at the word, the lines of it still wet, bleeding through the page.

"Soon," he said, voice dry as dust.

Ren nodded. "Yeah," she said. "But probably not soon enough."

And for a moment, the kitchen held its breath, all three of them waiting for the next cue.

THIRTEEN

The severed head was back.

Not in the existential sense—Vincent had already lost that particular game of metaphysics—but in the very literal, very real, very damp sense of a human cranium on his top fridge shelf, perched between the value tub of Greek yoghurt and the Sriracha with the crusty nozzle. It rested on a fresh sheet of wax paper like a butcher's special, the slow ooze of what was once neck seeping through the folds and pooling in a small, dignified lake inside the cherry tomato container below. Someone (almost certainly Vincent, though plausible deniability was all he had left) had nudged the head's chin upwards, so its cloudy, half-lidded eyes stared directly out whenever the fridge was opened.

Which is how Ren found it at 19:42, on her way to steal what she assumed was the last edible banana in the building.

She stood there, door agape, the cold light painting her face the kind of blue usually reserved for embalming fluid and first-date nerves. For a long moment, she said nothing. Then she reached in, grabbed the banana, and closed the door with a soft, patient click.

Vincent was already in the kitchen, propped against the counter, arms folded and face set to "nonchalant," which fooled no one but the man himself. He watched her with the wary politeness of a housecat who's just toppled a priceless vase and is waiting to see if anyone's noticed.

Ren pointed a thumb fridge-ward. "Is there an explanation for the severed head, or do we just roll with it?"

Vincent's mouth worked for a second. Then: "It's not mine."

Ren considered this. "You've said that before. It keeps not being true."

He gave a shrug that could've doubled as a seizure. "I can explain the provenance, if you want. I just didn't want to spoil your dinner."

Ren regarded the banana, then the fridge, then Vincent. "Mate, it's a bit late for 'spoil' as a concept." She made her way to the table, dragging a chair out with a booted foot. "I'm assuming it's recent?"

Vincent nodded, grateful for the implied timeline. "Appeared again a couple of hours ago. Wrapped, as you saw. Mrs Barley has already disposed of it once. The night you darkened our doorstep, in fact."

Ren perched on the edge of the chair, arms folded over her chest like a court stenographer at a particularly lively inquest. "Was it addressed to you? Or is this a generic threat?"

"Just the head. No card. No context. Not even a witty Post-it."

The fridge hummed on, content in its role as the world's coldest trophy case.

Ren picked at the banana, but her attention was fixed on Vincent. "Who is it?"

Vincent closed his eyes. "The head? Ex-cultist, I think. Name of Maximus. Or at least, that's what he called himself in the emails. He was heavy on the Carmine glyphs, light on basic grammar."

Ren whistled, low. "So, prophecy drama?"

"Almost certainly."

She considered, then said: "Are you going to do anything about it, or is this just the new normal?"

Vincent tapped his fingers against his elbow, a fidget that had worn a dent in the skin over centuries. "I was giving it an hour. Sometimes they reattach, or sprout legs, or just—" He made a vague, upward gesture, "evaporate."

Ren made a face. "Has that worked before?"

He thought. "Once, in 1910. But it left a stain."

Ren took a bite of banana. "We could just call the police."

Vincent's laugh was all throat. "Yes, let's. Hello, officer, someone has sent me the decapitated head of an occultist, again. Oh, and by the way, please don't look too closely at the bite marks on the skull."

Ren chewed, undeterred. "What would you do if you weren't... y'know. Undead, implicated, etcetera?"

"I'd drink," Vincent said, deadpan. "But you seem to be on a sober streak, so let's brainstorm."

Ren threw the banana skin into the bin, then paced the kitchen, trainers squeaking against the tiles. "Okay. First, we need gloves. Maybe tongs."

Vincent's eyebrows made a spirited dash for his hairline. "You want to move it?"

She gestured, exasperated. "It's in the fridge with the food, Vincent. The cucumbers are already fucked. If we leave it, Mrs Barley 'll just incinerate the whole kitchen and us with it."

He considered. "She would, at that."

Ren opened a cupboard and retrieved a box of latex gloves. She slipped them on, snapping the wrists with the smugness of a television coroner. "We bag it, bin it, and bleach the shelf. Sound good?"

Vincent nodded, and for a brief moment, the kitchen felt almost like a normal workplace: colleagues, task, mild occupational hazard.

Ren opened the fridge and extracted the head, cradling it in her hands like a gruesome rugby ball. The expression was stuck between confusion and surprise—a look Vincent had seen on many a cultist before things turned irretrievably weird.

She set it on the table, then frowned, leaning in. "There's something on the back. Looks burned in."

Vincent squinted. Sure enough, above the ragged neck stump, a new symbol had been branded into the flesh: a triangle inside a crescent, lines radiating outward like a crude sun. The edges were still raw, the shape clean and deliberate.

Ren pointed at it. "This mean anything?"

Vincent's pulse skipped, a physical impossibility that still managed to disconcert. "It's an invocation mark," he said, voice thin. "Old one. Pre-dates Carmine. Whoever left this—left him —wanted me to find it."

"Lucky I'm here then, isn't it," Ren said.

She prodded the head, careful not to touch the wound. "So it's a message. But why deliver it in person? Email's faster."

Vincent didn't answer right away. He studied the mark, the way the burn cut into the scalp, the way the symbol seemed to crawl under the skin. "Sometimes the medium is the message," he said at last. "And sometimes it's a warning."

Ren leaned back, gloves smeared with residue. "What, like a love note? *'Roses are red, blood is divine, here's a severed head, now please be mine'*?"

Vincent didn't laugh. "Worse," he said, barely above a whisper. "It's a threat. And now I think I know who left it."

The fridge hummed louder, as if eager to get in the last word. Ren watched Vincent with a look that suggested she had, in fact, expected all of this, but had hoped for at least a day off before the next crisis.

The head didn't blink.

Vincent let the silence stretch, holding it between thumb and forefinger like a relic, before finally giving it up for lost. He sat at the kitchen table, elbows planted either side of a chipped cork placemat, hands steepled as if in prayer to a god he had long since written out of his own canon. The fridge, that chthonic idol, whirred behind him. The head was back inside now, double-bagged and zipped into the salad drawer, but its presence lingered: an audience of one, awaiting confession.

Ren cleared her throat, the first to blink in their staring contest with the void. "You going to tell me what that symbol was?" she said, voice tight with the effort of pretending this was Tuesday business as usual.

Vincent's eyes dropped to the table. He ran his thumb over a burn mark, the crescent of an old cigarette, and let his mind tumble back through the decades.

He didn't speak for a long time.

"I was young," he began, which, coming from Vincent, could cover anywhere from the Black Death to the tail end of the 1890s. "Stupid, in the way only immortals get. When you realise you can outlive consequences, you start treating history like a blackboard."

Ren watched, unmoving, as he wound the story out. The kitchen light flickered above him, casting deep bruises under his eyes.

"The Order of the Veil," he said at last. "You've heard of them?"

Ren nodded, slow. "Human cultists. The ones who think vampires are, like, misunderstood saints."

Vincent's lips twisted, the memory soured. "They were never vampires, not really. Just Renfields with ambition."

"Renfields?"

"Human fixers, feeders, fanatics. They wanted to serve. To be part of something." His voice dropped, the words scraping up his throat like dry bread. "They wanted a prophecy. A real one. So they found me."

Ren blinked. "You?"

He shrugged, self-mocking. "I was good with words. Had a reputation, back then. If you wanted to invent a messiah, you hired a proper ghostwriter."

She considered, then: "So you made the prophecy?"

Vincent barked a laugh, sharp and hollow. "No one makes a prophecy, Ren. You just take the stories people already tell themselves and give them a plot twist and slap on some compelling cover art." He flexed his fingers, knuckles creaking. "They had a whole setup: secret meetings, an underground press, elaborate rituals with too much incense and not enough self-awareness. I thought it was all a joke. Performance art. Until it wasn't."

He let the memory fill the room. The kitchen dropped away, replaced by the recollection of a crypt: a low, airless vault beneath a derelict church, the ceiling so close you could touch the mildew with your breath. Dozens of them, faces painted white, hoods drawn tight, candles burning to stumps in a ring around the altar. They hung on his every word, hungry for meaning, for magic, for a reason to exist beyond waiting tables and lurking on message boards.

He could see himself, ninety years younger, standing at the centre with a sheaf of pages in one hand and a glass of cheap communion wine in the other. Reading aloud the gospel he'd written for them: the legend of Carmine, the Great Bloodline, the triple-crescent mark. The part where the world ended, but only after the right people had been let in on the secret.

"They treated it like scripture," Vincent said. "I kept thinking they'd break character, laugh, go home to their tenement flats. But they didn't."

The air in the crypt had been thick with sweat and anticipation. He'd seen it then, a moment too late: the shift from theatre to liturgy. The way the crowd's collective gaze fixed not on him, but through him, as if the script had taken on a life of its own.

"One of them tried to stage the first ritual," Vincent said.

"Real blood. Real death." He looked at Ren, a rawness in his eyes that the kitchen light couldn't bleach out. "They didn't even get the words right. They just wanted it to mean something."

Ren's voice was very small. "What happened?"

He gave a little half-shrug, the gesture of a man whose skeleton was mostly composed of old regrets. "I walked out. Burned every copy, every note. Left them with nothing but a rumour."

He hadn't expected it to survive him. But then, immortals never did.

Ren let him have the quiet for a bit. She'd stopped pacing, arms folded so tight her hands dug into the soft of her sides. "So that new mark," she said. "You recognise it."

Vincent nodded, the motion heavy. "They called it the Unmasking. Sign of the End Times, or at least the end of the story. Supposed to summon the author, so he can write the last act."

Ren glanced at the fridge. "And the head is..."

"A calling card." Vincent forced a smile, brittle as the ice in the freezer. "They want me to finish what I started."

The fridge clicked, compressor grinding into a higher gear. Somewhere in the pipes, air bubbles raced and popped, as if the building itself was bracing for bad news.

Ren picked at the edge of the table. "Do you want to?"

Vincent looked up, sharp, as if the question itself was an accusation. "God, no. I never wanted to. But they don't care." He hesitated, the weight of old words pressing down on his tongue. "They never did."

He let his head fall forward, the heel of his hands digging

into his brow. "I should have seen it coming," he muttered. "But it's always the sequel that ruins the franchise."

Ren snorted, a sound that came out more like a sob. "So what now?"

Vincent's mouth twisted into something like resolve. "Now? We bin the head again, and maybe change the locks."

Ren stood, fetched a bin bag, and held it out with the businesslike composure of a hospital orderly. "You do the honours," she said. "I'll get the bleach."

Vincent took the bag, hands steady now. The light overhead flickered once, then held, the kitchen briefly brighter than it had been all morning.

He opened the fridge, cradled the ziplocked head in both hands, and deposited it in the bag, careful not to let it roll or spill. As he cinched the plastic tight, he caught a last glimpse of the branded symbol—still raw, still glistening, still waiting for its cue.

Ren returned with the bleach and a rag. They worked in silence, scouring away every trace of the visitor. The fridge, at least, would remember nothing.

When the job was done, Vincent stood at the back door, bin bag in one hand, the other braced against the frame. He stared out at the night sky, then back at Ren. "You don't have to stay with me," he said, not quite a whisper.

Ren shrugged, slumped into a chair. "Not like I've got somewhere better to be. Besides," she added, "somebody's got to make sure you don't start writing again."

Vincent gave her a look. "If I do, please shoot me."

Ren grinned, a thin slice of mirth. "Deal."

The fridge was clean, the head gone, but the story lingered, hovering in the air between them.

Somewhere, in the city's deepest archive or its shallowest grave, the Order of the Veil was waiting. And Vincent, for all his protest, knew he would answer.

But for now, he watched the sky brighten by degrees, felt the burn of bleach on his hands, and tried very hard not to remember how good it had once felt to be worshipped.

FOURTEEN

The first thing Vincent noticed about Ren's flat was the smell. Not the usual landfill bouquet of unwashed cups and tragic curry, though those lingered like a recurring trauma, but something sharper and older—incense, he guessed, though not the aspirational kind that promised serenity or cheap enlightenment. More like patchouli mixed with printer toner and a note of burnt hair.

He stood just inside the door, arms crossed, observing as Ren made a circuit of the room, trailing chaos in her wake. There were books, thousands of them, all occult or pseudo-occult or the sort of self-published treatise that came with a warning and an aftertaste. Notes wallpapered every vertical surface; yellow stickies colonised the fridge, the TV, even the inside of the window blinds. At the centre of it all, a battered encyclopaedia sat open, bleeding scraps of lined paper like a gut-shot animal.

Ren didn't pace so much as ricochet, bounce, and collapse

in increments. She was still in the hoodie she'd been in all week, but now she'd layered a T-shirt over it, bearing the slogan "Cult Survivor – Ask Me How," and paired with leggings that might once have been black. She had a biro clenched in her teeth and a phone in each hand, thumbs flickering between a Generative AI chat window and what appeared to be a Romanian message board for insomniac conspiracy theorists.

Vincent tried not to touch anything. "Have you considered the possibility," he said, "that your filing system is itself a summoning ritual? There are at least three chaos sigils within reach of my left elbow."

Ren didn't look up. "Don't be precious. I've seen your flat. Your idea of filing is 'stack until collapse, then hope you die first.'" She stabbed at her phone, scrolling with the urgency of someone negotiating a ransom. "Besides, this is active research. Don't touch the blue folder. It bites."

He studied the piles. The blue folder was wedged at an angle between a German monograph on blood rites and a battered paperback called *Vampires: Real, Imagined, or Just Really Good at Lying?* The latter had been annotated in three colours and was bristling with enough index tabs to flag an entire bookshop for demolition.

Ren stopped dead, then reversed course and plucked a dog-eared pamphlet from the bookshelf. "Here," she said, waving it at Vincent like a loaded wand. "Found another match for the invocation. Third paragraph, second line. Carmine triple-crescent plus the old phoneme for 'devour'." She flipped it open, then shoved it at him without warning.

He took it gingerly. The page in question was crowded with runes, some of which had been circled with a heavy, angry hand. At the margin, someone had written in all caps: "IF THIS IS A JOKE, IT'S NOT FUNNY."

Vincent said, "You know most of this is nonsense, right? Half of it was written by bored Victorians on laudanum."

"Good," Ren replied, already back at the whiteboard, which had been repurposed from a failed home fitness regime. "So you'll feel right at home."

He let her have that one. "I mean it," he said, following her with his eyes. "There are more fake grimoires in circulation than there are people who've ever actually done magic. Or whatever you want to call what I do."

Ren spun, marker in hand, and jabbed at a cluster of words in the top-right corner. "You don't do magic. You just make everyone else believe you do. It's the same as writing, just with more self-loathing."

He grinned, despite himself. "That's cruel. Accurate, but cruel."

She chewed the biro, then uncapped the marker and added a fresh circle around the phrase *Vessel: mutable?* "There's a pattern," she said, speaking mostly to the air. "Every time this sigil turns up, it's in the context of a transfer. Blood, text, sometimes both. But the thing I can't figure out is what happens to the vessel. Does it survive? Does it even want to?"

Vincent shrugged, affecting indifference. "It's a metaphor, usually. They want to believe in immortality, so they graft a story onto someone else and hope the audience is buying."

She turned, and her eyes were sharper than her voice. "Have you ever actually seen it used?"

He hesitated. "Once. Maybe twice. It's not the sort of thing you forget."

Ren waited, arms folded, her posture an open dare.

Vincent examined the marker in his hand as if hoping for answers. "Last time I saw the sigil used properly, it was at a crypt in Lyon. Nineteen... forty-two, I think." He paused, letting the memory fill the room, pushing out some of the incense. "The guy who hosted was a priest, or claimed to be. Whole congregation, all in on the show. The vessel was a woman from the Balkans—Serbian, maybe. She didn't speak, just let them draw the mark. They did the ritual, drank the blood, tore up the script, the usual fanfare."

Ren's voice was thin. "And then?"

He looked up, mouth twitching. "And then she exploded."

Ren blinked. "You mean—?"

Vincent nodded, relishing her discomfort just enough to take the edge off his own. "Well. Technically, she imploded first, then exploded. Details matter."

A beat passed, in which both tried to process the logistics of spontaneous cultist combustion.

Ren picked up her coffee, took a long sip, and grimaced. "What happened to the priest?"

Vincent considered. "He survived. Lasted another two years before the Nazis shot him. Claimed it was all performance art. The locals didn't agree."

She scrawled a note on the whiteboard, the word "combustion" underlined twice. "So what happens if this lot actually pulls it off? What if they're not just cosplaying?"

He watched her, the way her fingers drummed the marker, the way she never quite met his eyes when the questions got big. "You're worrying about the wrong outcome," he said. "The risk isn't the vessel going off. The risk is the story gets out, and people start believing. That's always when things go bad."

Ren didn't answer. Instead, she moved to the window, peeled the blinds back with two fingers, and stared out at the city. The view was rubbish: another estate block, streaked with the weather, and an endless parade of pigeons looking for a place to die.

"Do you think they're watching us?" she said.

Vincent said, "They always are. Especially when you think they're not."

She shut the blinds, turned back, and looked at the sprawl of notes and books. "If this is all a game," she said, "why does it feel like we're losing?"

Vincent smiled, but it didn't quite reach his eyes. "Because we are. That's how you know it's real."

She made a fist of the marker, held it tight. "I want to burn it. All of it. Just walk away."

He shrugged. "You could. But someone else would pick it up. Stories don't go away just because you stop telling them."

Ren slumped onto the sofa, the springs protesting under the new weight. "So what's our move?"

Vincent leaned against the wall, surveying the battlefield. "We keep reading. We keep watching. And when the next head shows up, we hope it's not ours."

Ren snorted, a sound halfway between laugh and sob. "That's bleak."

"Realistic," he corrected. He checked the time, though he already knew it was far too late for anything healthy. "Want me to make tea?"

She shook her head. "There's whisky in the cupboard. Top shelf, behind the cereal."

He retrieved it, poured two fingers into a mug with the slogan "I'd Rather Be Cursed Than Mundane," and passed it to her. She accepted with a grateful nod, then sipped, grimaced, and said, "So. You've seen people die for this before. Think it'll be different this time?"

Vincent stared at the far wall, where a spider was mounting an expedition across three competing Post-its. "It never is," he said, and finished his own drink.

They sat in silence, the only sound the low, percussive hum of the radiator and the distant, echoing siren of an ambulance late for its appointment. The room was warmer than before, and the incense had faded to a background note of something almost like comfort.

Ren yawned, curled into the corner of the sofa, and let her eyes slide shut. Vincent watched her for a moment, then made his way to the door, careful to step around the blue folder.

He paused at the threshold, one hand on the frame.

"They won't win," he said. "Not if we stay ahead."

She didn't open her eyes, but her lips curled into a tired, wry smile. "I'll hold you to that, Lupo."

He closed the door gently behind him, the words hanging in the air like a binding contract.

Outside, the world was damp and directionless, the streetlights burning holes in the night.

He walked home, not hurrying, and let the city tell itself the next chapter.

The club had no name. If it ever did, it had drowned years ago under the tide of graffiti, blood spatters, and the kind of notoriety that made Google Maps mark the building as "Private Event—Do Not Enter." Vincent never needed directions, anyway; like all things feral and forbidden, the club called to him on a frequency just shy of audible, a pulse in the base of his skull that sharpened the closer he got to the river.

The entrance was a shipping container welded onto the rear of an abandoned warehouse. The bouncer was built like a siege engine, arms folded tight enough to deform his own tattoos. He clocked Vincent, looked past him, then back at Vincent as if recalibrating the threat assessment.

Vincent gave him a nod, a baring of teeth, and the bouncer stepped aside without a word. There were perks to being a known quantity in a scene where "known" rarely ended well for any party.

Inside, the club was a long, wet corridor leading to a hole-in-the-floor staircase, its descent marked by increasingly desperate attempts at decor. Every metre traded fire safety for atmosphere: exposed wires, bare bulbs, velvet ropes stained with old joy, walls sweating condensation that dripped in time with the bass. By the time he reached the bottom, the air was half oxygen, half expectation, and entirely hostile to sobriety.

Vincent paused at the threshold, letting his eyes adjust to the red. Blood-red, the colour of memory, the colour clubs all aspired to but rarely earned. The music was industrial, or something pretending to be—slammed-together beats and sampled screams, vibrating through the floorboards, rewriting the bones of anyone close enough to feel it. The crowd was a chorus of pale, sharp faces and sharper teeth. Even the ones who weren't vampires had learned to dress like they wanted to be asked.

He scanned for Lucien, found him immediately. Some people never change, even if they switched gender, wardrobe, or personal mythology every other week. Lucien was sprawled in a corner booth, glass of something viscous and crimson in one hand, a phone in the other. His look was pure vampire magpie: mesh vest, silver chains, enough piercings to warrant a metal detector. Under the lighting, his skin shimmered with the faint iridescence of the newly-turned, or the dangerously bored.

Vincent threaded the crowd, ignoring the hands that grazed his arm or the invitations tossed with every sideways glance. He didn't belong here, not anymore, but belonging was overrated and never paid well.

He slid into the booth across from Lucien, the pleather seat sticking to the backs of his thighs like a thirsty leech.

Lucien didn't look up at first, but the grin was already waiting for him. "Vincent. As I live and un-breathe. Thought you were off the menu."

"I was," Vincent said, signalling the bartender for a drink. "Then someone left a head in my fridge. Twice. Thought I'd return the favour."

Lucien laughed, sharp enough to take a thumb off. "You always did have a way with gifts." He sipped his drink, licked a bead of it from his lower lip. "So what brings you to my little oubliette? Slumming it, or just hungry for the nostalgia?"

Vincent watched the dance floor, where a couple in identical latex catsuits were trying to out-murder each other with their eyes. "I need information. You're still plugged in, aren't you?"

Lucien made a performance of weighing the question. "Depends on the market. Depends on the payment. Depends if you plan on actually paying, for once."

The bartender arrived, set down a glass with something the consistency of cough syrup and the provenance of a biohazard. Vincent sniffed it, made a face, drank anyway. "Heard of the Order of the Veil?" he said.

Lucien's eyes flicked up, the smile sharpening. "Old blood. Very old blood. You're a few centuries out of date, darling. That lot's just a cautionary tale now."

Vincent fished into his coat, pulled out the glyph. He'd copied it onto a napkin, but even the napkin looked afraid to be in the same postcode as its own ink. He slid it across the table, watching Lucien's fingers twitch as he reached for it.

Lucien picked it up, held it to the light. "You shouldn't have brought that here," he said, voice suddenly flat. "You really, really shouldn't have."

"And yet," Vincent said, "here we are."

Lucien set the napkin down, careful to avoid skin contact. "There are people in this room who'd murder you for less."

"I know," Vincent said. "I'm counting on it."

Lucien sipped, chewed the inside of his cheek. "There's a rumour. The Old Work is coming back. Someone's trying to finish what Carmine started, only this time, it's not about prophecy. It's about architecture."

Vincent blinked, slow. "Go on."

Lucien nodded. "They're building something. Something

sacred, something violent. The blueprint is in blood, the bricks are bodies, and every foundation needs a cornerstone."

Vincent felt the room tilt, just a touch. "Who's running it?"

Lucien shook his head. "No names, just a title. The Bloodbard." He smirked. "Thought that would amuse you."

It didn't. If anything, it made Vincent's stomach drop through the seat and into the nearest storm drain. "That's not possible."

Lucien grinned, too many teeth, all for show. "Isn't it? You wrote the prophecy. Maybe the story just wants a rewrite."

Vincent palmed the glass, knuckles white. "So what—this Bloodbard wants to finish the old script? Start a new one? Bring the end times with a better soundtrack?"

Lucien leaned in, dropping the camp. "They think you're a god, Vincent. Or a demon. Honestly, I'm not sure there's much difference anymore."

He wanted to laugh, or scream, or throw the glass in Lucien's face, but all the energy drained out of him like water through a sieve. "You believe any of it?"

Lucien shrugged, elegant. "I believe in self-interest. But if you're asking whether people are going to die for this—" he gestured at the napkin, "—then yes. It's already started."

The music peaked, a howling wall of distortion. Vincent let it shake through his bones, flattening any resistance he might have been saving for later. "What's the next step?"

Lucien leaned back, flashing a pair of canines that had not been store-bought. "You're the writer, Lupo. What would you do?"

He didn't answer. Not here, not now, not with the ghosts of a hundred failed drafts drifting through the club's recycled air.

He stood, leaving the drink unfinished. "If anyone comes asking about me, tell them I'm dead. Or that I'm in the market for a better ending."

Lucien inclined his head, a parody of respect. "Always a pleasure. Try not to get yourself beheaded."

Vincent walked out, feeling the weight of the club's gaze on his shoulders, the napkin burning a hole in his pocket. The bouncer at the door eyed him, then nodded as if nothing in the world could surprise him anymore.

Outside, the river was a slick, black artery under the streetlights. Vincent stood at the edge, fished a cigarette from his coat, and lit it with hands that didn't quite stop trembling.

He thought about the Bloodbard. The name tasted like a punchline, a joke he'd made up in a fit of literary pique two hundred years ago. Now it was stalking the city, building a cathedral of corpses, and dragging him back into the centre of the story.

He smoked down to the filter, flicked it into the river, and watched the ember spiral out before the darkness swallowed it whole.

Then he walked, fast and purposeless, letting the city catch up with him.

FIFTEEN

Vincent was at the window, looking out over the silent street, when the front door slammed open and Ren barrelled through, bringing a microclimate of North Circular drizzle with her. She tracked muddy prints across the hall, shrugged her coat onto the banister (directly atop his, which twitched with residual damp), and shouldered her way into the lounge without so much as a "hello." In her wake, the flat's faint aura of bleach and surrender was instantly replaced with the reek of wet wool and the brighter, more reckless energy of someone who'd just found evidence and was absolutely about to use it as a bludgeon.

She carried her laptop clutched under one arm like a reliquary, the other still gripping a Red Bull can that, from the looks of it, had been drained and refilled with an even more sinister substance. She took a swig, wiped her mouth with her sleeve, and glared at Vincent as if he were personally responsible for the weather, the bins, and every locked door in her life.

"Could have texted," he said. "Or, you know, knocked."

Ren's eyes sparkled, feral. "No time for pleasantries. We've got a situation." She flung herself onto the sofa, boots up, limbs splayed with proprietary disregard for the upholstery. "And I'm not even going to try and sugar-coat it, because frankly, you don't deserve it."

Vincent leaned against the wall, arms folded, already resigned. "I'm not sure I can handle a crisis before dinner."

"Good," she snapped, "because you're about to lose your appetite." She swung the laptop round, thumbed the trackpad with the flourish of a game show host, and spun it to face him. "Recognise this?"

Vincent squinted. The screen showed a scan of a battered, yellowing playbill, its headline in gothic font: *THE CRIMSON MASQUE—A Play in One Act*. Below, a listing of cast members ("V. Lupo as Himself" in first billing), a rehearsal photo, and—just beneath that—a hand-drawn glyph, three crescents in the exact configuration he'd last seen branded on the back of Maximus's skull.

He blinked. "You're joking."

Ren's grin was all teeth. "Wish I was." She jabbed the screen. "Turns out your mysterious murder cult is, and I quote, *'an avant-garde performance collective from the late nineteen-twenties.'* They were meant to do one show, a sort of proto-immersive theatre thing, but the company imploded before opening night. Because, and this is my favourite part, three actors vanished during the final dress rehearsal. No one knows if it was a stunt, a mass resignation, or a publicity-seeking death pact. But the script survived, and so did the legend."

Vincent ran a hand through his hair. "You're saying this is all just bad theatre?"

Ren shrugged. "Isn't everything?" She drained the can, crushed it in her fist. "But here's the kicker: the invocation sigil, the blood rituals, all of it—straight out of the script. They even used your bloody name."

He tried to laugh, but the sound caught in his throat. "Theatre people. They're even worse than cultists."

Ren flicked to the next page, where a tattered scan of the original script was annotated with a fury of red pen and highlighter. "I spent half the night trawling through university archives and conspiracy blogs. Turns out there's an entire subculture obsessed with reconstructing the lost play. They call it 'Bloodbard's Folly.' Some believe it's cursed. Others think it's the key to immortality. The only thing they all agree on is that it's supposed to be staged in full, with no interruptions, and that anyone who tries to disrupt the narrative gets—" She pointed to the programme, where three names had been slashed through with a literal razor, "—removed from the cast."

Vincent looked away, suddenly cold. "This is insane."

Ren grinned. "Welcome to your own afterparty." She closed the laptop, hugging it to her chest. "I thought you'd get a kick out of it. Your legacy, not just undead, but recast as dinner theatre."

He rubbed his eyes. "Was any of it real?"

She shrugged again, less flippant this time. "Does it matter? Someone's making it real now."

They sat in silence, the hum of the fridge competing with the gentle, rhythmic clack of Ren's boots tapping against the coffee table.

Vincent broke first. "When did you find this?"

"About three hours ago. I was trying to work out how the

glyph travelled from the Romania to Camden Town, and the earliest mention was a fringe theatre review in 1926. The reviewer hated it. Called it 'self-indulgent, blood-soaked self-aggrandising nonsense.'"

He winced. "That tracks."

"But then it pops up again in Vienna, and then in Marseille, and each time, there's a rash of unexplained deaths or disappearances. It's like someone's been shopping the script around Europe for a century, looking for the perfect audience."

He slumped onto the nearest chair, which wheezed under the sudden weight. "And the best anyone could do was a severed head in my fridge."

Ren wagged a finger. "You joke, but the fridge thing? That's a stage direction. *'The author's head shall remain on ice until the penultimate act.'*" She pulled up the scanned script and read, "*Scene Twelve: 'The scribe's hunger outlives the body. The story feeds, even as the ink curdles.'*"

He stared at her, then at the wall behind her, as if the old plaster might start seeping stage blood in protest. "It was supposed to be parody," he muttered. "They were supposed to laugh."

She looked at him, softening slightly. "Well, they didn't. And now someone's taking it very seriously."

Rain started up again, beating against the window in double time. Ren watched the droplets trace desperate routes down the glass, then said, "You ever think about what happens if they succeed? If they finish the script?"

He thought about it. Thought about the last time he'd seen the play performed, the way the audience sat in stunned silence, not sure whether to applaud or start praying. Thought about all the words he'd written that were never meant to outlive him.

"I don't know," he said. "Maybe nothing. Maybe the world ends with a whimper and a bad review."

She snorted. "You're such a downer."

He managed a weak smile. "Occupational hazard."

Another silence, but this one less oppressive, more a shared hiding place. Ren opened the laptop again, this time scrolling past the scanned script to a digitised archive of clippings, letters, grainy photos of the original troupe—men in blackface paint, women in veils, everyone wearing masks that were neither period nor tastefully ambiguous.

"There's one other thing," she said. "You said you never finished the last act."

He shook his head. "I left it blank. Figured the world could do without another tragedy."

She pointed at the screen. "Well, someone found a copy. Or thinks they did. And they're putting it together now, scene by scene, murder by murder."

He looked at her, suddenly frightened in a way he hadn't been since the vampire purge of 1814. "How do you stop a play?"

She grinned, a little wicked. "Bad acting?"

He actually laughed, the sound surprised out of him. "If only."

They both stared at the laptop for a while, watching as the cursor blinked on the last page of the script—a page still blank, waiting for someone to fill it in.

Eventually, Vincent said, "If they've got the play, they've got the map."

Ren didn't ask, but the question hovered between them anyway.

"To what?" she said, finally.

Vincent looked out at the rain, the dark nothingness of the city. "To everything I've ever regretted," he said, and let the words settle like dust in the gaps between sentences.

They watched the rain together, neither moving, both knowing that as soon as the weather cleared, the real performance would begin.

SIXTEEN

The local cabbies' café at four a.m. was less a business than a holding cell for the freshly released and the terminally restless. The sort of place that replaced sleep with carbs, and social boundaries with communal, caffeinated misery. Vincent and Ren had claimed the back booth by virtue of not giving a damn who else needed it. The table looked like it had been rescued from an archaeological dig and then vandalised by the descendants of everyone who'd ever suffered bad service. Its surface was a palimpsest of keys, knives, and existential sharpies—"*Kill Me*" layered over "*Arsenal 4ever*" layered over "*Angela iz a bitch innit.*" Even the salt shaker had an attitude.

The lighting, a symphony of jaundiced fluorescence, made everyone look like a corpse who'd just heard the world's worst joke. The ceiling flickered in Morse code; the staff, three-quarters asleep and the rest in denial, refilled the filter machine on autopilot. Every thirty minutes a new shift of misfits would slouch in: cabbies, off-duty bouncers, the rare academic up late for reasons unrelated to wisdom. At this hour, the only witness to your secrets was the next insomniac down the line.

Ren wore exhaustion like a badge. Her hoodie was zipped to her chin, hair a defensive explosion under the strip-lit onslaught. She sipped the house blend with theatrical disgust, then topped it up with four sugars, as if daring the diabetes to make a move. In her hands, a freshly printed page: grainy, half-obscured by the original's creases and the forensic enthusiasm of a university scanner. Across the image, red biro arrows, question marks, and a diagonal line that ended in *"OPENING NIGHT APPROACHES"* written in block capitals.

Vincent's first impulse was to order a whisky, but he settled for a flat white, which tasted of ash and something less pleasant. He watched Ren hover the printout above the tacky table, then slide it across like a warning.

"This is your fault," she said.

He scanned the page. The old playbill looked unchanged from the last time he'd seen it, except for the new stigmata of annotation. "You're making me nostalgic for the 1920s," Vincent replied. "And that's not a thing I want to be."

Ren jabbed at the photo. "Look at the names."

He looked. There, beneath the title—*The Crimson Masque, A Tragedy in Blood in One Act*—was a cast list: the usual suspects, half of whom had been dead long before the playbill even circulated. A few names were circled, some crossed out, others punctuated with "?" and *"Alive?"* in increasingly desperate script. The bottom of the sheet bore the legend: *"Troupe de Carmine, in association with Order of the Veil."*

"They're staging it again," Vincent said, voice flat as the coffee.

Ren arched an eyebrow. "You think it's just theatre?"

He sighed, massaged the bridge of his nose. "With this crowd? There'll be bloodletting in the wings, a body count in the stalls, and a glowing portal somewhere between Scenes Ten and Eleven."

She grinned. "That's oddly specific."

"I've seen things, Ren."

She believed him, which was why they were here instead of sleeping. "So, what's the next move?" she asked.

Vincent drummed his fingers on the tabletop. "Either we ignore it and hope the story eats itself, or we try to find the cast and cut them off before opening night."

"Option two," Ren said, sliding a napkin and borrowed pen across the field of battle.

They worked in the sullen silence of co-conspirators. Ren wrote down every name, every alias, every city she could think of—Lisbon, Paris, Cluj-Napoca, Hackney—then began drawing lines like it was an exorcism rather than a flow chart. Vincent supplied details where memory permitted, but most of what he knew had blurred into the general fug of his centuries. The big names were all dead, technically, but "technically" didn't mean what it used to.

After ten minutes, the napkin looked like a murder board designed by a particularly angry spider. Most of the lines ended in "?" or "*Probable*" or "*Missing*." Two names had been high-lighted by accident, via a collision with a ring of coffee. Ren pointed to one. "What about the Bishop?"

"Last seen in Florence," Vincent said. "If he's in London, he's not advertising."

She pointed at another. "the Turkish Princess?"

Vincent shook his head. "Retired to Monaco. Allegedly." He leaned in, voice barely above a whisper. "If this is the Order, they'll use proxies. New faces with old debts."

Ren looked unconvinced, but then, her default mode was to expect the worst and be pleasantly surprised by anything less. She sat back, stretched her legs under the table, and watched the lights war with the darkness beyond the window. The city outside was a slab of black and sodium yellow, the streets running with rain and the echoes of better decisions.

"We could infiltrate," she said.

Vincent nearly choked on his espresso. "You want to audition for the world's most cursed play?"

Ren shrugged, the movement pure North London. "I could pass for a stagehand. Or an understudy."

He shook his head. "Cult theatre people can smell outsiders. It's like cats, but more prone to ritual sacrifice."

Ren grinned, showing the kind of teeth that made her a favourite among people who hated small talk. "You're one of them, though. You wrote the script."

He grimaced. "Which means I'm the last person they'd trust."

She flicked the napkin at him. "You have to go. See how close they are. At least get a look at the new cast."

He toyed with the pen, watching the ink leak onto his fingers. "You realise this is a setup, right? Opening scenes, I get drawn in. the Midpoint, someone gets murdered. The Final scene—"

"We improvise," she said, finishing his sentence. "It's what you do best."

He couldn't argue with that. He'd built a career on improvising—when the plot fell apart, when the money ran out, when the last safe house turned out to be a trap. His life was a series of cold readings and desperate rewrites.

He finished his espresso, set the cup down with a finality that was only slightly undercut by its wobble. "Fine," he said. "I'll go. But if I end up on stage, you have to promise not to heckle."

Ren raised three fingers, Scout's honour, then immediately broke the pledge to flag down the waiter for more coffee.

Vincent stared at the annotated playbill announcing rehearsals at St. Martin's Crypts, the red ink seeping into the old paper, the words vibrating with the urgency of a threat that wasn't quite real until it killed you. The café lights flickered, settled, then flickered again. A chill ran up his spine, but it was the familiar, almost comforting chill of a story coming to life.

He pocketed the napkin, stood, and looked out into the night. Rain hammered the pavement, washing the city clean for the next batch of sinners.

He turned back to Ren, who saluted with her coffee mug. "Break a leg," she said.

He almost smiled. "That's how it always starts," he said, and walked out into the storm.

St. Martin's Crypts stood on the border between dereliction and demolition, a Victorian relic held upright by inertia and petty bureaucracy. Its stone facade was pocked with the scars of old protests, new vandalism, and one memorable attempt to burn the building down in the sixties. Moss smothered the carved cornices. Rain sluiced off the broken roof, pooling in potholes large enough to swallow the local fauna. Even the council had given up, surrendering the entrance to rust and a perimeter fence that suggested "keep out" but delivered it with a sigh rather than a threat.

Vincent skirted the main entrance, shoes squelching through a puddle that had colonised half the pavement. He found the side door unlocked, as expected, and ducked inside. The darkness was immediate and absolute, except for the sliver of light that filtered down the main corridor. He could hear the building breathe: the expansion and contraction of tired wood, the drip and splatter of water working its way from roof to basement, the brittle shiver of spiderwebs disturbed by nothing more than the memory of movement.

He moved with deliberate quiet. His senses stretched out, catching the low hum of voices from the assembly chamber—a blend of ordinary human murmur and something pitched just above, a harmonic that vibrated in the hollow of his skull. It was the sound of people trying to be silent and failing, of secrets rehearsed in whispers.

The corridor opened into the main hall, a rectangular cavern lined with cracked pillars and the ghosts of many hundreds dead and buried. The ceiling, painted with an allegory of an idyllic afterlife, now wept brown tears onto the parquet floor. The temporary stage at the far end was dressed with makeshift curtains—bedsheets dyed a disturbing red—and lit by a motley array of candles and what looked like a pair of battery-powered floodlights, one of which was on the brink of death.

On the stage, a semicircle of figures in crimson masks. They wore street clothes under the costume, but the effect was unnerving: an army of blank faces, mouths frozen in permanent grins. In the centre, a young man in a navy suit, barefoot, mask rimmed with what looked like gold leaf. He held a script, but when he spoke, he didn't read. He performed.

Vincent recognised the monologue before the second word. He'd written it as a joke, a bit of self-indulgent pastiche to pad out a dull expositional scene. Here, the words were weaponised. The cadences were sharper, each phrase slicing through the silence and lodging somewhere unpleasant.

"Blood is a script," the young man intoned, "and all are cast in its shadow. We are born audience, but die as actors, drowned by applause that is not for us."

The others joined in, a call-and-response from the back pages of Vincent's memory:

"Let the ink run. Let the vein open. Let the story feed."

He felt it then, a chill that ran down the line of his spine and settled in his feet. The air in the hall thinned. The candles guttered, drawing long, impossible shadows behind each masked face. The words weren't just words, not anymore. They'd been given teeth.

The monologue built, spiralled, twisted back on itself. Vincent watched as the young man's hands began to shake, the paper trembling in time with his voice. The mask cracked, just a little, at the corner. Sweat darkened the fabric over his mouth. The rest of the troupe drew closer, their own lines echoing, overlapping, a chorus that blurred meaning into rhythm.

Then the boy reached the final line. He spat it, not at the audience—of which there was, at least overtly, only Vincent—but at the empty space above the stage.

"The story ends when you bleed it dry!"

The air shimmered, as if the sound had ripped open a seam in the world. For a second, Vincent saw the ceiling warp, the heavenly mural twisting into something obscene and hungry. The candles burned blue for a heartbeat, then snapped back to orange.

Vincent clung to the wall, knuckles white. He'd been to a thousand rituals, suffered through a hundred bloodlettings, but never had he felt the power so raw, so utterly indifferent to the people wielding it.

He realised, with something like awe and a lot like fear, that these weren't cultists in the old sense. They were fans. The performance was the ritual. Every line, every stage direction, was a spell disguised as a script.

On the stage, the troupe broke their circle. The young man sagged, mask askew, but his eyes were bright and alive and staring directly at Vincent. Around him, the others rearranged the space—set out a chair, a prop skull, what looked like a punch bowl of suspicious provenance. They moved with the efficiency of people who'd practiced this a hundred times, who knew they were being watched.

From the wings, a new figure emerged. Masked, but the mask was black, not red, and the suit it wore was tailored with an extravagance bordering on satire. The figure paused, then turned its face to Vincent. It bowed—slow, mocking, deliberate. Vincent's throat closed.

He knew that bow. He'd seen it in old photos, in memories that wouldn't die even when you staked them through the heart. He'd invented it.

The figure straightened, then vanished backstage.

Vincent made a snap decision: he left before the curtain call.

The corridor was suddenly freezing. He felt the static on his skin, the way the words clung to him like damp. He half expected the moss on the outside walls to be waiting, to embrace him as he fled.

He stumbled out into the car park. The rain was biblical now, an assault from all directions. Ren's battered Peugeot idled at the curb, wipers losing the battle to keep up. She was in the driver's seat, engine running, hood up against the cold. She saw him, flashed her hi-beams and gestured with a tilt of her chin to get in.

He slid into the passenger seat, slammed the door. The warmth inside was an instant relief, but the memory of the hall hung around his shoulders like a soaked blanket.

Ren looked at him, her hands clenched on the wheel. "Well?"

He was silent for a moment, watching the rain bead and race across the windscreen. The wet city glowed in smeared reflections, streetlights running like fresh wounds.

"They're not rehearsing a play," Vincent said, voice low, even.

She waited.

"They're rehearsing an apocalypse."

They sat in the car, listening to the engine, the rain, the dying world outside. Neither spoke, because there was nothing left to say.

In the distance, somewhere beyond the storm, the old crypts exhaled candle smoke and triumph.

The story, for once, was right on schedule.

SEVENTEEN

Vincent woke twenty minutes earlier than he would have liked because someone was sliding paper under his front door. Not in the metaphorical sense (though, as always, the universe was compiling its own list of grievances), but with a literal scrape-and-sigh against the wood, calculated to travel directly along his spine and pin him to the mattress.

He lay perfectly still, listening to the city's evening-cycle: the sirens arguing with the river fog, office workers heading home after a quick pint, and, now, the stealthy movement of a messenger with strong opinions about stationary. Vincent resisted the urge to turn on the lamp. His eyes—never entirely human—were designed for this. The pitch-black of the flat was, to him, a milky twilight; the faintest source of streetlight, the softest LED glow from a forgotten appliance, pooled just enough photons for his pupils to process the entire room in ghostly relief.

He listened for footsteps in the corridor. Nothing. Whoever

had delivered the envelope was either an Olympic-level sneak or had simply dissolved into a shadow, which, in his line of work, wasn't as unlikely as one might hope. He rolled out of bed, feet hitting the cold floorboards, and padded to the door with the measured tread of a man who'd once set off a pressure-sensitive glyph at three a.m. and learned to never, ever repeat the experience.

The envelope, when he retrieved it, was heavier than it looked—thick, creamy paper, a swatch of texture that probably had a five-generation family tree and a trust fund. It was sealed with wax, the red so dark it was almost black, and pressed with a sigil he'd last seen on the back of a severed head.

Vincent held it up, turning it in the weak light coming from the kitchen. The seal was a triple crescent, overlaid with a thorny script that wound in and out like the world's most pretentious barbed wire. He resisted the urge to crack it with his teeth.

Behind him, the sofa gave a groan that could only be manufactured by the shifting weight of a grown human, and a moment later, Ren shuffled into the hallway, wrapped in a blanket and the sort of moral outrage only available to people who still had a functioning metabolism. Her hair was a riot, flattened on one side and levitating on the other, and her face bore the creases of someone who'd been sleeping with her phone pressed to her cheek.

She regarded the envelope, then Vincent, then the envelope again. "So," she said, voice thick with sleep, "is this the part where you get expelled from Hogwarts for crimes against the postal service?"

Vincent brandished the envelope. "Special delivery. No signature required."

Ren leaned in, squinting at the wax. "Nice. Very 'we know where you live.'"

He cracked the seal with a thumbnail and slid the card out. The contents were simple—a single rectangle of card, ivory, with handwriting so immaculate it probably belonged to a machine that had been programmed to simulate madness. The message read: "You are cordially summoned"—the cordially underlined twice, presumably for irony—"to the Orpheum Theatre." There was no time, no date, not even a dress code.

Ren peered over his shoulder, propped on tiptoes to get a better look. "It's a trap," she yawned, then immediately ruined the effect by yawning again.

Vincent held the card at arm's length, then flicked it with his finger so that it spun, tarot-like, onto the kitchen table. "They've stopped pretending, at least. That's progress."

Ren fished a mug from the draining rack, poured herself a generous serving of yesterday's coffee, and sipped it with the fortitude of a coal miner staring down a flooded shaft. "You gonna go?" she asked, not quite meeting his eyes.

He shrugged, trying to play it off, but the movement was too sharp. "When lunatics summon you to their lair, you show up. It's basic vampire etiquette."

Ren considered this, then nodded. "Want backup? I can do menacing. Or fetch you if you need a quick exit."

Vincent shook his head. "If it's what I think it is, they want me alone. You'd just end up as collateral." He softened, a fraction. "But if I'm not back by sunrise, call Mrs Barley. Tell her to burn the place down."

Ren grinned, then ruined it by spilling coffee on her dressing gown. "That's not a thing you say to a person with pyromaniac tendencies."

He watched her, the way she busied herself with the spill, the way she pretended not to care. "You really want to tag along?" he asked.

Ren's look was pure incredulity. "I'm not missing the chance to see you out-awkward an entire vampire cult."

Vincent smiled, a tight, inward thing. "Good. Wouldn't want succeed without an appreciative audience."

He glanced again at the card. The Orpheum Theatre. It had been derelict since the nineties—closed after a botched exorcism and a series of unfortunate leaks. Rumour had it that every performance since 1973 had ended in at least one minor possession, and that the ghost of a failed illusionist still haunted the catwalks, occasionally flinging sandbags at the living in a fit of professional envy. Vincent had once been hired to catalogue the theatre's archives, but found the stench of nostalgia overwhelming even for him.

Ren drained the mug, then reached for her phone. "You want me to Google the Orpheum, or do we just assume the entire night is cursed?"

Vincent hesitated. "Cursed is predictable. I'm hoping for merely fatal."

She punched at her phone for a few seconds, then held it up for him to see. "Orpheum Theatre. Still condemned. But the reviews are spectacular." She scrolled. "'Saw an alternative production of Phantom of the Opera here. Phantom was real. Four stars.' 'Nice venue, would not recommend to the easily spooked.' 'Best deathtrap in Shoreditch.'"

Vincent squinted at the address. "That's the back entrance. The old artist's door."

Ren nodded. "You want me to bring a crowbar?"

He thought about it, then shook his head. "If you have to use a crowbar, the plan's already failed."

She yawned again, then collapsed onto the sofa, letting the blanket tangle around her like a cocoon. "You want me to drive, at least?"

He considered. "Yes. If this goes pear-shaped, you're my exfiltration."

Ren saluted, the movement exaggerated and, given the state of her pyjamas, faintly obscene. "Aye-aye, captain."

Vincent watched her for a moment, then turned back to the envelope. He ran his finger over the broken wax, the faint indentation left by the sigil. He could feel the shape of it in his mind, the way you could feel a bruise from the inside. It wasn't just a summons. It was a claim.

He left the card on the table, retrieved a clean shirt from the laundry pile (the closest he had to formalwear), and began preparing for the evening with the resigned efficiency of a man laying out cutlery for his own wake. He'd faced down worse than theatre cultists, but rarely on an empty stomach and with this little information.

In the hallway, he paused. The flat was silent again, save for the mechanical hum of the fridge and the soft, arrhythmic snores from the sofa. He looked at the closed door, the envelope, the way the night gathered at the window in sheets of liquid dark.

Vincent thought about leaving a note for Mrs Barley, just in case. Something pithy, like "Gone to get murdered, back by dawn," but decided against it. She'd know. She always did.

He shrugged on his coat, buttoned it against the predawn chill, and slipped out the door with the envelope in his pocket, the wax seal cold against his palm.

On the way down the stairs, he checked his phone. No new messages. Nothing from the Order. No frantic calls from Zara or the archive. The silence was, in its own way, more terrifying than any curse.

At the street, he found Ren waiting, wrapped in a blanket and eating an apple like it was a challenge. She tossed him the keys to the car, then clambered into the passenger seat, feet up on the dashboard. "You drive. I'll navigate. If we hit a detour, it's because the satnav is possessed."

Vincent started the engine. It grumbled awake, shivering in protest. The car smelt like wet wool and Red Bull. He reversed out of the parking spot, tyres squealing in the damp, and aimed the bonnet at Shoreditch with the grim resolve of a man who'd already died once and had no plans to do it again.

"Final thoughts?" Ren asked, voice muffled by the blanket.

Vincent thought about it. "If I don't make it, tell Mrs Barley I still owe her for last month's cleaning. And she's in my Will."

Ren grinned, eyes already closing as the city's lights blurred past. "Noted."

They drove in silence, the world beyond the windscreen melting into a mess of neon and night. Vincent let the road carry him, the invitation's weight pressing against his chest, and wondered what sort of monster would go to this much trouble for a man who hated the theatre.

But then, he thought, monsters rarely needed an excuse.

The Orpheum waited, its doors as black as the gap between seconds, and Vincent pressed onwards, the city closing in behind him like an audience hungry for its opening act.

The Orpheum was visible from two blocks away, which was impressive considering it had spent the last thirty years slowly collapsing into its own legend. Its brickwork, once late-Victorian pride, had split into tectonic plates that threatened to shear off and flatten the next Instagrammer with a taste for urban decay. The windows were jaundiced with nicotine-stained plastic, and the stone steps at the entrance were colonised by moss and the ghosts of a hundred unsuccessful council renovation schemes. A faded "Demolition Pending" banner hung like bunting from the rusted balcony.

Vincent parked round the side, half on the kerb, and let the engine idle. He sat for a moment, eyeing the building, and exhaled. The envelope in his pocket radiated the kind of energy normally reserved for radioactive isotopes and the sort of hate mail that comes with its own restraining order.

Ren, blanket still draped over her like a superhero cape, watched him from the passenger seat with a studied lack of concern. "You need a pep talk?" she offered, tone neutral as Switzerland.

He considered. "Unless you have a how-to guide for suicidal diplomacy."

She pointed at the theatre. "Go in, don't die, text if you need backup. If you start monologuing, I'm giving you half an hour before I crash the party."

Vincent smiled. "You're a national treasure, Ren."

She grinned, a full display of teeth. "Break a leg. Or someone else's, if you get the chance."

He left her there, eyes closing as she adjusted the radio to some tinny late-night R&B, and jogged up the weed-choked service alley to the back of the Orpheum. The stage door stood where it always had, padlocked at the handle but, as tradition required, with half a dozen other entries unbarred in case of fire, rats, or actors with a mortal dread of punctuality.

He slipped inside, boots squeaking on the damp linoleum. The interior was worse than the outside. Most of the lighting had been stripped for copper years ago, leaving only shadows and the occasional moonlit puddle. The air reeked of old wax, mildew, and the long, slow exhalation of failing architecture. The backstage corridor led to the green room, still painted in a colour that could only have been named "Institutional Anxiety," and then to the wings.

He paused here, letting his eyes adjust. Beyond the gap in the curtains, the main stage yawned, lit only by candles and the residual glow from the three ancient, battery-powered spotlights he'd seen at rehearsals. On the boards, a dozen figures stood in a crescent formation, backs to the stalls, facing the darkness from which Vincent now watched.

Every one of them wore a mask. Not the knockoff Halloween variety, but full-face, hand-painted, the sort used in productions where the audience was expected to be both terri-fied and emotionally manipulated. The masks glimmered— porcelain, lacquer, a few leather; each one a different, florid expression of hunger or ecstasy or sorrow, as if the casting director had raided the personal effects of a hundred dead actors.

At the centre stood the tall woman in the blood-red cloak, her mask a Venetian affair with black glass eyes and a mouth fixed in a constant, lipless smile. The set behind her was minimal: just a single iron lectern, a floor scattered with white rose petals, and a threadbare curtain that tried and failed to suggest grandeur.

Vincent stepped out of the wings, letting his shadow fall long across the stage. The figures did not move. The silence was total, save for the faint sizzle of candlewax and the rumble of traffic outside.

He walked to centre stage, careful not to trip on the warped boards. The masked figures shifted as one, turning to face him, the movement synchronized and too fluid by half.

The Cloak Woman spoke, voice amplified and distorted by the space. "Bloodbard," she said, the title delivered with such relish it made his neck itch. "You have answered."

Vincent nodded, affecting a casualness he didn't feel. "You do realise I was drunk when I wrote most of the script."

The Cloak Woman ignored him, stepping forward. Up close, the mask's eyeholes were pure black; whatever lay behind did not reflect the candles. "Your words have brought us here. Your vision will guide the rite."

He looked past her, to the masked congregation sitting in the stalls. It was a full house. "Did you all lose a bet, or is this an immersive dinner theatre thing?"

The audience did not laugh, but a few shifted, a ripple

passing through the half-circle as if the same thought had brushed them all at once.

"Are you ready to begin?" the Cloak Woman asked.

Vincent considered making a joke, but his mouth was dry and there was a fresh, icy dread under his skin now. "If you're expecting a monologue, I haven't memorised the lines."

The Cloak Woman turned to her followers and gestured. Two broke formation and vanished into the wings. They returned moments later, dragging between them an ancient trunk, battered and iron-banded, the kind that survived fires and, more alarmingly, amateur theatrical tours of Eastern Europe. They heaved it to the centre of the stage.

"Your work," the Cloak Woman intoned, "is not lost." She snapped her fingers; one of the masked figures popped the trunk with a crowbar.

The lid fell back, and Vincent's heart stopped. Inside, hundreds of pages—some bound, most loose—lay in stained, precarious stacks. He recognised the script immediately, not just the flourishes and edits and crossed-out lines, but the actual texture of the paper. His paper, the good stuff, the batch he'd thought he'd burned back in 1947 after the Lyon incident. The top layer was yellowed, curling at the edges, but beneath that he saw clean, white sheaves, as if someone had kept writing long after he'd stopped.

He bent to pick one up, then thought better of it.

The Cloak Woman stepped closer. "The ritual is incomplete, Bloodbard. You must finish the story."

Vincent made a show of examining the script. "Last time someone tried to stage this, the entire cast exploded. You really want a sequel?"

She cocked her head. "You ended it wrong. The chorus was denied. The vessel unfilled."

He let the words roll around his skull. They were the same phrases the cultist in Prague had used, the same as the head in the fridge. The story had spread, mutated, evolved, but always the same core: finish the ritual, complete the play, give the audience what it wants.

Vincent looked up at the gallery. He could sense them now—not just the masked actors, but others, in the dark. More masks. More watchers. Some human, some not. The Orpheum's acoustics carried their breath down to the stage, a susurrus of anticipation.

He picked up a page. His own handwriting glared at him, venomous. He read the top line, and his stomach plummeted. This wasn't his draft. It was his worst ideas, the fragments and discarded curses, sewn together by someone who hated him enough to do it properly. The next page was worse: an invocation he'd scrawled and then sworn never to repeat, written out here in perfect, meticulous script.

He kept his face neutral. "You did all this for a table read?"

The Cloak Woman did not blink. "Tonight we finish what was begun."

She gestured to the trunk. "Read."

Vincent glanced at the audience, then back to her. "No intermission?"

She ignored the jab. The other masked figures now formed a full circle, trapping him in with the trunk, their candlelit faces leering down like spectators at an execution. From the wings, two more entered, dragging with them a battered, old lectern and a goblet that looked like it had been stolen from a cathedral in the 1200s.

Vincent weighed his options. Ren was outside, but there was no chance she'd survive the opening monologue if she tried to force her way in. He looked at the pages again. If he refused, they'd kill him; if he complied, they'd probably kill him anyway, but with better production values.

He thumbed to the marked page and began to read.

At first, the words felt clumsy—self-parody, bad poetry, the sort of stuff he'd have shredded in a fit of pique. But as he spoke, the room shifted. The air thickened, the candle flames bent inward, and every masked face seemed to lean closer. The words became heavier, each one falling into the pit of his stomach and lighting up with an old, unwelcome fire.

He could feel the theatre responding. The cracks in the walls flexed, the peeling paint seemed to sigh, and somewhere up in the gods, a spectral hand set a trap for the curtain. He kept reading.

The Cloak Woman began to echo his words, amplifying them. The others joined, chorus-like, the sound building in volume until it was a wall of overlapping voices, impossible to distinguish one from another. Vincent tried to stop, but the script would not let him—his tongue tripped over itself, his mouth shaped syllables he'd never meant to write, never mind utter in front of witnesses.

He tried to drop the page, but his fingers were locked, every muscle in his arm wired to the performance. Around him, the masked cultists swayed, arms raised, and the circle began to close further. He saw now that their masks weren't fixed—they moved, a little, the expressions warping with every line, teeth extending, eyes opening or narrowing depending on the word. The faces changed with the story.

Vincent choked out the last line. "Let the heart open, let the vessel fill. The story ends when the blood runs free."

The Cloak Woman shrieked, a sound that began as joy and ended as pure, lacerating agony. The masked chorus screamed with her, but did not break the circle. Instead, the scream folded back on itself, quieted, became a hum.

He staggered back, the page falling from his hand at last. The trunk was moving, the pages inside stirring, shuffling, crumpling as if chewed from within by something eager to escape.

The Cloak Woman stooped, picked up the page, and held it to the candle. The paper went up with a hiss, and every single mask in the room turned to watch it burn. The eyes behind them were now visible—red, black, some pure white. Some were just holes.

"It is done," the Cloak Woman intoned, voice a full octave lower. "Now, Bloodbard, you will take the stage."

She ripped off her mask. The face beneath was featureless, blank as a sheet of new paper except for a mouth—a perfect, vertical slit that widened, and widened, and widened. She lunged at him, arms impossibly long, the cloak unfurling into a shadow that engulfed the candlelight.

Vincent reeled, stumbled into the trunk, and felt hands— dozens, hundreds—clutching at him, dragging him down into the mass of pages. He tried to scream, but the words caught in his throat, choking him with the taste of ink and salt and old, bad memories.

The stage faded. The audience went black. He fell through words, through time, through the endless, hungry silence of a story that would not end.

EIGHTEEN

Vincent knew theatrical staging, and he knew the real thing. The two rarely overlapped, but tonight the distinction was academic. Vincent woke and found himself seated at a battered trestle table on the Orpheum's stage.

The masked ensemble had a workmanlike approach to ritual, more convention than coven. They filed in, half a dozen strong, faces hidden behind those same porcelain masks he'd seen on stage earlier—some pale and smooth as soap, others lacquered with flourishes and the odd tasteful bloodstain. None of them made a sound beyond the necessary, and none so much as acknowledged his existence. He could have been a prop, or a mark, or (more likely) a necessary irritant in the running order. They moved around him, careful, choreographed.

Cloak Woman, the director of this particular melodrama, stood at the head of the table with her hands folded over her stomach. The cloak fell in rigid lines, the hood shadowing her face so completely she might have lacked one. When she spoke, it was without preamble. "We've restored your work to its pure form. You will complete the script tonight."

Vincent looked at the array before him: a stack of his old drafts, cleanly unburned despite his best efforts; a bottle of ink with a quill stabbed into its gullet; a silver chalice with a lid, steam condensing on its rim. He gave the tableau a slow nod, as if mentally assigning points for effort.

He said, "You do realise I haven't written a single word without an advance in decades?"

Cloak Woman did not respond, but one of the chorus slid the chalice an inch closer to his right hand. The movement was rehearsed, the tilt of the wrist betraying a touch of performance anxiety. Another nudged the quill until it rolled to a stop, perfectly aligned with the scar along Vincent's index finger.

He made a show of ignoring the blood. "Bit early in the evening for refreshments, isn't it?"

He lifted the lid on the chalice, expecting an offering of cheap Shiraz or, at best, a theatrical syrup. Instead, the air was abruptly thick with the scent of fresh human blood—young, warm, the kind that hadn't seen an embalmer or a morgue. Vincent's fangs, always dormant but never gone, throbbed with a warning pulse under his gums. He snapped the lid shut, hoping nobody clocked the tremor in his fingers.

Cloak Woman's voice followed the motion like a predator tracking prey. "The act must be consummated in spirit and in body. All else is theatre."

Vincent glanced at the scripts, feigning boredom as his eyes darted over the top page. He took a moment to study the paper —good cotton rag stock, none of that Amazon "artisan" shit— and then let his gaze roam over the words.

The familiar lines of his own handwriting stared back at him—only these weren't exactly his. The margins crawled with a hand that was not his own, annotations and cross-outs in red, blocks of glyph and runes pressed into the paper's grain as if applied with a soldering iron. There were instructions, too, but they moved when he tried to read them, like a news ticker composed of insects.

He licked his lips, tasted copper and bile. "I can tell you put in the hours. So: is the dress code always 'blood sacrifice chic,' or just for me?"

A ripple moved through the cultists, but none took the bait. The bulb above him swung wider, strobing the faces in a sequence of mask, shadow, mask, shadow. They watched, but only with the patience of predators waiting for a dying animal to stop twitching. Even the Orpheum's backstage ghosts seemed to have given the evening a miss, as if aware this performance had an all-or-nothing clause in the contract.

Vincent looked at Cloak Woman. "If I do this, what happens to me?"

"Your role is to finish the work. After that, you will not matter," she said, and it had the comforting cadence of ritual.

He opened the ink, sniffed it. Cheap stuff, but at least it wasn't red. He uncapped the pen, poised it above the script, then let his hand hover. Every muscle in his arm wanted to rebel, but the air was heavy with the expectation that only cults and publishing houses could manage.

He looked up, eyes catching the bulb's reflection in half a dozen masks. "Just so we're clear: you're all literate, right? I'd hate for this to be a waste of time if nobody can actually read the ending."

Still nothing. He suspected they'd all taken a vow of silence, or maybe it was just a side effect of being this invested in cosplay.

Vincent drew a deep breath, then flicked through the stack. The words shifted under his gaze, lines that should have been throwaway poetry bristling with new intent. The marginalia was no longer content to sit on the sidelines: it bled into the main text, curved over the edges, wrapped around letters in ways that were definitely not typographical. He'd written spells before—on purpose, by accident, and in at least one regrettable fanfic—but this was the first time he felt the script was writing him in return.

He said, "If you want this to be authentic, you have to let me improvise. That's how it works."

Cloak Woman inclined her head, the slow nod of a stage manager who's already bought the insurance for fire and flood.

Vincent dabbed the quill in the ink. The scratch of the nib on the page was immediately, alarmingly loud. He hesitated, then wrote:

The author sits, surrounded by masks and the promise of violence. He knows the ending, but writes it anyway.

A physical wave passed through the cultists—barely perceptible, but unmistakable. The air around him thickened, the bulb's hum shifting from whine to bass. Even the rain falling on the roof went momentarily quiet, as if the city itself was holding its breath.

The Cloak Woman stood at his left shoulder, hands folded neatly in the style of a dowager prepping a firing squad. Her mask was new: not the Venetian number from earlier, but a simple slip of raw linen, stained with the kind of patterns you got from years of handling red wine and other, less social fluids. She never quite met his eyes; Vincent could respect that. Around them, the masked ensemble loitered in a semicircle, each with their own private drama: the Lizard (a mask of scales and lacquer, chipped at the chin from too many headbutts), the Twins (conjoined at the temple by a bolt of black ribbon), the Poet (mouth sewn shut with silver thread, eyes ringed in kohl). There were more, of course, but he'd run out of creative insults by the time he'd made it to "the Punchline" (the smallest, mask painted as a literal clown, who for some reason radiated an air of imminent violence).

They were silent, except for the breathing, which came in syncopated bursts—inhale, exhale, pause, repeat—like a choir that had lost the melody but was determined to keep time.

Vincent flexed his hand, forced the pen down, and began to write.

Ren had managed to kill the car battery, half her dignity, and a jumbo box of Fruit Adventure Tic Tacs in the hour since Vincent had gone inside. The night was not so much cold as predatory, a damp West London kind of chill that snuck in through the seams of her coat and worked its way up the back of her neck like a slug with boundary issues. The dashboard clock glared a baleful 02:07 at her, while the back alley's only working streetlight cast the Peugeot's interior in the colour of wet cardboard and despair.

She checked her phone for the tenth time in as many

minutes. No texts, no calls, not even a passive-aggressive "still alive" from Vincent. She thumbed the screen off and stared at the windscreen, watching her breath leave sticky spirals in the condensation. At some point she'd tried to wipe it clear with the sleeve of her hoodie, but the effect was closer to Venetian glass after an earthquake.

Ren could have stormed the Orpheum, but she'd inventoried her assets and come up short. She was down to a Swiss Army knife, a discount can of "premium" energy drink, and the sort of street-level self-defence techniques that worked best when the opponent had not, in fact, spent centuries perfecting their own murder choreography. She reasoned that if Vincent needed rescuing, the smart money was on him texting for help.

Instead, she reached into the footwell for her laptop. It was one of those models marketed to "creative professionals," which was a polite way of saying it ran hotter than hell and had a battery life measured in "episodes of *Bake Off*." The thing juddered to life, fans screaming, as Ren tethered to the nearby Pret's Wi-Fi and launched into research with the desperation of someone who really didn't want to just sit and stew.

First up: the Orpheum. She'd done the basics already—old theatre, closed for decades, a magnet for ghost hunters and people who pronounced "aesthetic" with the maximum number of syllables. But she'd skipped the deep dive, the sort of research that turned up the stuff even Vincent didn't know. She started with the council's property records, which were as navigable as the Sargasso Sea but with more sunken hopes.

She found what she was looking for within minutes: two years back, the Orpheum's lease had been quietly purchased by an entity called Orbis Malvorn Ltd. Registered in the Channel

Islands, because of course it was. The directors were anonymous, but the paperwork trail was just faintly sloppy—enough to show someone had tried to clean up after themselves, but not with the conviction of a true paranoiac. She cross-referenced the address with Vincent's old notes, found three hits, and felt her heart pick up an extra beat.

She dug deeper. Orbis Malvorn was linked to a string of holding companies, all in the names of dead poets or minor Catholic saints. It was the sort of shell game Vincent would have appreciated, if only for the commitment to theme. Ren clicked through document after document, her eyes glazing, until a signature stopped her cold.

Bartholomew Archer. Company secretary.

Ren sat back, the damp seat sucking heat through her jeans. She blinked twice, sure she'd misread it. But the name was there, stamped in digital permanence.

She knew it, not from her own life but from Vincent's: Bartholomew, the Renfield, the daylight man, the first person Vincent had trusted after Carmine. The man who'd once saved Vincent from being staked in a Soho bedsit, only to vanish a few years later. They'd never spoken of him, not in detail. But Vincent's reaction to the name—when Mrs Barley had mentioned him, drunk and half-dreaming in the dead zone between midnight and sunrise—was all the proof she'd needed that it mattered.

She scrolled back, reread the lines. There was no doubt.

Bartholomew was alive. And he was running the cult.

Ren closed the laptop, her breath frosting in the air. She felt the urge to throw up, or punch something, or maybe just call

Vincent and scream down the line. But instead, she sat, motionless, letting the knowledge harden around her like winter.

She didn't know what this meant for Vincent, or for herself. But she knew the next move wasn't going to be his.

Ren looked at the theatre, the cracked facade now looming in the orange sodium as if the whole building was holding its breath. She took out her phone, opened a new message, and started typing with numb fingers.

Inside, the story had changed. And she was the only one who'd read the footnotes.

She pressed send and waited for Vincent to come out.

He always did, in the end.

NINETEEN

Vincent began writing with the expected: *SCENE XII: The Mask Falls.*

Then, with the flourish of a man about to destroy his own career, he added a note in the margin: *Director's Cut: All stage directions to be taken with extreme prejudice.* If he had to be the cult's scribe, he would at least be its saboteur.

He wrote with intent, but every line he scribbled felt wrong, like carving graffiti into his own headstone. The ritual demanded precision—the old Latin, the sigils, the idiotic iambic pentameter—but Vincent layered it with landmines: contradictory stage cues, parentheticals that looped back on themselves, dialogue so arch it risked spontaneous gothic collapse.

He felt the magic kick in almost immediately. It was like being in a lift with bad wiring and a worse soundtrack: the world wobbled, lights dimmed, and somewhere in the plumbing a pressure valve screamed in protest. The candles flared, each flame a hungry tongue. The air turned wet, then dry, then wet again. Vincent glanced up, half expecting applause, but the audience only watched, their collective hunger pressing in on his skull like an inflating bicycle inner tube.

Cloak Woman pounced on the moment. "Very good," she purred, voice bright as broken glass. "You feel the resonance, yes? The chorus stirs."

Vincent managed a lopsided smile. "I always did like a responsive crowd."

"Keep writing," she said, and, just for a moment, he glimpsed the edge of her real mouth—a slash of red behind the linen.

So he wrote, faster, more recklessly, letting the pen do the bleeding. He wove in jokes that only a seven-hundred-year-old nihilist could appreciate. He slipped in allusions to failed revolutions, cheap lager, reality television, and the entire collected works of Sir Terry Pratchett. He wrote in lines that could not be spoken and stage directions that only made sense upside down and in ultraviolet. And, just to see if the universe was paying attention, he inserted the phrase: *"Let the curtain call be a curtain fall, and may the author survive only in the footnotes."*

The magic responded like a wounded animal. The room went cold, then searingly hot. The owl skulls rattled, and the stage lights began to dim and brighten to match the emotional intensity of the writing. The masked cultists began to hum, a deep vibration that Vincent felt in his molars. The page beneath his hand bucked like a living thing, but he pressed down, forcing the words through.

A minute passed. Then another. The humming built to a fever pitch.

And then, with the precision of a hammer coming down on a thumb, a hand slammed onto the desktop.

The shockwave nearly knocked the pen from Vincent's grip. He looked up, blinking, and found the Lizard looming over him, mask split at the jawline, breath hot and wet on his face. The hand—long, veined, almost reptilian in its delicacy—splayed over his draft, pinning the page.

"This is not the line," Lizard rasped. The voice was deeper than before, fractured in the middle like glass left out in a hailstorm.

Vincent considered his options, found none of them satisfying, and decided to make a new one. He met Lizard's gaze—at least, the shiny black hollows where a gaze might one day be installed.

"It is now," Vincent said, calm as you like.

Lizard's fingers dug into the paper, claws threatening to tear it down the middle. "The rite will not tolerate falsehood," it warned. This was not a committee; this was the voice of the blood-drenched id, the bit of every cult that just wanted to watch the world burn and eat the ashes for dessert.

He leaned in, close enough to see his own face reflected in the mask's green sheen. "Neither will I," he said.

A tense beat hung in the air, thick as glue. Vincent braced for violence—a thrown chalice, a ceremonial dagger, a spontaneous combustive event. Instead, the Lizard's mask cracked, literally: a fine fracture webbed out from the left temple, and the breath that escaped was tinged with something metallic and sweet.

Cloak Woman intervened, her hand landing on Vincent's shoulder with the softness of a feather duster and the certainty of a guillotine blade. "The Bloodbard will find his voice," she announced, faux-soothing, to the audience. "He always does, in the end."

There was a murmur from the crowd, half-reluctant, half-religious. Vincent caught the mood: half of them wanted to see him fail, and the other half wanted to see how far he could go before he set himself on fire.

He licked the corner of his mouth, where sweat or blood had pooled. "You don't get to improvise in this company?" he asked the room, faux-casual.

The Poet, mouth sewn shut, wept a single tear of ink. The Twins exchanged a look and shrugged in tandem. The Punchline made a sound somewhere between a giggle and a death rattle.

Cloak Woman's fingers kneaded Vincent's shoulder, and for a moment, he imagined she might pop his head off like a dandelion. Instead, she bent low, linen mask brushing his ear.

"Finish the final scene," she whispered. "Tonight, we open the gates."

Vincent's pen hesitated. He looked down, at the trembling page, at the growing chaos in his own handwriting, and thought about all the times he'd sabotaged a reading for the sake of a cheap laugh. This was different: the stakes were real, and so was the magic.

He wrote:

Curtain. Mask drops. Chorus, bereft.

The page responded with a flicker, the ink writhing for a second before settling in place. He risked a glance at the Lizard, who was still looming but now seemed unsure whether to tear out Vincent's throat or ask for a signed copy.

Vincent tried not to look at the blood chalice, but the smell was aggressive, rising through the ink's own chemical reek. He wondered, briefly, if there was a metaphorical point to all this, or if the universe was just playing out an elaborate, mean-spirited joke at his expense.

He wrote another line:

The chorus tightens its circle. The script is nearly done.

The room groaned, a sound from the floorboards or the stones beneath. Cloak Woman remained behind him, so close he could feel the chill radiating off her. He kept writing, hoping that the faster he went, the sooner the punchline would arrive and he could go back to pretending his existence had some margin of autonomy.

He tried for another joke. "You know, most publishers just ask for an outline and a sample chapter. This is a little... intense."

He glanced back, and saw her face at last—only there was no face, just a mask behind the mask, layered so many times that the notion of an original was laughable. In the centre of the eyeholes, he glimpsed a wet, glistening red, as if something was waiting to pour out at the right cue.

He wrote:

The ink runs. The blood fills the cup. The story feeds.

The bulb above him flickered, then steadied. Cloak Woman placed her hand on his shoulder again—cold, but not dead—and squeezed, once, a gesture of both encouragement and finality.

He wrote the last line:

The vessel empties. The mask falls. The hunger is not sated, only shared. Lights out.

He stopped, pen hovering. The script was done, but the

energy in the room had reached a fever pitch. The cultists began a low, wordless chant, a vibration that burrowed in through Vincent's teeth and rattled his jawbone. The pages in front of him shimmered, the ink bleeding into the paper until the letters floated free, forming patterns that moved, alive, in the dim light.

He leaned back, every nerve singing with adrenaline and dread. The air was electric, charged with the kind of power he hadn't felt since the last time he'd tried to undo a curse by writing it backwards.

Cloak Woman leaned in, her voice suddenly soft and close. "Drink."

He looked at the chalice, the blood inside still warm, still steaming in the cold air. Every cell in his body screamed to refuse, but Vincent was nothing if not a slave to ritual. He raised the cup, the silver already slick with condensation, and drank.

The blood was sweet and bright and impossibly alive. It ran down his throat and into his veins, and with it came the memory of every word he'd ever written, every line of script that had outlived its speaker. The room spun, the bulb's afterimage burning into his retinas.

The chorus's chanting rose, then snapped to silence.

Vincent dropped the cup. It clattered to the floor, rolling until it wedged itself under the table, out of sight.

He gasped, breath ragged, and looked at the finished script.

He slumped forward, forehead hitting the edge of the table with an audible thud.

Cloak Woman let go of his shoulder, and with her touch gone, the room's temperature shot up, the sweat on Vincent's face going instantly cold.

Vincent sat, motionless, until the blood settled in his gut and the taste of metal faded from his mouth.

He looked up at Cloak Woman. "All done. You want it read aloud, or shall I just staple it to your next victim?"

"You'll perform it," she said. "On stage."

Vincent suppressed a sigh. "Of course I will."

Vincent felt the disturbance in his dressing room before he heard it—the air thickening, the taste of old secrets rousing from the dust in the curtains. The backstage of the Orpheum had a rhythm all its own, but this was something imported: a cadence from another century, steady as a metronome and twice as piti-less. The masked figures responded as if to a conductor's silent downbeat, parting with synchronised economy to either side of the corridor. Even Cloak Woman, unflappable in her shroud of cult-leader chic, straightened with a snap, folding her hands behind her back and adopting the posture of a junior usher awaiting the arrival of an Ofsted inspector.

Bartholomew Archer entered as if he owned the place, which, for all practical purposes, he did. He'd traded in his favoured bone-white suit for a black one, crisp enough to give Savile Row a crisis of confidence, but the effect was the same: he looked like a banker on his way to foreclose on the afterlife. Age had not been especially cruel, but it had sharpened his features and put steel in the lines of his jaw. His hair had gone from gunmetal to snow, slicked back in the same geometric pattern Vincent remembered from the twenties, and his eyes—oh, the eyes—were still two perfectly machined holes for pouring in light and wringing out your intentions.

He stopped just short of Vincent's dressing table, running a gloved fingertip over the loose pages of dialogue and scene directions from the newly penned final scene. The touch was almost tender, as if reacquainting himself with a pet he'd once left on a roadside. The silence stretched, brittle and intentional, until Bartholomew looked over and said, "Vincent. Or should I say, Bloodbard. It's been… what? Ninety years? I see you've kept the cheekbones."

Vincent resisted the urge to bare his teeth. "And you've kept the habit of stealing my work."

"Not stealing," Bartholomew said, producing a sheaf of paper from under his arm and flicking it open with a magician's showmanship. "Perfecting." He tapped the margin, where the script was annotated in a precise, red-inked hand. "You never had the patience for revision, old friend. Or for closure."

A subsonic rustle rolled through the cultists who stood in the corridor—approval, or maybe hunger. Vincent caught the movement: the Twins leaning in, Lizard's tongue flicking at a broken canine, Punchline's painted smile creasing upward.

Bartholomew read the room, then turned the full force of his attention on Vincent. "We never did finish our little project. But I think you'll find tonight's audience is rather more... dedicated than the usual West End crowd."

Vincent made a show of relaxing, slouching in the battered chair. "If you wanted a reunion, Bart, you could have just sent a courier. Preferably one without the murder-hobo dress code."

Bartholomew set the script down in front of him, pages fanned like a hand of cards. "You always did think everything was a joke. Maybe that's why you never understood the stakes." He nodded at Cloak Woman, who stepped forward. "The ritual is in your hands now. Quite literally."

He glanced at the masked troupe, all waiting for a cue, and said, "Take him to the stage. It's time."

Vincent considered, briefly, whether to resist. He calculated the odds—twelve masked psychos, Cloak Woman's right hand already flexing for a grab, Bartholomew probably packing more than a sense of occasion—and decided against it. Besides, he wanted to see how it ended.

The Twins moved in first, each grabbing a wrist with the cold confidence of people who'd done this before. The others closed in, a blood-coloured scrum, their robes hissing over the floorboards and their masks creaking like old teeth. Lizard hissed in Vincent's ear, a wet, reptilian sound that carried a single, clear warning: cooperate, or lose something vital.

He looked over his shoulder as Cloak Woman and Bartholomew fell in behind, the two of them watching like a producer and a director who'd finally solved the casting problem. The corridor ahead was already lit by flickering candles—each one spelling out, in subtle shadow, the promise of a performance that would leave stains on both the architecture and the soul.

As they marched him toward the stage, Vincent caught a final glimpse of the green room: the costumes, the owl skulls, the circle of masks left behind. He wondered, briefly, if anyone would remember what was written here tonight.

He doubted it. But then, he'd always preferred footnotes to curtain calls.

TWENTY

Ren had seen more than her fair share of botched stakeouts—usually from the inside of this very Peugeot or, once, in the back of a riot van that she'd escaped by vomiting so convincingly the arresting officer chose to retire. But this, she decided, was a new genre: paranormal waiting game, feet going numb, watching the city's second-worst theatre die by inches while her boss tried to commit career suicide via interpretive ritual.

She checked her phone for the seventeenth time, just to confirm that time was still linear and she was not, in fact, stuck in some personal hell dimension where nothing happened but bad R&B and condensation. Vincent had not texted. The dashboard clock was edging toward three a.m. She could almost hear her mother's voice, somewhere in the back of her head, laying out the precise number of life choices that had led her to sitting outside a condemned playhouse in a neighbourhood where even the foxes were carrying blades.

Enough was enough. If Vincent wasn't dead, he was at least

overdue a rescue attempt. She zipped up her hoodie, pulled the drawstrings so tight she had to mouth-breathe, and slid out of the car with the quiet efficiency of someone who had once burgled a church (long story, mostly legal, absolutely deserved). She walked the perimeter, boots scraping the kerb, and kept her hands in her pockets—partly for warmth, mostly so she didn't look like she was casing the joint, which, to be fair, she absolutely was.

The Orpheum was less a building than a vertical landfill with delusions of grandeur. Every inch of it screamed "heritage site" in the same way a corpse screamed "formerly occupied." The front doors were chained shut, festooned with warning notices: UNSAFE STRUCTURE, NO PUBLIC ACCESS, CCTV IN OPERATION, which, Ren noted, was a lie. She counted at least four bricked-up windows, three pigeons, and a line of what she sincerely hoped was ketchup trailing from the main steps to a gutter full of wet cigarette ends.

She found her entrance at the side: a rusted steel fire door, chained shut with a padlock that would have given a discount locksmith an aneurysm. The chain, though, was looped through a steel ring that was more decorative than functional, and Ren knew from experience that old metal gave way under the right kind of pressure. She scouted the alley for a lever, found a length of steel rebar in a skip, and went to work.

She set her shoulder, wedged the bar between the chain and the frame, and leaned in, putting her weight behind it. For a second, nothing happened; then, with a groan and a spatter of rust, the ring sheared loose and the chain collapsed to the tarmac with all the subtlety of a dropped anchor. Ren winced, checked over her shoulder for witnesses, and slipped inside.

The interior was a mausoleum: all soft rot, old velvet, and a smell that was part damp, part mouse, part the kind of chemical you used to preserve bodies in the fifties. The foyer was thick with dust, the air shivering with the echo of every footstep. There were footprints in the carpet, some recent, some so ancient they'd become part of the design. Ren flicked her phone to torch mode, then immediately flicked it off again—better not to be a beacon. Her eyes would adjust.

She moved slow, letting her feet map the dips and swells of the floor, hands brushing the wall for bearings. The deeper she went, the more she realised the place wasn't abandoned at all: there were fresh cigarette butts, a scattering of empty Red Bulls, and, ominously, a child's juice carton jammed into the hollow of a radiator. People were here. They were just hiding.

The main corridor forked left and right. From the left, a faint thrum—music, maybe, or chanting. From the right, a clatter and a brief, shushing hiss. Ren grinned, old instincts kicking in. She went right, tracking the sound, body hunched, every nerve buzzing with the thrill of a really good trespass.

She slipped through a door marked "Wardrobe," then into a warren of smaller rooms—dressing spaces, wig stores, the kind of windowless cubes where, once upon a time, someone named Mildred had wept into their gin before the second act. The floor here was better kept. The footprints were fresher. Ren stopped, closed her eyes, listened. There: the wet click of tongue against teeth, a shuffle of fabric, a stifled cough. Someone was just around the corner.

She risked a glance. Saw a sliver of light and, in it, a sliver of face: white, featureless, a mask of painted porcelain with a black smear where the mouth should be. The mask lingered, then vanished—silent, unsettling. Ren pulled back, heart hammering. She waited, counted to twenty, then moved on.

The dressing room was empty, but the mirrors told a different story. Each was cracked, as if someone had tried to shatter their own reflection and failed. The countertop was littered with powder, lipstick, and a forest of empty vials. The air was heavy with the ghosts of hairspray and old sweat.

Ren crept to the nearest mirror, traced her finger through the dust, and saw the symbols etched into the glass: circles, crescents, the triple-glyph she'd seen on Vincent's summons. Someone had gone to the trouble of painting them on every available surface, layering them over the remnants of old graffiti and newer, sharper knife-marks.

She took a quick inventory: no Vincent, no sign of a fight. She kept moving.

A few rooms down, she found a crate labelled "Props." Inside: a stack of masks, each painted with different faces—animal, human, cartoon, even one that looked like it had been modelled after Vincent's worst hangover. There were red cloaks, too, the kind that would have done a Hammer Horror proud, and a neat bundle of scripts, all identical, each stamped in the corner with the Carmine sigil.

She fished one out, flicked through. It was a copy of *The Crimson Masque*, or at least the last few scenes. The lines were annotated, pages marked with "BLOOD" or "CHORUS" or "SEE PAGE 8 FOR RITUAL." On the last page, someone had scrawled: "THE BLOODBARD DIES HERE." The handwriting looked suspiciously like Vincent's, only sharper, meaner.

Ren snapped a few pictures on her phone, then stowed the

script in her bag. If nothing else, Zara could have a field day with it.

She was about to move on when the air shifted. A footstep in the hall, not hers. Ren ducked behind the crate, holding her breath.

A shadow slid across the doorway, then stilled. There was a pause, a slow intake of breath, then a measured voice, careful and warm like a radio host trying to sell you both philosophy and insurance.

"Our guest is resisting. Prepare the contingency."

The shadow moved on. Ren exhaled, trying to keep her own voice from escaping as a squeak. The phrase stuck in her head, and so did the accent: old-school, maybe Eton, with a hint of the kind of posh that didn't need to show off. It was the sort of voice that didn't ask for permission, only results.

Ren waited, counted to sixty, then rose and ghosted out into the hall. She crept in the direction of the voice, following the echoes as they pinged off the cracked plaster. A few turns, a flight of stairs, and she found herself on the upper balcony, overlooking the main stage.

Below, the theatre was alive: masked figures moving in the orchestra pit, setting out candles and painting lines on the floor. At centre stage, a table was laid out with all the trappings of a nightmare: knives, goblets, a book that pulsed when the candlelight flickered. On the stage apron, a woman in a long red cloak stood, arms folded, mask gleaming in the dark.

And next to her—Ren had to squint, but when the figure turned, she caught the edge of his face, the crisp jaw, the hair slicked back in perfect, serial-killer geometry. His mask was off, for now. He wore a suit, tailored, a lapel pin that looked suspiciously like a masonic symbol.

"Bartholomew Archer," Ren whispered, and immediately hated herself for doing it aloud.

She'd only ever heard the name in passing from Mrs Barley —never from Vincent, not directly. He'd called him "the familiar," or "Bart," or, once, "the reason I don't trust anyone who wears cufflinks." She'd assumed he was dead. Most of Vincent's acquaintances were.

Ren watched as Bartholomew (it felt wrong to think of him as "Bart") leaned over, said something to the Cloak Woman, and then moved to the edge of the stage. His voice rolled out, unhurried:

"The Bloodbard has completed the final scene. Curtain in fifteen."

The cultists responded with a collective hiss, not quite applause, but something more animal. Bartholomew smiled, turned, and strode offstage, his steps so light they barely registered on the boards.

Ren slunk back, chest tight. The realisation landed with a nauseating clarity: this wasn't just a performance, and it wasn't just a ritual. It was personal. She'd thought Vincent was the main character in a drama he'd written for himself, but Bartholomew—Archer, whatever—was the director, the critic, the audience and the executioner all at once.

She needed to move. Fast.

Ren retraced her steps, hugging the walls, every sense screaming that she was being watched. On the stairs, she passed a cultist in a fox mask, who paused, tipped its head, and then vanished. In the corridor, she ducked into a storage closet when she heard laughter—two voices, both disguised, both giddy with anticipation.

She waited, thinking.

The ritual was about to kick off, and Ren had, in her bag, exactly one set of car keys, a phone with fifteen percent battery, and a stolen script. No weapons, no backup, and—she checked, just in case—no sudden ability to teleport.

She considered calling Mrs Barley, but knew it would be pointless. The old woman would have told her to handle it herself, and besides, she doubted anyone outside the Orpheum could get there in time.

She had to do something. Anything.

Ren slipped out of the closet, walked fast but not so fast as to attract attention. She moved through the Orpheum like a burglar in a house already halfway burgled. Every corridor was a hazard course of rotten carpet and tripwire-grade extension leads, but she made better time than she'd hoped, the echo of applause guiding her to the action like a lighthouse for the terminally unwise. The theatre was a warren; it had been designed by Victorians who believed that a truly great venue should allow the actors to enter from anywhere, including the roof and possibly the underworld. Ren exploited every shortcut she remembered from her single failed attempt at drama school, and a few she invented on the fly.

She'd lowered the hood of her hoodie because it was hard to hear, and she wore her hair tucked under a beanie that might have once belonged to a minor criminal or an even minor-er poet. Her breath stayed shallow, her steps measured, her pulse somewhere between the rhythm of a nightclub and the death rattle of a dying appliance.

She reached the grand drape—a curtain thick enough to stop a low-calibre bullet, or at least a hail of popcorn—and eased her head around the edge just as Vincent was paraded onto stage. Two cultists flanked him, twins, she guessed, from the identical fuck-you angles of their elbows. Behind them, in full Master of Ceremonies mode, was Bartholomew. He'd added a red silk cravat and a single white rose in the buttonhole, as if to suggest the evening would climax in either a duel or a funeral.

Ren fished her phone from her back pocket, thumbed the camera to video, and started filming.

She kept low, using the darkness of the wings as cover, and focused in. The shot was a bit Blair Witch—wobbly, half the frame taken up by the curtain's mouldering brocade—but she got the essentials: Vincent, all angular resignation, hair plastered to his skull by what looked suspiciously like blood. His face was composed, set in that "I'd rather be anywhere else, but especially not here" mode. The cultists looked worse: some in bespoke horror-wear, others in a kind of post-apocalyptic charity-shop couture, all topped by those grotesque masks.

She panned over the audience—every seat filled, each patron masked and robed, hands folded in anticipation. The house lights had been dialled to "serial killer documentary." On stage, a circle of salt or something whiter marked the performance area. The centrepiece, of course, was the battered desk with Vincent's script; above it, the backdrop had been painted with a crude copy of the triple-crescent sigil.

Ren kept filming, but her thumb was already hovering over the upload button. If she had to, she'd stream the whole damn thing to every cult forum and supernatural subreddit in Europe.

Bartholomew moved to the front of the stage, the real spotlight now on him. He raised his hands, the hush that followed as precise as a sniper shot. "Ladies and gentlemen," he said, "tonight we resurrect more than art. Tonight, we summon the original voice, the truest word. Tonight—" and here he grinned, that wolfish arch in his eyebrows "—the Bloodbard will reveal the last act."

A round of applause. A few hisses. Somebody in the front row threw up a hand signal Ren didn't recognise, but she filed it away for future paranoia.

She zoomed in on Vincent's face. He rolled his eyes. Classic.

Ren ducked away from the curtain, blinking the phone's afterimage out of her retinas. If there was going to be a bloodbath, she wasn't about to record it on a phone built for cat videos and dodgy Wi-Fi. She needed an edge. A weapon. Something. She darted into the wings, scanning the chaos for anything she could repurpose as a deterrent.

The prop table was a junkie's fantasy of options: stage daggers (dull, but probably effective if you got the drop), real daggers (hidden among the fakes for maximum confusion), a coil of plastic chain, two garish clown wigs, a length of piano wire, and—miracle of miracles—an antique revolver, the kind that looked like it came with its own suicide note. She palmed the revolver, checked the cylinder (fully loaded, because why not), and slid it inside the waistband of her jeans. For show, she took the sharpest of the daggers and tucked it into her sleeve.

She checked the phone again. Still recording. Still uploading. Her signal bounced between two bars and a declaration of "Emergency Calls Only," but the video was out there, now. If she didn't make it, at least the internet would know who to mock.

A fresh volley of applause yanked her focus back to the stage. Vincent had been shoved forward, to a white X taped on the floor. He blinked against the light. Cloak Woman appeared stage right, carrying the script in both hands like an offering. Bartholomew bowed, took the script, and handed it to Vincent with all the ceremony of a papal coronation.

Vincent took it, scanned the top page, and sighed. He looked up, caught Ren's gaze through the gloom, and, for a split second, she thought he might laugh. Instead, he mouthed something—hard to tell, but it looked like, "I hope this is being recorded."

Ren gave him a thumbs up, then flipped it into a middle finger for luck.

Bartholomew cleared his throat. "Our author will now perform the final scene."

The masked audience snickered, a weirdly polite sound, like pensioners at a dirty joke in a church hall.

Vincent straightened, took a deep breath, and began to read.

It started simple enough: the usual blood and thunder of Vincent's early drafts. The language was more baroque than Ren remembered reading in the kitchen—either Vincent was ad-libbing, or Bartholomew had revised the script into self-parody. The air in the theatre changed, though; the further Vincent read, the more electric it became, as if every consonant was a spark and every word a fuse. The audience leaned in, the cultists closed the circle tighter, the house lights dipped to sepulchral.

Vincent's voice grew louder, more confident, more... inhuman. The mask slipped, just a bit. His fangs—subtle, but visible now—flashed with each syllable. He gestured with the script, and the wind of the gesture carried real weight. The Twins flanked him, but even they seemed wary.

Ren slithered closer to the stage, staying low behind the stacks of scenery. She could see the arc of where this was going: Bartholomew would force the end, Vincent would resist, and someone was going to get their head caved in. She counted the shots in the revolver, worked out which cultists looked like they'd go down the easiest, and reviewed the exit routes. There were none. It was all or nothing.

Vincent reached the final page. His hands trembled—not with fear, but with the anticipation of a man about to blow up the pub quiz with a trick answer. He glanced at Bartholomew, then at the audience, then—once more—at Ren.

He read the last line: "The vessel empties. The mask falls. *The hunger is not sated, only shared.*"

A ripple tore through the cultists. Several dropped to their knees, others clutched at their masks as if the words had scalded them. The audience in the stalls convulsed, a tidal movement of bodies reeling as the ritual's effect washed over them.

Bartholomew staggered, caught himself, and glared at Vincent. "What have you done?" he spat, voice stripped of its calm. "That's not the ending."

Vincent grinned, all teeth. "It is now."

The Twins lunged, but Vincent was ready. He twisted free, swinging the rolled up script like a cudgel, catching one in the jaw. The mask split, the cultist howled. The other reached for Vincent's throat, but he bit down—hard. Blood sprayed, dark and arterial.

Ren launched herself onto the stage, revolver drawn. She levelled it at Bartholomew, who backed away, hands up. "You think you can stop this?" he hissed, face mottled with rage.

Ren flicked the safety off. "Worth a go."

She fired a shot into the ceiling—mostly for effect—and shouted, "Nobody move!" The effect was mixed, but it bought her a second.

Cloak Woman appeared at Bartholomew's side, a sacrificial knife gleaming in her hand. She moved fast, but Vincent was faster: he vaulted the desk, and tackled her, but not before she threw the knife at Ren.

The hilt of the knife hit Ren's temple hard, and her body dropped to the floor in a heap.

Vincent and Cloak Woman tumbled in a tangle of velvet and viscera. The cultists on the stage and in the stalls screamed, some joined in putting the boot in, others stood and watched, transfixed by the carnage.

The tumble ended badly for Vincent. Cloak Woman twisted like smoke, sliding on top of him with predatory grace. Her weight bore down hard, velvet clinging slick with blood as she wrenched his arm behind his back. He snarled and thrashed, but she moved with the unhurried certainty of someone who'd already decided the ending. Around them the stage dissolved into chaos—cultists jeering, others baying for blood, the air thick with the stink of sweat and candle smoke— yet on the boards it narrowed to two figures: predator and prey, and for once Vincent wasn't the one with fangs.

Cloak Woman had him down. Vincent's cheek pressed hard against the stage boards, her knee grinding between his shoulders, one velvet-gloved hand wrenching his wrist back until the joints creaked. The knife she held gleamed inches from his throat, a theatrical mockery turned lethal. Bartholomew approached with all the languid triumph of a man reclaiming centre stage. He peered down at Vincent—his old employer, the once-feared apex predator—and let a slow smile spread. "How the tables turn," he purred. "Once you dictated the story. Now you're just another line, waiting to be cut."

Vincent snarled, twisting hard enough to throw Cloak Woman off balance. Her velvet sleeve tore in his grip; she hissed and vanished back into the melee. Free at last, Vincent rose in a single, brutal motion, eyes on Bartholomew.

"Footnote this," Vincent growled, and with a sudden burst of feral strength, he seized the cult leader by the collar and belt. Gasps erupted from the stalls as Vincent heaved Bartholomew bodily off the stage. His scream cut short in a bone-crunching thud as he disappeared into the orchestra pit.

For one glorious moment, Vincent stood tall—bloodied, furious, almost triumphant. Then came the hollow whump of wood on skull. The Cloak Woman, wielding a stage-prop oar with theatrical flourish, cracked it across the side of his head. Stars burst behind Vincent's eyes; his knees buckled.

The stage tilted, swimming, as if the whole theatre were drowning. Vincent dropped to one knee, clutching at the boards. Cloak Woman loomed above him, shadow long, oar raised again.

TWENTY-ONE

For one horrifically plausible second, Vincent was certain that this was how it ended: kneeling on the scorched wood of the Orpheum's main stage, surrounded by a riot of masked cultists, their knives and "magickal" club badges glinting with the kind of anticipation usually reserved for serial divorcees at a bank holiday wedding. He risked a sidelong glance at Ren, who had come to, but was bleeding from the temple and still clutching the antique revolver with an optimism Vincent had never known her to possess. She met his gaze, eyes wide and electric, and mouthed, "Any last ideas?"

Vincent considered, briefly, the merits of a moving confession, then remembered he'd never had the energy for sincerity.

"Negotiate?" he whispered.

Ren grimaced. "They're not even unionised."

Before Vincent could craft a retort, Cloak Woman strode forward, hands raised in the universal gesture of "Behold, I am about to say something regrettable." The mask she wore was new, fresh from the back pages of a surgical horror catalogue, the mouth pulled into a perfectly round 'o' as if trapped in permanent surprise.

"Bloodbard," she intoned, projecting to the sticky upper circle, "by the authority vested in me by the Charter of Eternal Darkness, I pronounce you anathema, obsolete, and about to be recycled into your constituent narrative elements."

Vincent stifled a sigh. "You see what I'm up against?" he stage-whispered to Ren. "Even their banter is copy-pasted."

Ren gave a minute nod, then braced for impact.

The cultists surged as one, an avalanche of velvet and stolen bravado. Vincent tensed, ready to go down with at least one of the more floridly dressed in his teeth, when the theatre doors exploded open with a sound that split the air.

A silhouette filled the entryway, backlit by the sodium haze of the city beyond. It was tall, it was irate, and it wore a sensible cardigan over a shirt emblazoned with the crest of the Greater London Authority.

Mrs Barley entered, carrying a battered satchel, an umbrella that looked like it could be used as a battering ram, and the air of a civil servant who had found the overdue forms and was going to staple them to your soul.

At her side, not so much walking as gliding, was Zara Delacourt. Her suit was perfectly pressed, her hair slicked back and streaked with argent, her expression one of absolute, undiluted disapproval. She carried nothing but a slim volume of what might have been legal code, but glared with the intensity of a woman who considered magic a regrettable subclause of reality.

The cultists halted, several tripping over their own capes. Even Cloak Woman took an involuntary step back.

Mrs Barley surveyed the carnage, the ruined chandelier, Bartholemew who was still reassembling himself in the orchestra pit, and the twenty-odd masked enforcers ready to commit acts of mythic unpleasantness. She tutted, clicked her tongue, and advanced with all the subtlety of a Social Services audit.

"Council enforcement," she announced, flashing a lanyard that expired nearly twenty years ago. "This gathering is in contravention of local byelaw 17B, subsection 3—public nuisance, ritualistic slaughter, and failure to register a public event with Environmental Health."

No one moved.

Mrs Barley, ignoring the silence, plonked her satchel on a toppled chair, unzipped it, and removed a battered tin marked "council-issue vampire compliance kit." She opened it with practised precision.

"Right then," she said, to no one in particular, "let's get this farce cleaned up."

The first cultist to approach did so with a degree of caution, the sort one reserved for traffic wardens and unexploded ordnance. He drew a ceremonial dagger. Mrs Barley met him with a smile, palmed a garlic lozenge from the tin, and popped it into her mouth with a crack.

The cultist hesitated, then lunged.

Mrs Barley's response was a blur: she jabbed a sharpened umbrella stake into his thigh, caught his mask as it tumbled off, and then, in a single, fluid motion, flicked her wrist so that a silver knitting needle flashed between her fingers and embedded itself in the man's ear.

He went down, whimpering.

Mrs Barley whacked him once more with the umbrella for good measure. "Conduct unbecoming," she said. "Next."

Vincent, against his better instincts, was impressed. "That's... actually quite good," he muttered, as three more cultists closed in on Mrs Barley.

Ren, always the pragmatist, took advantage of the distraction to haul herself to her feet and unload two rounds from the revolver into the nearest masked figure. One bullet grazed the man's shoulder, the other punched through his mask and left a blooming flower of red across his lapel.

The theatre erupted in chaos. Cultists fanned out, some descending on Mrs Barley, others on Vincent and Ren, still others clustering around the pit where Bartholemew was reconstructing his own shoulder joint.

Amid the violence, Vincent caught a glimpse of Zara, serene at the foot of the stage. She opened her book, licked a finger, and began reading in a clear, unhurried monotone. Her voice didn't project, but it didn't need to; the words she spoke seemed to rewrite the very air, and wherever her gaze landed, the cultists' movements faltered, as if someone had swapped out their choreography mid-dance.

Mrs Barley's compliance kit was a marvel of repurposed government surplus. She wielded a spray bottle marked "Consecrated Water – Do Not Drink" with ruthless efficiency, spritzing the eyes of her assailants and following up with a biro to the windpipe. One masked woman attempted a hex; Mrs Barley countered by whacking her on the knuckles with a reinforced ruler, then binding her hands together with a length of red tape labelled "EVIDENCE – DO NOT TAMPER."

Ren, fuelled by adrenaline and the rage of a woman who

had, quite frankly, had enough supernatural interference in her life, fought with a fury that surprised even her. She used the revolver as a bludgeon, then resorted to biting, scratching, and, in one memorable moment, hurling a fire extinguisher into a cluster of advancing cultists. The extinguisher discharged on impact, coating the enforcers in a blizzard of white foam and instant existential doubt.

Vincent, for his part, decided that dignity was overrated. He ducked a wild swing, caught a mask by the chin, and tore it free, revealing a young man with the face of someone who'd expected this to be a much less hazardous night out in the West End. Vincent shoved him into the orchestra pit, then turned and rammed his elbow into the face of the next opponent.

The magic in the room was unravelling. With every line Zara read, the boundaries between scene and reality blurred further. The remaining cultists began to flicker—one moment they were menacing, the next they looked lost, uncertain, as if they'd been summoned to the wrong rehearsal. A few stood in place, reciting lines from what sounded like different plays entirely. One, wearing a mask that appeared to be a tragic pig, bellowed, "Out, damned spot!" then collapsed in a heap.

Bartholomew, still limping from his fall, surveyed the carnage with mounting horror. His mask had cracked, revealing one wild eye and a jaw clenched so tight it seemed liable to snap. He made a last, desperate gesture to Cloak Woman.

She advanced, lips working behind the mask, and chanted a phrase that left scorch marks on the air.

Zara's head snapped up. "Oh, for heaven's sake," she muttered, and flipped to the back of her book. "Vincent! Duck!"

He did, just as a bolt of black energy split the space he'd

been occupying. The force of it knocked two cultists over and left a smoking furrow in the floorboards. Ren, never missing an opportunity, kicked Cloak Woman in the back of the knee, then decked her with a right hook that would have made her mother proud.

Mrs Barley, seeing the Cloak Woman fall, made straight for Bartholomew. She withdrew a heavy, metallic clipboard from her satchel, inscribed with the sigil of the City of Westminster. She swung it like a mace, catching Bartholomew in the ribs and sending him sprawling.

"Improper use of public property," Mrs Barley declared, standing over him. "I'm afraid that won't do. That won't do at all."

Bartholomew tried to speak, but only managed a strangled gurgle.

Vincent, battered but upright, used the moment to gather the survivors. "Ren, Zara—stage right. Mrs Barley, cover the exit."

The four converged near the shattered backdrop, ducking behind the remains of a prop archway. Mrs Barley dabbed her brow with a monogrammed handkerchief, then set about reorganising the contents of her compliance kit with the air of a woman reshelving books after a riot.

Zara, for the first time, looked tired. She blinked, her eyes slow to refocus. "That's the limit of what I can do," she said, voice hoarse but steady. "Their reality is... fragile now. If you can disrupt the ring leader, it should unravel the rest."

Vincent peered over the arch, took in the state of the theatre. The remaining cultists, no longer coherent as a group, milled in confusion. Some wept, some chanted, a few simply removed their masks and stared at their hands as if expecting to find answers in the creases.

Bartholemew was standing now, in the centre of the pit. He flexed his hands, enjoying the attention. When he spoke, it carried—less with sound than with intent.

"Is this all?" he called, disdain curdling the syllables. "Are these the champions of the age?"

Vincent felt the words burrow into his skull, old habits dying hard.

He drew a breath, then turned to the others. "I suppose," he said, "it falls to us."

Mrs Barley eyed him up and down, unimpressed. "If you're quite done bleeding everywhere, we have a job to finish."

Ren cocked the revolver, though, truth be told, it was more effective when used as a cosh. "After you, mate."

Zara nodded, then whispered, "Try not to let him monologue. It only encourages the dead."

Vincent straightened his tie, wiped a streak of blood from his lip, and stepped out onto the stage. The others followed, forming a line that was more school assembly than Avengers, but he'd take it.

Bartholemew regarded them with a sneer. "You presume to challenge me?"

Vincent shrugged. "I've got nothing better to do."

The theatre stilled. Even the city outside seemed to pause.

Vincent looked at the faces beside him: Ren, jaw set, ready to do violence; Mrs Barley, knuckles white on her umbrella, as calm as a judge at a cake competition; Zara, eyes like live wire, fighting through the fatigue to spin up the next spell.

Zara forced herself upright. Each breath came ragged, thick

with the copper tang of burning herself out, but still she raised her hand, fingers trembling like faulty antennae. The pew splintered further as power whipped through her, a crackling arc of violet light tearing across the stage.

Bartholomew didn't flinch. He lifted Vincent's script in both hands, pages fluttering, and the words themselves rose up to meet her strike. Sentences coiled in the air like serpents of ink, binding themselves into a wall of narration that caught her blast, absorbed it, and rewrote it into harmless sparks. He sneered. "Do you see? Even your brilliance is nothing when set against the will of the story."

Zara's jaw clenched. She spat blood, then hurled another spell—harder, sharper, a spear of raw will that cut through the curtain of words with a scream of tearing paper. Bartholomew reeled back, slammed against the table centre stage, script torn and smouldering at the edges.

She had him. For a heartbeat, she had him.

But her body faltered, half-solid, half-not. She staggered, lungs seizing, her silhouette flickering like a bad reel. The killing blow fizzled in her palm, dying before it could form.

And Bartholomew, eyes blazing with borrowed Carmine fire, raised his arms. The words leapt back into place, not a shield now but a weapon, jagged lines snapping forward with the force of a whip. "My turn," he said, and unleashed the curse.

Vincent never claimed to be an expert in loss, but he knew the taste. Metallic, intrusive, clinging to the gums for hours after the event. So when Bartholemew's strike hit Zara and she staggered back, like she was twelve Pornstar Martini's deep into an all-weekend hen do in Blackpool, he recognised the moment for what it was: an invoice due for payment.

She was half-there and half-not, a glitch in the meat of the world. Her hand went right through the varnished rail, then flickered back into existence, nails digging splinters before her palm ghosted away again. Her suit jacket lost all definition, collapsing into a shifting silhouette that revealed the lapels of the blouse beneath, then the memory of skin, then nothing but outline.

"Zara!" Ren hissed, breaking the spell with a shout. She moved to grab Zara by the elbow, but her fingers closed on nothing but the chill.

Zara's eyes found Vincent. "It's fine," she said. "Just... takes a second to adjust."

Vincent reached out, meaning to steady her. His hand passed clean through her shoulder, which felt like pushing into a deep freezer full of secrets and library dust. He pulled back, shivering.

The cultists, what few remained, sensed the change and bolted. The effect was instant and complete—a dozen masked fanatics, reduced to disoriented drama students, running for the exits as if the police had finally shown up to break up the party. Bartholemew simply stared at Zara in disbelief, as though he'd never once considered the possibility of someone dying in a new and original way.

Zara looked down at her hands, flexed them, watched as each finger went translucent at the tip and then slowly bled back into colour.

Ren, still too shocked for wit, said, "Are you—are you—?"

"Halfway through a reclassification," Zara said, managing a weak grin. "Don't suppose there's a benefits package for this one."

Mrs Barley watched from the footlights, face set. She withdrew a fresh knitting needle from her sleeve, examined it for straightness, then tucked it into her compliance kit with a decisive snap. "Bloody stupid risk," she said, voice as dry as shredded cardboard. "You could have warned us."

Zara managed to bow, or at least to approximate one; the top half of her body followed the gesture, the bottom half lagged behind by a fraction, like a badly encoded animated gif. "I had to improvise. There wasn't time for a health and safety briefing."

Vincent shook his head, struggling for a phrase that would capture the absurdity, the horror, and the faint, sour pride. "That's going to make our coffee mornings awkward," he said.

Zara was fading faster now. Her feet blurred into the floor, the outline dissolving from heel to knee as though someone had started erasing her from the ground up. Her hair floated around her head in a silver-grey nimbus, every strand individually detailed, the effect somehow more vivid than before.

Ren tried again to reach her, succeeded only in producing a faint ripple in the air. "What do we do?" she asked, turning to Vincent, then to Mrs Barley. "Is she—can we fix it?"

Mrs Barley shrugged, the gesture more formal than dismissive. "She's not lost. Just—" she paused, searching for the word, "—untethered."

Zara smiled, teeth now the most solid thing about her. "It's not so bad," she said, her voice carrying strangely—softer, but somehow in stereo, as if every echo in the theatre had decided to harmonise. "All the paperwork's digital, and I can read the foot-notes in real time."

Vincent couldn't tell if it was a joke or a warning. "Can you help us?"

Zara nodded. "More than before, actually." She stretched her arms, or what was left of them. "I can see the narrative. Where it's weak, where it's stitched. I can follow Bartholomew's script and even edit around it. So long as you don't mind a little haunting."

Ren snorted, which was as close to a blessing as she'd give.

The last of the cultists had vanished, leaving only dropped masks, empty goblets, and the stink of disappointment. Bartholemew, buoyed by the change in fortune, made a final, half-hearted lunge at the group, but found his way blocked by Mrs Barley's umbrella, which now shone with a faint blue shimmer.

"I'm not done with you yet, sunshine," Mrs Barley told him, and with a single, efficient push, sent the bastard straight back into the stage curtain.

Zara hovered now, inches off the stage, her body shedding little sparks of memory—fragments of old files, unfinished research, the ghost of a library catalogue. She wavered, then stabilised, a perfect spectral secretary, still taking notes in the afterlife.

Ren sat down hard on the lip of the stage, hands trembling just enough to rattle the revolver in her grip. "Next time you decide to die, maybe give us a heads up," she said.

Zara's voice came from everywhere at once, gentle as a librarian's whisper. "Next time, I'll do it by the book."

Vincent looked up, and caught Zara's eye, or whatever sense substituted for eye contact in her new state.

"Ready for the last act?" he asked.

Zara grinned, a perfect crescent of light and mockery. "After you," she said, her voice trailing off like the end of a sentence nobody wanted to finish.

Vincent squared his shoulders, and gestured to the others. "Let's finish the story," he said.

And somewhere in the ether, the city braced itself for whatever came next.

TWENTY-TWO

The Orpheum's main stage was a murder scene for metaphors. What wasn't bleeding was broken, and what wasn't broken had already been trampled into a mulch of velvet, powdered paint, and the kind of regrets that only ever got cleaned up with strong spirits and an Arts Council grant. In the centre of this ruin, two monsters circled each other with the lack of ceremony usually reserved for bin day in Hackney.

Bartholomew, still in what was left of his suit (now mostly rags and bad intentions), moved with the cold focus of someone who'd rehearsed this particular grudge for half a century. Vincent could see the man's hands flexing, bloodless and pale, fingertips blackened from old rituals or just a surfeit of nicotine. In a better-lit world, he might have passed for a retired bishop or a minor aristocrat fallen on hard times. Here, framed by the smoke and intermittent flicker of flames, he looked like a villain whose only regret was not killing more efficiently.

Vincent, for his part, stood with his back to a toppled

lighting rig and tried not to wobble. His shirt was ruined, his jacket long since surrendered to the mechanics of staged violence, and his left arm had gone from "fashionably pale" to "worrying shade of Victorian consumption." The adrenalin rush had faded, leaving behind only cold resolve and the sort of philosophical clarity that came from knowing every mistake was about to be called in for payment.

Bartholomew feinted right, then vanished entirely—a classic move, but always a bastard to counter. Vincent braced, waited, and—predictably—felt the impact at his flank, where Bartholomew had re-materialised with a flying tackle that could have earned a slow-motion replay on any television channel worth its salt. They both went down hard, skidding through a puddle of congealed candle wax and what Vincent sincerely hoped was stage blood.

Bartholomew was on top immediately, one hand clamped around Vincent's throat, the other pinning his wrist with supernatural force. "You never learned to stay down," he hissed, the accent pure boarding school but the delivery all gutter.

Vincent gasped, tried for wit, and got only a wheeze. "Why would I, when you make getting up so much fun?"

Bartholomew's lips curled, baring a set of teeth that glinted with unfamiliarity. It took Vincent a second to process: the bastard had silver caps. Every canine, every bicuspid—sterling and polished to a point. It was both grotesque and, on a certain level, deeply funny.

"Did you get those fangs done on Harley Street, or did you pop over to Turkey?" Vincent choked, managing a weak grin.

Bartholomew's reply was a growl and a downward plunge. The bite landed just below the crook of Vincent's elbow, where the flesh was thin and the nerves were close to the surface. The pain was immediate and unignorable: less puncture and more white-hot soldering iron, a spreading chemical agony that made Vincent see not just stars but entire unlicensed constellations.

He howled, jerked his arm away, and managed to plant a knee in Bartholomew's ribs. The ex-Renfield rolled, but didn't release the grip, instead digging in with the tenacity of a dog bred for bad decisions. Vincent twisted, managed to slam the heel of his hand into the bridge of Bartholomew's nose—nothing broke, but the head snapped back, and that was enough.

He got his legs under himself, staggered upright, and braced against a half-collapsed stage riser. His left arm was numb from the biceps down to the wrist, the skin already blistered and angry. The blood, which should have gushed, instead oozed out in a slow, silvery trickle, each drop hissing as it hit the floorboards.

Bartholomew licked the wound, eyes rolling back in momentary ecstasy. "Do you know how long I've waited for this?" he asked, voice echoing through the wreckage.

Vincent wiped his mouth on the back of his hand, spat blood onto the parquet. "Judging by your hairline, at least two world wars and the death of irony."

Bartholomew lunged again, this time with less grace, more brute force. Vincent sidestepped, caught a flying elbow to the ribs, and countered with a right cross that connected to Bartholomew's jaw with a satisfying crunch. The other man barely flinched. Instead, he smiled, the effect made more ghastly by the blood pooling at the gumline and the way it made the silver teeth shine like loose change in a wishing well.

They broke apart, circled. Somewhere in the balcony above,

the crystal of the shattered chandelier caught a breeze and sang a single, sweet note before collapsing to the ground in a tinkle of despair.

"Let's be honest," Vincent said, trying to keep the tremor out of his voice. "You could have settled this with a phone call and saved the cleaning bill."

Bartholomew's eyes narrowed. "You never could take responsibility, Vincent. Not for your words. Not for your consequences." He kicked a chunk of scenery at Vincent's feet. "You write the script, but someone else always cleans up the mess."

Vincent bent, picked up a jagged length of two-by-four, and weighed it in his palm. "Let's skip to the part where you tell me I'm my own worst enemy, shall we?"

Bartholomew obliged by rushing him again. They collided, wood against flesh, and for a moment Vincent had the upper hand—he caught Bartholomew under the chin with the plank, knocking him backwards into a stack of faux-marble pillars left over from the theatre's final production of Macbeth. The impact was suitably theatrical: pillars toppled, the scenery folded in a slow-motion collapse, and Bartholomew disappeared beneath the avalanche of plywood and fibreglass.

Vincent leaned on the plank, breathing hard, waiting for the punchline.

He didn't wait long. Bartholomew exploded from the wreckage with a shriek, one hand brandishing a splintered banister rail, the other clutching a prop skull. He hurled the skull first—cliché, but effective. Vincent ducked, caught the rail across the chest, and went down with a thud that vibrated through his sternum and into the root of his teeth.

Bartholomew straddled him, pressed the splinter to

Vincent's throat, and leaned in close enough that Vincent could smell the mix of aftershave and halitosis. "This is how it always ends," Bartholomew whispered. "With you, on your back, waiting for someone else to write you an ending."

Vincent smiled, or tried. "You really should have quit while you were ahead, Bart."

With the last of his strength, Vincent bucked his hips, knocked Bartholomew off-balance, and brought the splintered end of the rail up—catching his foe in the side, just above the kidney. Bartholomew hissed, but did not let go. Instead, he clamped down, sunk his silver teeth into Vincent's collarbone, and twisted.

Vincent screamed, clawed at Bartholomew's hair, and finally, in a move born more of desperation than strategy, bit back. He sank his fangs into the soft flesh of Bartholomew's neck and clamped down until the world went grey at the edges.

For a moment, the two men were locked in a grotesque parody of a lover's embrace: biting, tearing, desperate not to let the other go. The taste was salt and iron and static, a flavour that threatened to unmake Vincent from the inside out.

Bartholomew wrenched free, leaving a ragged piece of skin in Vincent's mouth. Vincent spat it out, rolled clear, and tried to stand, but his legs buckled and he went down on one knee.

"You see?" Bartholomew croaked, staggering upright, one hand clutching at his bleeding neck. "You're nothing but hunger and spite with a larger than average vocabulary. You always were."

Vincent shook his head, tried to laugh, and failed. "You say that like it's a bad thing."

They circled again, slower this time. The fight had devolved into a series of feints and exhaustion, each man too battered to risk a full assault but too angry to walk away. Every breath Vincent took was laced with pain and the coppery taste of his own mortality. He watched Bartholomew for any sign of hesitation, but the man was pure intent now—no room for banter, no space for regret.

They closed again, this time less spectacularly—just a grim, desperate grapple, hands on throats and knees to groins, both straining for the upper hand. They crashed through a balustrade, the wood snapping under their combined weight, and rolled onto the boards below, locked together like a pair of rats in a bin fight.

"Give up," Bartholomew hissed, breath hot against Vincent's ear. "It's already over."

Vincent laughed, the sound wet and raw. "I can't. You know that."

Bartholomew hauled back, threw a punch that rattled Vincent's teeth in their sockets. Vincent returned the favour with a headbutt, the impact sending a shockwave through both skulls and leaving him half-blind with the afterimage of pain.

The next exchange was less fight, more slow-motion demolition. They clawed, bit, and raked at each other with hands that were more weapon than limb, each landing blows that would have felled a lesser being. Vincent's vision swam with red, and he realised, distantly, that it was his own blood running into his eyes.

He wiped it away, saw Bartholomew advancing, and readied himself for the last, stupid charge.

"Need a better dentist next time," Vincent muttered, teeth bared.

Bartholomew grinned, and for a second Vincent saw the boy he'd once mentored, before the ambition and the rot had set in. It was almost enough to make him hesitate. Almost.

They collided one last time, bodies slamming together, and in the collision something gave—whether it was a bone, a will, or just the patience of the universe, Vincent wasn't sure.

When they broke apart, Vincent found himself still standing, just, while Bartholomew staggered back, clutching at the balustrade stake protruding from his chest. The wound above the pectoral pulsed, blood welling between his fingers. His face twisted, equal parts rage and disappointment.

"You think this matters?" Bartholomew gasped, voice bubbling with fluid. "You think any of it matters?"

Vincent steadied himself against a broken pillar, breathing through the pain. "That's the point," he said. "None of it does. Not unless you make it."

Bartholomew's knees buckled, but he refused to fall. "You never did understand. You never saw the story for what it is."

Vincent took a step forward, legs trembling. "And you never saw the end coming, did you."

They stood, two ruined titans, at the heart of the world's worst closing night.

Vincent waited for the punchline, but Bartholomew just glared at him, hate burning through the fatigue.

It was a stalemate, the kind that only ever ended with a trick, a cheat, or a miracle.

Vincent was fresh out of miracles.

He glanced around the wreckage, searching for something—anything—that could end it.

Bartholomew, bleeding out and still unbroken, took a shaky breath and prepared for one last lunge.

Vincent braced, blood pooling at his feet, and readied himself to improvise—because that, if nothing else, had always been his talent.

It was the stench that did it in the end—a bouquet of scorched velvet, wet ink, and the dying breath of a thousand candles. Vincent's head was swimming with the aftermath, but also with the knowledge that if Bartholomew didn't bleed out before he charged, he was going to have to do something spectacularly stupid to finish the job. He was out of weapons, out of breath, and—if he was being honest—out of good lines.

He reached for something to steady himself and his hand closed, miraculously, on a shaft of black. At first he thought it was a chunk of ruined scenery, but the texture was wrong: too light, too cold, too deliberate. He looked down and saw it was the quill he'd used to complete the last act of the play. It had rolled beneath the riser in the earlier chaos, surviving both fight and dramaturgy by sheer narrative perversity. The feather, which should have been charred to nothing, was intact. Its nib, once ceremonial, now glimmered with a wet shine that could only be fresh prophecy ink.

Vincent turned it in his hand, watching the surface shimmer. This was the sort of thing that got you killed, or worse, sued by the estate of a dead poet. Still, it was all he had.

He squared up, took a running lurch, and caught

Bartholomew full in the chest with the quill, just above the sternum.

The effect was instant. Bartholomew's body jerked, the ink leaping from the quill onto his skin, blossoming into lines of script that wrapped around his torso, arms, and neck. Each letter burned with a blue-black fire, chaining him not to the world but to the page, the rules of the story itself. Vincent could feel the pull, the weight of narrative gravity—this was not violence, but an edit.

Bartholomew howled, the sound climbing an octave with each new shackle, until his voice broke entirely and he was reduced to mouthing silent protests as the script overwrote his outline. His hands clawed at his chest, but the fingers passed through his own ribcage as if he'd gone suddenly two-dimensional, a smear of villain pressed between vellum sheets.

The runes reached his eyes, which rolled white, then black, then vanished altogether. Bartholomew's outline flickered, then collapsed into a cloud of loose punctuation, which drifted gently to the floor and evaporated with a faint scent of old library and missed deadlines.

Vincent stood over the empty patch, quill still in hand, and waited for his vision to catch up with the rest of him.

He got three breaths before the world punched him in the gut. Blood was soaking through his shirt in half a dozen places, each one leaking in time with a pulse that was rapidly losing its argument with entropy. The numbness in his left arm had become full-on dead weight, and his legs weren't so much "standing" as "remembering how to stand."

He staggered backwards, slumped onto the nearest flat

surface (a trunk labelled "PROPERTY OF ORPHEUM – DO NOT SIT"), and tried to take stock.

He'd done it. He'd written the ending.

It felt like shite.

The cold was crawling up his spine now, more a suggestion than a threat, but absolute in its intent. Vincent closed his eyes, let the stage lights burn orange imprints into his lids, and prepared for the traditional parade of regrets. He didn't get far.

A pair of hands, warm and unsteady, cupped his chin. Ren was there, somehow—clothes torn, one eye swelling shut, but more alive than she'd looked since this whole sorry production had started.

"Jesus Christ," she said, voice trembling, "you look like you've been through a blender."

Vincent tried to smile, managed a twitch instead. "I'd pay extra for that, but they say you can't improve on the classics."

She ignored him, crouched low, and inspected the wounds. Her fingers were gentle, tracing the edge of the collarbone where Bartholomew had bitten deepest.

"You're dying," she said, deadpan.

Vincent looked down at the river of blood pooling on the stage. "I've had worse hangovers."

Ren snorted, but her eyes were wet. "You need to drink."

He shook his head, or tried. "I'm not going to feed. Not from you."

She laughed—a single, explosive sound, halfway between joy and rage. "You absolute bastard. After all that, you're going to be noble?"

He closed his eyes again, feeling the edges of consciousness fray. "It's not nobility. It's fear. I wouldn't be able to stop. I'd take you with me."

She sat down next to him, thigh pressed hard to his. "Too late for that. You already did."

They sat in silence, the ruined stage settling around them like the aftermath of a very expensive funeral. Somewhere behind the scenery, the antiquated fire suppression system finally kicked in, spraying a half-hearted rain that did nothing for the ambiance but gave everything a smell of damp bandages and chlorine.

Ren pulled a penknife from her boot, flicked it open, and pressed the blade to her own palm. The cut was neat, just below the thumb, and the blood welled instantly.

She shoved her hand against Vincent's mouth.

"Drink," she said. "I am not having you die on me, not after all the crap you've put me through."

Vincent tried to turn away, but she was stronger than he was now. "I mean it," she said, pressing harder, "I will break your fucking jaw if you don't."

He opened his mouth, tasted her blood—sharp, new, a rush of life so intense it nearly stopped his heart altogether. He sucked, just once, then recoiled, terrified at the taste of her, at what it would mean if he lost control.

She held him there. "Trust me," she whispered, and the words were more intimate than any spell or confession.

Vincent drank.

The sensation was nothing like the baroque erotica he'd ghostwritten for decades. It was hunger, but also grief, rage, memory—everything raw and unfinished, flooding into him until he wasn't sure where he stopped and she started. Her pulse beat against his lips, and he tried to measure it, to ration, but the blood told its own story and refused to slow down.

When she pulled her hand away, her wrist was shaking, and her face was pale, but she smiled. "You good?" she asked.

He nodded, not trusting his voice.

She sagged against him, arm thrown over his shoulder in the world's least convincing version of a victory hug. "You're a menace," she said. "But you're my menace."

Vincent looked at her, saw the unvarnished truth in the exhaustion, the dirt, the blood. He tried to say something profound, but what came out was, "I think I've ruined these clothes."

She laughed again, and the sound was enough.

The rain from the sprinklers had gone cold, washing away the blood but not the memory. They sat together, Vincent's head on Ren's shoulder, her hand still pressed to the wound, and waited for the next disaster to arrive.

Neither of them said it, but the story had changed.

This time, they both got the last word.

TWENTY-THREE

Mrs Barley had always despised the way prophecies made themselves at home in a place. She could still recall the acrid aftertaste of the last one she'd exorcised: a mid-tier apocalyptic job wedged behind the utility meters at the Camden Civic, whose only discernible effect was to turn the custodian's evening sherry into battery acid. This one—whatever Bartholemew and the Cloak Woman had summoned—was far worse. Even the ruined shell of the Orpheum, down to its smouldering upholstery and flop-sweat stench, seemed to be holding its breath.

Mrs Barley gave the theatre a professional once-over, taking in the debris with the long-suffering forbearance of a housekeeper cleaning up after toddlers. Torn velvet curtains drooped from the fly space like the tongues of dying animals; the chandelier, last seen in pieces, was now only a bitter memory and a collection of glass teeth on the pit floor. Candles, guttering in uneven ranks, provided the only lighting, which in turn cast the

Cloak Woman's silhouette up onto the plaster like the city's worst Rorschach test.

Cloak Woman staggered up from the parquet, slowly at first, and stood at the edge of the stage, arms held wide, cloak in full pageant mode. Shadows rippled around her, animated by an intelligence Mrs Barley recognised from every ill-advised seance and Ouija experiment she'd cleaned up since '76. But it was the words—actual words, shreds of text torn from a thousand forgotten stories—that disturbed her most. They visibly hovered, luminous and jittery, around the Cloak Woman's head like moths with a taste for punctuation.

Vincent and Ren huddled together in the front row, casualties of their own plot but still too alive to shut up. Ren clutched a makeshift tourniquet round Vincent's arm with the grim intensity of someone who'd learned first aid from a YouTube playlist called "Fix Your Mates in a Riot." Vincent, for his part, was contributing little beyond snark and the occasional dribble of blood. They looked, Mrs Barley thought, like the promotional poster for a very unlicensed stage adaptation of *Trainspotting*.

"Right, you," Mrs Barley said, her voice carrying a tone that, even now, brooked no contradiction.

She unlatched her satchel—battered, monogrammed, and technically an artefact of the Greater London Authority's Department of Nuisance Containment—and withdrew her compliance kit. The kit had begun life as an overengineered doctor's bag, but years of emergency upgrades had rendered it a museum of quick fixes and legally ambiguous weaponry. She produced a vial of garlic spray, a length of reinforced umbrella with a sharpened ferrule, and—her personal favourite—three silver-plated knitting needles, size 10.

Mrs Barley advanced onto the stage. The Cloak Woman watched, impassive behind her mask.

"Do you really think," Mrs Barley asked, "that anyone's impressed by this kind of carry-on? I've seen better productions at the local primary school."

The Cloak Woman's head tilted, the mask's carved lips twisting into a sneer.

"You have no idea, old mother, what is at stake," she said. Her voice wasn't a voice so much as a chorus, every syllable doubled with the resonance of something that had been rehearsed too many times for comfort. "This is prophecy. Not your council busywork."

Mrs Barley tutted, and launched her first attack.

The umbrella, wielded one-handed, was less a weapon and more a statement of intent. She jabbed it at the Cloak Woman's chest, quick and surgical. The point met the cloak and was deflected, but Mrs Barley anticipated this, pivoted, and followed with a cloud of garlic spray directly into the villain's mask-slits. The Cloak Woman reeled, or at least gave a passable impression of someone unprepared for aerosolised alium.

"Council-issue," Mrs Barley remarked, voice dry as a lecture. "Available in all good supply cupboards."

The Cloak Woman lashed out with a claw of shadow, but Mrs Barley batted it aside with the umbrella and, using the same motion, whipped a knitting needle into the woman's shoulder. It stuck, just below the seam; a line of black-red ichor welled around it, then froze into beads that hovered in the air.

"Jesus. She's good," Ren cheered from the stalls.

The Cloak Woman dropped the performative composure. Her next move was pure anger: she flicked her hands, and a volley of prophecy fragments shot outwards like shrapnel. Each one was a line of text, jagged and luminous, reciting itself as it travelled.

Mrs Barley ducked the first, let the second score a line across her jacket, and blocked the third with the umbrella. It left a smoking brand in the fabric, but not much else.

She closed the distance. Another needle—this one underhand, straight for the ribs. The Cloak Woman sidestepped, but Mrs Barley had already pivoted, landing a chop with the umbrella across the back of the knees. The villain went down on one, cloak bunching in a dramatic puddle.

"Is this really what you wanted?" Mrs Barley asked. "All this drama for what? Fancy dress and bad poetry?"

The Cloak Woman's eyes narrowed behind the mask. She clapped her hands, once. The stage floor answered, splitting wide with a sound like tearing parchment.

From the new chasm, more prophecy poured forth—dozens, maybe hundreds of scraps of narrative, each one a different shade of incandescent. They clustered around the Cloak Woman, feeding into her outline, making her taller, broader, more than she'd been a moment before.

Mrs Barley braced, umbrella held two-handed now, but she could feel the weight of the magic pressing against her will, the air thickening with every recited line.

"Stay back," she called over her shoulder. "It's escalating."

Ren tried to stand, made it to the edge of the stage, but the shadows pushed her down as if gravity had doubled. Vincent, too, tried to rise, but his left leg betrayed him, and he slumped back into his front-row seat, muttering a litany of what might have been curses or just excerpts from unfinished manuscripts.

The Cloak Woman—now nearly two metres tall and wrapped in a cocoon of living prophecy—loomed over Barley, arms lifted in victory.

"This is not your story, Housekeeper," she intoned. "This is the city's reckoning. The play must finish."

Mrs Barley bared her teeth. "Try it."

The next attack was less elegant: a broad, hammering sweep of shadow designed to flatten. Mrs Barley sidestepped, but the edges caught her, sending a spike of numbness up her left side. She compensated, lashed out with the umbrella and managed to clip the Cloak Woman's ankle.

Barley's movements were slower now, the umbrella feeling heavier, her vision tunnelling. Sweat beaded at her temples. She gritted her teeth and made herself count out loud—one, two, three—every time she inhaled.

The Cloak Woman pressed the advantage, raining down a hail of prophecy shards. Each one stung, some drawing blood, others just bruising the will.

From the periphery, Ren's voice: "You got this, Mrs Barley!"

"Look out, left!" Vincent warned.

Mrs Barley rolled under the next sweep, came up on her knees, and—using her last knitting needle—hurled it underarm into the Cloak Woman's thigh.

There was a pause. Then, the villain howled.

The prophecy fragments shivered, their orbit losing coherence. For a brief, beautiful moment, Mrs Barley could see the woman beneath the cloak: pinched face, eyes wild, hair cropped short and slicked to her scalp with sweat. She was younger than Mrs Barley had expected. Not a true immortal, just a bureaucrat of fate with ambitions beyond her station.

Mrs Barley planted her feet, gripped the umbrella like a halberd, and lunged. The tip caught the Cloak Woman in the solar plexus. For a second, both women stood locked in place.

"You know," Mrs Barley hissed, voice trembling from effort, "if you'd put half as much effort into civic engagement, you could have run this city."

The Cloak Woman's mask twitched. "You can't stop what was written."

Mrs Barley forced the umbrella deeper. "Then I'll write a new ending."

The world shivered.

Something gave way inside the Cloak Woman. The prophecy fragments lost their structure, flitting away like startled starlings. She staggered backwards, clutching at the umbrella still lodged in her middle.

Mrs Barley pressed forward, one step at a time, boots slipping on the cocktail of wax, blood, and liquefied narrative that coated the boards. The Cloak Woman tried to summon another fragment, but her voice failed. All that came out was a strangled gasp and a flurry of half-formed sentences.

With a final, decisive motion, Mrs Barley twisted the umbrella free and jabbed it into the villain's shoulder, pinning her to the proscenium arch.

The effect was instant. The prophecy, stripped of a host, exploded outwards in a shockwave of pure, unmediated story. For a split-second, Mrs Barley was everywhere—every moment she'd ever lived, every regret, every memory she'd tried to box away in the years since the city council dissolved the old order. Then it was gone, and she was herself again, standing over a defeated enemy and feeling, for once, nothing but cold satisfaction.

The Cloak Woman slid down the arch, cloak tangling around her knees. She looked up at Mrs Barley, face pale and lips pulled into a snarl.

"Housekeeper," she spat.

Mrs Barley nodded. "Exactly."

She turned to Ren and Vincent, both of whom had managed to crawl onto the lip of the stage. Ren and the ghostly Zara managed a weak clap. Vincent just wheezed and gave her a thumbs-up.

Mrs Barley straightened her jacket, retrieved her knitting needles, and wiped the worst of the prophecy off her umbrella.

"Let's get you two out of here," she said, voice as brisk and clear as the morning after.

They made it four steps before the floor opened up beneath them, shadows reaching, snaring Mrs Barley's ankles and dragging her off her feet.

Ren screamed, lunging after her, but the darkness was too quick. Mrs Barley's last sight before she was pulled into the black was Vincent's face, mouth open in a warning she couldn't quite hear, and the Cloak Woman's mask, still fixed on her with a gaze of absolute, unkillable contempt.

Then the world snapped shut, and Mrs Barley was gone.

Mrs Barley surfaced into the void with the reluctant clarity of a woman arriving late for her own funeral. The world was stripped of colour and noise: a blank stage, no audience, the dust not even bothering to settle. She took inventory. Both legs were cocooned in bands of shadow, cold as ice and twice as unyielding; her arms were pinned behind her back, wrists welded together by the same material. She tasted metal, and—less welcome—a distant sweetness like burning plastic.

The Cloak Woman hovered above, every inch the high priestess of other people's disasters. Her mask, now fused to her face, glistened with a damp, unblinking sheen. Around her, the prophecy shards circled, hungry for a denouement.

Mrs Barley craned her neck and caught sight of her world on the other side of the veil: Ren and Zara, standing over Vincent, who sprawled sideways, blood haloing the theatre floor. She saw Ren smashing at the stage floor with the hilt of the pistol, trying to break through and keep fighting, and felt a rush of perverse pride at the girl's refusal to stand down. The Cloak Woman didn't even notice. Her focus was on Mrs Barley, and on the story that needed finishing.

"You are a stubborn relic," the villain said, voice ringing with the authority of every rejected ballot and failed council motion. "You are irrelevant. The prophecy will feed, and I—" she hesitated, mask twitching, "—I will become what I was always meant to be."

Mrs Barley shifted, feeling the pain in her shoulders blossom and subside, replaced by a cold resolve.

"'Irrelevant' is what they said when they closed the libraries," Mrs Barley replied, her voice astonishingly steady for someone tied up in a hostile footnote. "Didn't stop me. Won't stop me now."

The Cloak Woman leaned in, eyes blazing from behind the

mask. "You are already erased. I looked for you in the record, and found only redacted lines."

Mrs Barley bared her teeth in something that wasn't quite a smile. "You should have looked in the margins."

The pressure grew, the shadows thickening around her, squeezing air and thought into a single, jagged line. Mrs Barley could feel her own story being read—page by page, paragraph by paragraph—by the prophecy. She felt the edits, the omissions, the moments when her name had been X'd out by bureaucratic decree.

If they wanted her erasure, she'd give it to them.

She closed her eyes and let her mind wander, not to the glory days of the order or the pride of a perfectly-judged tea service, but to the moments they'd deleted: the birthdays skipped over, the letters that came back "recipient unknown," the faces that, in the end, never called her "mum" or "sister" or even "friend." There were blank calendars, and yearbooks with photos blurred out, and a single box of documents at the back of a locked office, each file stamped "irrelevant" in triplicate.

She brought these up, one by one, and laid them out in the black. The prophecy fragments hesitated, hovered, then swirled in a vortex around this new offering.

The Cloak Woman screeched, the sound raw and animal. "No. You cannot feed it nothing. It is impossible—"

Mrs Barley's lips twitched. "It's not nothing. It's what you left behind."

The prophecy—hungry, self-correcting, desperate for closure—latched on. It slurped up the erased birthdays, the inked-out signatures, the shredded council memos. The more it took, the more the Cloak Woman faltered, her outline growing thin, the shadows losing integrity.

"You will die empty," the villain spat, panic flooding her tone.

Mrs Barley shook her head. "I'll die how I lived: with the paperwork finished, the dinner plates washed and left on the draining board, and the bin out on the right day."

The prophecy fragments, gorged on deletion, grew bright and hot, then collapsed in on themselves. They circled Mrs Barley in a perfect ring, cutting her free from the shadows. She rolled to her feet—awkward, unpractised, but upright—and faced the villain, who now clutched at her chest as if trying to hold her story in.

Mrs Barley felt the void eating away at her—every memory, every accomplishment, every time someone had used her name in a sentence. She knew the cost, and it was fine. It was more than fine: it was, for the first time in her long, professionally anonymous life, worth it.

She stepped up to the Cloak Woman and, with two fingers, flicked the mask from her face. It shattered on the ground, leaving nothing beneath. The villain's body, without a story to bind it, wavered, then collapsed inward, folding over and over until it was the size of a thumbprint and then, less than that, the afterimage of a sigh.

Mrs Barley turned, the prophecy ring still whirling, and walked out of the void. Each step left less of her behind. By the time she reached the light, she was lighter by many things— regret, ambition, all the weight of unspent legacy—but she was still walking.

She found herself in the Orpheum again, on the stage, Ren

staring at her like she was an apparition, Vincent rising unsteadily behind.

Mrs Barley opened her mouth to speak, found her voice quieter, a shade thinner. She coughed, once, and tried again.

"Right," she said. "Let's get this place cleared up before the authorities arrive. Who wants a cup of tea?"

Ren grinned, eyes bright with tears. Vincent, still leaking from several places, gave a two-fingered salute.

Mrs Barley smiled back, not quite sure what else there was to do.

She pressed a hand to her throat, feeling the hollow where her voice used to carry more weight. She would be fine. Or, at least, she would be enough.

TWENTY-FOUR

The Orpheum looked like the aftermath of a particularly vindictive production of *Titus Andronicus*: everything was sticky, nothing was upright, and the air was so thick with smoke and loose magic you could have bottled it and sold it to disaffected teenagers. The city had gone eerily quiet outside, but within the theatre, history and prophecy were still squabbling over the bill.

Ren, never one to be idle in a crisis, was the first to start picking through the debris. She waded into the carnage with a bin bag and a pair of latex gloves filched from the makeshift St. John's Ambulance kit Mrs Barley kept in her satchel. She scooped up handfuls of parchment, most of it still flickering with residual ink, and threw them onto the centre of the stage, where a ceremonial brazier (likely last used to roast chestnuts for a Christmas panto) had been pressed into service as a bonfire. The flames were already hungry, crackling with a blue-green tongue and a smell that managed to be both intoxicating and deeply wrong.

Vincent sat on the proscenium steps, cradling his left arm and watching the fire with the particular fascination of a man who suspected it might be hungry for him, personally. His suit had bled through to the lining, and the pale shirt beneath was ruined beyond even his standards for sartorial neglect. Every so often, he plucked a page from the stack beside him, read a line aloud in mock-sermon, and then, with exaggerated drama, consigned it to the flames.

"'The city shall rise, clothed in its own ashes...'" he intoned, then flicked the scrap into the fire. "Let's hope the fashion suits."

Mrs Barley, restored to a veneer of professional calm by the rhythm of cleanup, stalked the aisles with a dustpan and brush, tutting at the mess and muttering about proper disposal protocols. Each time she found a torn-out chunk of prophecy, she would examine it, purse her lips as though weighing its threat to public order, then snap it in half and pass it to Ren for incineration. Sometimes the torn pieces would fight back, trying to glue themselves to her fingers or sprout tiny fangs that nipped at her sleeves. Mrs Barley never batted an eye, just gave them a quick jab with a recovered knitting needle and moved on.

Zara, the late and apparently posthumous arrival to the team, floated above the stage like the world's most judgmental lighting technician. She drifted through the rafters, translucent and wreathed in a halo of static, occasionally poking her head down to point out a missed scrap or, once, a wriggling chunk of prophecy that had attempted to disguise itself as a spent fuse. Her voice carried in the uncanny way of those unburdened by flesh, but her sense of sarcasm had, if anything, only been enhanced by death.

"Left, Vincent," she called. "By your knee. That's a live one."

Vincent bent, winced, and picked up a ragged corner of vellum. It writhed in his hand, trying to snake up his sleeve, but he shook it off with a flourish. "My hero," he said. "You always did have a knack for catching the bits everyone else missed."

Zara's ghostly brow arched. "It's called attention to detail. Some of us actually finished the paperwork."

Ren shot Vincent a look. "You all right to keep going? I can do this solo if you want to be useless and play victim for a bit."

He gave a theatrical sigh, then pitched another scrap into the fire. "If I stop, I'll stiffen up," he said. "And besides, I'm hoping the smoke will cauterise something important."

Mrs Barley, still methodically sweeping the stalls, said, "If you're not careful, it'll cauterise your sense of perspective. Some of these fragments are still active. Try not to inhale them."

Vincent considered this, then shrugged. "Could be worse. At least it's not glitter."

For a while, they worked in something approaching harmony. The prophecy burned with a vindictive eagerness, each page igniting in a gout of green or a howl of bottled regret. The brazier filled the theatre with a shifting light, casting the figures on stage as giants or shadows depending on the flicker of the flames. Even the ancient boards seemed to shudder with relief each time a page was reduced to embers.

But after half an hour, the prophecy began to notice.

The first sign was the sound: not the crackle of burning parchment, but the soft whisper of paper moving under its own power. A draught, maybe, or a memory of a draught, teased loose pages from the corners of the room. They slid along the floor, riding the currents of their own inevitability, and clustered at the base of the stage like an audience unwilling to go home. Ren noticed it first.

"Mrs Barley," she called. "We've got company."

Mrs Barley straightened, squinting into the gloom. "Just paper," she said. "Keep burning."

But the pages multiplied. Some fluttered from the ruined balcony, shedding ink like dandruff. Others fell from the fly space, where Zara had missed them in her circuit. Still more crept from beneath the seats, each one stitched with line after line of Carmine's worst and weirdest predictions.

Vincent watched as a dozen pages coalesced at his feet, then slowly assembled themselves into a rough effigy of a man. The paper figure tottered upright, arms pinwheeling, then made a grab for his ankle.

Vincent didn't hesitate. He stomped the thing flat and tossed the shreds into the brazier, where they vanished in a single, hissed curse.

Ren, undeterred by the mounting weirdness, started stuffing pages into the fire two-handed. She worked with the intensity of someone trying to outrun a deadline, and the prophecy answered her aggression with more of its own: pages leapt for her face, tried to wedge themselves between her lips, snaked up her sleeves in an effort to tattoo her from the inside.

Mrs Barley abandoned the dustpan and joined the fray, wielding her umbrella like a riot baton. She batted the worst offenders into a growing pile, then doused them in a measured splash of holy water from her hip flask. The liquid sizzled and steamed, but the pages only grew more desperate, fusing together into a single, wriggling mass that crawled for the fire.

"Zara!" Mrs Barley called. "Can you do something?"

Zara, who had been observing the chaos from above, shook her head in spectral dismay. "I'm incorporeal, remember? Besides, you lot seem to be enjoying yourselves."

Vincent looked up, hair wild and eyes red from smoke. "We're about to get buried in prophecy, and you're doing commentary?"

"Management," Zara replied, and then, with a sudden intensity, "Mrs Barley, behind you!"

Mrs Barley spun. A length of parchment, thicker than the rest, had wound itself around the haft of her umbrella and was climbing toward her hand. She jabbed at it with a knitting needle, but the needle snapped in half, the metal dissolving with a shriek.

Ren ripped the thing away, bare-handed, and hurled it into the brazier. The fire reacted as if it had been given rocket fuel: the green flames exploded outward, washing the stage in a pulse of light and sound that knocked everyone flat.

For a heartbeat, the theatre went silent. Then, in unison, every loose scrap of prophecy in the room shivered and took flight.

It was, Vincent reflected, the world's least welcome ticker-tape parade. The air filled with shredded lines and bleeding runes, each fragment circling the centre of the stage in a tightening gyre. The words themselves began to speak, a chorus of overlapping voices that alternately begged, threatened, and plagiarised themselves in real time.

Ren covered her head, swearing. Vincent, unable to do

much with one working arm, ducked behind Mrs Barley, who had crouched into a defensive stance and was swiping at the flying paper with the remains of her umbrella.

Zara, now a swirling spectre in the heart of the vortex, began to recite lines in counterpoint. "Don't let them touch you," she warned. "They'll rewrite your memories if they can."

Mrs Barley gritted her teeth. "Well, they're about to get the business end of my retention policy."

The next few minutes were a blur: Mrs Barley and Ren snatched at pages, tearing them out of the air and feeding them into the ravenous brazier. Vincent, struggling to stay conscious, improvised by using a burnt chair leg as a makeshift paddle, batting the more persistent fragments into the flames.

The prophecy, sensing its impending doom, escalated. The pages fused into shapes—a snake that slithered down a curtain, a wolf's head that snapped at Mrs Barley's hand, a swarm of black-red butterflies that clung to Ren's hair and refused to dislodge. Each creature died with a shriek or a curse, always in Carmine's voice, always with a fresh layer of melodrama.

Zara, dipping in and out of the vortex, began to collect the fragments herself—her ghostly hands passing through the paper, but somehow drawing the words into her outline. She pulsed with new light each time, her eyes crackling with stolen electricity.

"Zara!" Vincent called. "Are you—"

She turned, smile brittle. "It's fine. I always wanted to be a walking library."

The final, furious wave hit as the prophecy gathered itself for one last stand. Every surviving scrap in the theatre twisted together, forming a tower of pages that loomed above the brazier. At its summit, a rough paper mask of Carmine's own face glared down at them, lips twitching with recycled menace.

Vincent, dragging himself upright, met the mask's gaze. "You're overwritten, old friend," he said, and, with a last effort, hurled the chair leg at the base of the tower.

The blow toppled the whole structure into the fire. The mask screamed—a sound composed of every angry rejection slip Vincent had ever received—and then disintegrated in a cyclone of blue flame.

When Vincent's hearing came back, the stage was empty except for a few drifting embers. The prophecy, for the first time in centuries, had nothing left to say.

Ren sat up first, rubbing her head. "We finally done?" she asked, voice hollow.

Mrs Barley checked the perimeter, then dusted off her hands. "Done," she said.

Zara, now fully corporeal in her incorporeality, hovered over the remains of the brazier. "You lot make a hell of a mess," she said. "I'll be cleaning up the echo of this for a decade."

Vincent, leaning heavily on the ruined steps, managed a weak smile. "We can take turns haunting the next lot."

They sat for a moment, letting the relief soak in. The Orpheum, still battered and bleeding, felt lighter than it had in years.

Vincent looked around at his unlikely coven, and found that, for once, he had nothing clever to say.

The peace lasted just long enough for the Orpheum to remember its own structural integrity. The first warning was a groan from above, followed by the fall of plaster dust that gently snowed onto their heads, lending everyone a last-second touch of pantomime.

Then, with the perverse sense of timing only a condemned building could manage, the entire upper balcony lurched free of its moorings and caved inwards, flattening three rows of red velvet seats below with a sound like a thousand typewriters being thrown into the Thames.

Ren shot to her feet, eyes wild. "That's our cue."

Vincent tried to stand, but his left leg mutinied at the suggestion. "Regret to inform you that my dramatic exits are strictly limited to limp mode," he said.

Mrs Barley was already moving, herded by a deep-seated refusal to ever be the last to the fire drill. She grabbed Vincent's good arm and yanked, with the competence of someone who'd spent thirty years helping elderly relatives up ice-slicked church steps. "Out. Now. Ren, take his other side."

Ren slung Vincent's arm over her shoulder. He sagged against her, offering a wan smile. "You know, this is exactly how I pictured our first dance."

She elbowed him in the ribs, gently. "You weigh a ton and smell like bonfire."

"Flattered," he panted, half-dragged along as the dust thickened.

Zara hovered behind, trailing a shower of blue-white sparks. "I'd offer to help, but, you know—lacking the corporeal touch." She zipped ahead, her afterimage dancing in the smoke. "This way. And hurry."

The quartet pelted (or limped, in Vincent's case) up the centre aisle as the ceiling above them groaned in a language only load-bearing walls could speak. Chunks of painted plaster rained down, the cherubs and muses from the proscenium arch smashing to powder on the carpet. Each footfall threatened to pitch them through to the sub-basement, where the river's tide gurgled and the city's least sanitary rats waited for an encore.

A chandelier—last seen glittering above the stalls—picked this moment to break free, plummeting to earth with a hiss of broken glass and the musicality of a heavy metal album played backwards. It landed dead centre, missing Barley's head by a margin usually reserved for legal blood alcohol limits.

Ren swore and doubled her pace. Vincent tried to contribute with his good leg, but the effort sent a fresh wave of red blooming through his ruined shirt. "I'm afraid going any faster really isn't in my current repertoire," he gasped.

Mrs Barley, unruffled, snapped, "Neither is dying in a collapsing theatre, so move."

Zara called from the lobby: "Come on!"

They veered through the grand vestibule, which was already filling with smoke. The glass in the front doors had shattered inwards, the leaded panes now scattered like a jeweller's tantrum. Ren kicked the last door open, and together they stumbled out onto the cracked stone steps.

The night air hit them with the relief of a cold lager after a funeral. They gulped it down, blinking at the sudden quiet.

For a second, the world went slow.

Then the Orpheum gave up the rest of its will to live. The painted dome, that gaudy carousel of angelic disappointment, caved in, sending a gout of green-blue fire skywards. The noise rolled over them in a wave of pressure, flattening the hedges in the square and sending car alarms into full-throated hysteria.

The next disaster was more personal. The chunk of theatre that had formed the eastern facade, with its ornate crest and the words "HORATIO'S ORPHEUM" in ancient script, detached and plummeted directly onto Ren's beloved Peugeot. The car, which had survived three relationships, two MOTs, and a collision with a taxi driver, folded like wet cardboard.

Ren stared at the wreck, mouth open in a perfect O.

Vincent, bracing himself on a bollard, surveyed the carnage. "Well," he said, "at least it wasn't my deposit."

Mrs Barley, who had never trusted foreign cars, gave a short, satisfied nod. "You can bill the council," she said.

Zara drifted to Ren's side, offering a spectral pat on the back. "Look on the bright side. Parking's free for the rest of the year."

Ren managed a laugh, but it came out half-choked. "That's not how insurance works," she said, tears blurring her vision as she watched the final, dignified beep of the Peugeot's alarm fade to silence.

Vincent turned to Mrs Barley, a question in his eyes.

She caught it, and gave him a look that managed to combine commiseration, maternal exasperation, and an unspoken offer of tea. "Let's get you stitched up before you leak all over the pavement," she said. "And Ren, we're all staying in one place tonight. No arguments."

Ren just nodded, arms wrapped around herself as if afraid her organs might try to escape too.

They limped away from the smouldering ruin, a housekeeper, a vampire, a human, and a ghost, none of them quite fitting the description on their name tags. Behind them, the Orpheum finally collapsed, the flames licking up the last of Carmine's prophecy with a satisfied hiss.

"Next time," Mrs Barley said, adjusting her singed cardigan and giving her best glare to the heavens, "we're burning prophecies somewhere with proper fire exits."

No one disagreed.

They walked on, into the hush that follows a disaster, already arguing about whose turn it was to make tea, and whether Zara counted for the purposes of a tie-break.

The city, as always, carried on.

TWENTY-FIVE

Three days of theoretical rest had rendered Vincent Lupo into an exhibit of ambulatory morbidity, carefully arranged on the fold-out daybed in Zara's book-lined parlour. The effect was that of a minor saint or defrocked potentate, swaddled to the chin in percale and old hospital bandages, his hair slicked back from fever and convalescence. The only evidence of vitality was the permanent, if faded, stain of sarcasm clinging to his lower lip.

Mrs Barley, whose official stance on palliative care was that it should be administered briskly and, if possible, with enough force to dislodge malingering, stood at his elbow. She fluffed the pillows with an aggression usually reserved for electoral fraud, then leaned over him, holding a mug of something that smelled of Bovril, iodine, and, inexplicably, Pimm's.

"Drink," she said, "or I'll have it upended into you. Nothing grows back right if you let it dry out." She watched as Vincent made a show of sipping, then set the mug down with all the ceremony of a prisoner declining his last meal.

Ren watched from the doorway, arms folded and jaw set. Whilst the rest of Zara's flat was strictly clinical minimalist aesthetic, the parlour was barely recognisable as a living space: floor to ceiling in paperbacks, the air hazed with the warm, dry scent of old glue and colder, less sociable hints of formaldehyde and bandage adhesive. Someone had drawn the curtains against the daylight, but a halo of city glow seeped through the fabric, turning everything a shade less alive than it was.

"What's in that?" she asked, nodding to the mug.

Mrs Barley pursed her lips. "Electrolytes and beef stock. One for the soul, one for the cellular matrix. Both taste better than your last attempt at microwave dinner."

Vincent coughed—deliberately, for effect. "I preferred the morphine. At least that had a story."

"Well, you're not having any more," Mrs Barley snapped, and adjusted the bandage at his neck with something close to tenderness. "The last of it left your system yesterday, and it did nothing for your appetite. The beef will have to do."

Ren caught his eye and shrugged in silent agreement. Her gaze wandered the room, tracing the lines of the bookcases, which towered in untidy ranks up to the lath and plaster ceiling. There were academic sketches tacked to the wall, most of them anatomical in nature, a few depicting the muscular structure of bats and what looked suspiciously like the exoskeleton of a giant insect.

"It's like an old library got into a relationship with a morgue," Ren said, to no one in particular.

Vincent's voice was papery, but he managed to aim it at her.

"I'll take that as a compliment. Libraries are underrated places for romance."

From somewhere above, a faint crackle of static. At first, Ren assumed it was the heating—Zara's radiators were more promise than performance—but the sound resolved itself into speech, clear and precise, ringing as if through a long corridor.

"I hear we're doing post-mortems before breakfast now," Zara's voice called, cool and just the right side of spectral.

Ren jumped, glancing up. The ceiling was shadowed, but near the cornicing, a distortion shimmered: the outline of Zara's head and shoulders, flickering, more like a projection than a presence. She hovered there, her hair floating in a slow, viscous halo, eyes unblinking and a shade too large.

"I'd offer tea, but I can't touch anything that isn't at least 40% dead," Zara added, drifting downwards and coalescing at the threshold.

Mrs Barley's expression did not change. She set the mug down on the rickety table and went to retrieve a stack of clean towels from the airing cupboard, muttering about "premature hauntings" as she passed. Vincent watched her go, then glanced up at Zara's ghostly presence.

"Nice of you to manifest in time for visiting hours," he said.

Zara's mouth quirked. "You're not my only patient."

Ren, less accustomed to spectral visitations, edged around the sofa until she was at Vincent's side, using him as a very inefficient meat shield. "Can she see us? Or is this like a conference call?"

"I can see you fine," Zara answered, a faint echo in her voice. She regarded Ren with a disconcertingly unblinking stare.

Ren flinched at the scrutiny, but managed a brittle smile. "Still breathing. No thanks to some."

Vincent stifled a smirk, then winced as the movement pulled at the healing bite on his neck. "We're all a little less alive than we were."

Mrs Barley returned, towels in hand. She spared a look at the hovering Zara and said, "I suppose you'll want to have your say before we get him up and about."

Zara floated a little closer, her outline flickering like a faulty fluorescent tube. "Actually, yes," she said, voice dropping to the octave reserved for serious announcements and funeral directors.

"Ren," she began, "I need you to stay here. In the flat. Permanently."

Ren blinked. "You what?"

Zara's face didn't move, but the sense of a smile radiated outwards. "You always wanted a city centre address. I've always wanted someone to haunt. It's win-win."

There was a beat, then Mrs Barley snorted, not bothering to conceal the derision. "Given the price of property in central London, that's quite a gift."

Vincent sat up, grimacing as he propped himself on one elbow. "You're not planning on haunting me, then?"

"Don't flatter yourself," Zara replied, voice dry as new parchment. "You'd make a terrible ghost host. Too many unresolved issues, too many old flames."

Ren looked from the ghost to the others, mouth open in a perfect circle. "I'm not—I mean, it's not like I need—are you even allowed to sublet to the living?"

"I'm not renting, I own the place. I can do what I like."

Zara's attention never left Ren. "I need someone to keep the place in order. And I'd quite like the company."

Ren let her fingers drift along the nearest shelf, brushing dust from the spines of "Dreadful Doctrines" and "A Taxonomy of Urban Hauntings." The motion steadied her, a little. "You're serious."

"I'm dead," Zara said, "but yes."

A silence rippled out. In it, the city's noises crept back—an ambulance three streets over, the distant resonance of building work, the shrill peal of a bicycle courier who was, at that moment, being menaced by a flock of pigeons.

Vincent used the lull to rearrange his blankets with an extravagant sigh. "I think I'll need to stay for another month, at least."

Mrs Barley whacked him on the shin with a rolled-up towel. "You're not an invalid. Tomorrow, you'll be up. By Sunday, you'll be back in your own flat and I expect you to help with the chores."

Vincent mustered a flicker of his old charm. "If you wanted to see me naked, you could have just asked."

Mrs Barley ignored him. "You, girl—are you staying or not?"

Ren looked at the flat—at the dust motes, the anarchic bookshelves, the ghost who watched her with the patience of a librarian waiting for the overdue fee—and exhaled. "I'll stay," she said, the words steadier than she felt. "For a while."

Zara inclined her head, the gesture as formal as a benediction. "Good. There's work to do."

Mrs Barley nodded, as if this settled the matter. She started to clear away the medicine, packing up the bottles and mugs with the efficiency of a pub landlady at closing time.

Vincent slouched into the cushions, gaze drifting towards the ceiling where Zara's afterimage lingered, faint and blue in the light. "Is it always this cold when you're around?" he asked.

"Only if you're guilty," Zara replied, and faded from view, her outline dispersing like mist.

Ren turned to Mrs Barley. "How do you... how do you get used to it?"

Mrs Barley shrugged. "You don't. You just keep the tea hot and the curtains closed, and hope the ghosts are on your side."

There was a kind of finality in that, a sense that, after everything, the only thing left to do was to put the kettle on and pretend it all made sense.

Vincent, warming to the new normal, picked up his mug and cradled it like a talisman. "To the ghosts, then," he said, voice hoarse but sincere. "May they haunt responsibly."

Ren lifted her cup in echo, and Mrs Barley, too, raised hers, though she didn't bother to hide the scepticism in her eyes.

For a moment, the three of them sat in the hush of the flat—living, dead, and in-between—united by nothing more than the stubborn refusal to leave.

Outside, the city forgot about them. Inside, they did their best to remember.

After lunch (which was served at three in the morning and consisted of toast triangles and a small, resentful dish of tinned peaches), the survivors drifted into the living room. The flat's proportions were somewhere between "Edwardian salon" and

"Victorian oubliette," but the clean lines and designer furniture performed their usual magic, making it seem larger, older, and altogether more certain of itself than its inhabitants.

Vincent had made it off the daybed and onto a wing-backed armchair, one leg tucked under him in defiance of both medical advice and the current laws of physics. He looked less dead, or at least less likely to startle a passing pathologist. Ren took the other chair, which was slightly too upright for comfort, and immediately set about folding and refolding the hem of her borrowed sweatshirt.

Mrs Barley hovered at the window, making a production of dusting the ledge with a handkerchief. She'd drawn the curtains halfway, as if in negotiation with the weather, and now studied the dark street outside with the wary scrutiny of a war widow expecting a telegram.

It was Zara who broke the silence, her form appearing in the centre of the room, face composed but eyes bright. "You've all gone very quiet," she observed, her voice filling the space in a way that had nothing to do with acoustics.

"We're reflecting on our many failures," Vincent replied. He rummaged in the depths of the woollen blanket draped over his lap and produced a rectangular package, wrapped in brown paper singed at the corners and tied with a piece of ribbon that looked as if it had survived a house fire.

Ren clocked the present and groaned. "You didn't."

"I did," said Vincent, and held it out to her, his expression unreadable. "Go on, then."

Ren accepted the package with the delicacy of someone being handed a live animal. She peeled off the ribbon and sniffed at the charred edges, then opened the paper to reveal a notebook—hardbound, with a heavy, ivory cover. Across the front, in Vincent's familiar, looping script, were the words "Future Drafts." The letters were embellished with unnecessary flourishes and a few spots of blood, presumably authentic.

She turned it over in her hands, thumb tracing the edge. "It's empty," she said, more accusation than observation.

Vincent shrugged. "It seemed appropriate. You're the only one with an actual future."

Zara drifted nearer, arms crossed. "It's a high compliment," she said, voice gentler. "He only gives blank books to people he thinks will survive long enough to fill them."

Ren looked up, uncertain if she'd just been insulted or promoted. "I don't know what I'd write," she admitted, cheeks burning.

"That's the idea," Vincent said. His voice was softer than usual, almost lost beneath the hum of traffic and the occasional bark of Barley's dusting.

Mrs Barley, unwilling to be left out, stepped forward and set the handkerchief down on the table. "You can always start with a complaint," she suggested. "That's how the best stories go."

Ren, stalling, flipped to the first page. It was, indeed, blank, save for a small watermark in the corner: a stylised bat, grinning. She grinned back, in spite of herself. "You're all mad, you know that?"

"Occupational hazard," Mrs Barley replied.

Vincent watched her, the brittle humour in his face replaced by something closer to anticipation.

Ren closed the notebook, hugging it to her chest. "You write the first line," she said, and pushed it back to Vincent.

He took it, turning it over as if searching for a hidden

meaning in the marbled endpapers. After a moment, he accepted a pen from Mrs Barley and uncapped it with a flourish.

He opened the notebook to the first page, hesitated, then wrote:

She laughed, and the world didn't end.

He passed it back, and Ren read the line in silence. The room, for once, stayed still; even Zara seemed reluctant to break the hush.

Mrs Barley, never one for sentimentality, cleared her throat. "Well, that's nice and vague. Should last you at least a month."

Ren smiled, real and wide. "If I start with that, maybe nothing else will seem so bad."

"Or maybe it'll all be terrible, but at least you'll know why," Vincent said, reclaiming his usual optimistic streak.

Zara drifted overhead, looking down on them with the air of a chaperone whose charges have at last stopped setting fire to the curtains. "You'll do," she said, and her smile was the first truly warm thing to settle in the flat since their brush with prophecy.

As the first whispers of sunrise revealed themselves, Mrs Barley fetched more tea, and Ren started filling the blank book —notes at first, then sketches, then whole paragraphs, quick and slanting, the ink bleeding through as if eager to get to the next page. Vincent watched her work, less a mentor now and more a witness, and even managed not to correct her spelling.

TWENTY-SIX

Vincent had read somewhere that convalescence was meant to be an exercise in patience and gratitude, but the only thing he was exercising was the world's last remaining supply of passive aggression. He'd arranged himself on the sofa with the care of a museum archivist, layering blanket atop blanket until he resembled an archaeological dig site for extinct mammals. The sling, while technically necessary for his shoulder's continued structural integrity, was more of a prop: he made sure it was visible from every possible angle, just in case anyone doubted the extent of his suffering.

Mrs Barley bustled around him with the undivided focus of a one-woman NHS triage unit. Her movements, even now, were clipped and economical; she swept past the sofa, whisked an empty blood bag from the floor, and dropped it into a bin lined with a carrier bag from the Co-op. "If you're well enough to whinge, you're well enough to do the washing-up," she announced, not bothering to look at Vincent as she stripped the coffee table of abandoned plasters, prescription bottles, and the kind of crumbs that could only have originated from illicit toast.

Vincent managed a sound somewhere between a sigh and the death rattle of a disappointed marsupial. "You wound me, Mrs Barley," he said, reaching for the mug on the side table and failing, "truly, you do. The Hippocratic Oath used to mean something in this country."

Mrs Barley ignored him, setting down a new mug—this one, he noticed with some horror, contained a teabag floating in what looked very much like chicken stock. "Drink up," she said. "You lost a lot of fluids."

Ren was cross-legged on the floor, back against the radiator, wearing her third favourite hoodie (one had been lost to bloodstains and fire, and, the other, to an overzealous Shih Tzu). She held Zara's house keys in both hands, flipping them over with an air of disbelief and something dangerously close to sentiment. Every so often she glanced up at the ceiling, as if expecting the late Zara Delacourt to materialise from the light fixture with an update on the day's haunting.

"So," Ren said, "am I supposed to just... live here now? Or is this one of those 'the ghost comes back and tries to kill you' deals?"

"Only if you stop paying the utilities," Mrs Barley replied. She wiped the sideboard with a damp cloth, her glare never leaving the surface even as she dispatched a line of dust into oblivion. "Zara would prefer a housemate with basic hygiene."

Ren grinned, teeth bright against her cracked lips. "Well, that counts Vincent out, then."

Vincent, too weak for a proper retort, flicked a manuscript page at Ren's feet. "Don't listen to her. I'm the ideal roommate.

Silent after dawn, rarely in the bathroom, and fully up-to-date on my shots."

"Speaking of shots," Mrs Barley said, "your antibiotics are due." She reached into her cardigan pocket and produced a blister pack with the casual menace of a street dealer.

Vincent eyed the pills as if expecting them to attempt a hostile takeover of his bloodstream. "I'm not convinced these are even effective on my kind."

"Then consider it a placebo," Mrs Barley snapped, "and swallow before I escalate to suppositories."

Ren snickered, then sobered as she noticed a small stack of envelopes in the post pile, one of which bore a name she recognised from Vincent's bedside reading material.

She snatched it up, holding the envelope aloft like a game show prize. "Ooh, fan mail for Celeste Evermoon. Do you want me to open it, or are you worried about anthrax?"

Vincent's face went blank. "It's probably a royalty statement. Just bin it."

Ren tore the envelope open with her teeth and extracted a square of heavy card, lavishly printed in purple and black. "It's fan art," she announced, "from... let's see... 'Himari, age 39, Tokyo.'"

Mrs Barley, now disinfecting the door handles with a vinegar-soaked wipe, gave a low hum of approval. "International readership. Not bad for what's essentially self-published mummy porn."

Ren held up the drawing for all to see. It depicted a vampire, lushly rendered in digital ink, with angular cheekbones, a perpetual five-o-clock shadow, and an expression that could have passed for either ennui or terminal constipation. The resemblance to Vincent was not only uncanny; it was prosecutable.

"Why do all your main characters look like you?" Ren asked, waving the card. "You even got the eyebrow right."

Vincent sniffed. "I have a face built for archetypes. It's not my fault the genre has limited imagination."

Mrs Barley leaned over, examining the picture through her reading glasses. "That's not all it's limited in. I assume this one also pines after a doomed mortal girl half his age and sulks about the futility of eternity."

Ren thumbed through the rest of the card, giggling. "No, this one actually eats the mortal girl and runs off with her mum. It's progress."

Vincent tried for dignity, but it collapsed under the weight of the blanket pile. "I'm contractually obligated to deliver a minimum number of plot reversals per novel. My publisher likes a twist."

Mrs Barley finished her cleaning, then planted herself in the armchair opposite Vincent, hands folded over a clipboard that had not left her side since the Orpheum. "If you spent half as much time healing as you did cultivating your public image, you'd be walking by now."

Vincent fumbled with his sling, making a show of adjusting it. "You should know better than to rush a recovery. Besides, I'm enjoying the attention."

Ren rolled her eyes, then flicked the fan art into Vincent's lap. "Frame it," she said, "and put it over your bed. If it ever moves, you'll know your number one fan is on her way."

Mrs Barley pinched the bridge of her nose, as if staving off a migraine. "Children," she muttered, not bothering to hide her disgust. "The lot of you."

She stood, dusted her hands, and departed for the kitchen, where the sound of kettle-filling and mug-rattling was as reassuring as any heartbeat.

Vincent, left in the aftermath of her efficiency, shifted in his nest and inspected the fan art. He couldn't deny the accuracy; even the slouch in the shoulders was bang on. He considered, just for a moment, what it would mean to be immortalised not as a saviour or a martyr, but as the sulking anti-hero of a thousand torrid paperbacks. It was a legacy, of sorts.

Ren, meanwhile, pocketed Zara's keys and surveyed the room, its comfort and the promise of a brighter future. There wasn't a television, but she found she didn't mind.

It was a little-known fact that London's blood banks did a roaring trade in the after-midnight economy, and Vincent, with his customary dedication to plausible deniability, had always preferred the house brand: O-Negative, no additives, locally sourced. He popped the fridge open and fished out a bag with his good hand, taking a moment to appreciate the cold sting against his palm.

The fridge shelf, once reserved for old cheese and the occasional ill-fated yogurt, now bore the faint watermark of a headless vacancy. Vincent stared at the space where the severed head had once nestled among the condiments, a ghost shelf if ever there was one. Ren, in the act of unpacking takeaway kebabs onto the dining table, noticed his hesitation and followed his gaze.

Mrs Barley, who had just unscrewed the lid from a jar of gherkins, clocked the moment as well. The three of them stood, silent, in the triangle of fridge, table, and kitchen. No one mentioned the missing head, and that was perhaps the most telling thing of all.

Vincent broke the spell with a shrug. "I suppose we'll have to make do with leftovers."

Ren, who had already unwrapped her lamb doner and was busy picking out rogue bits of red cabbage, said, "The last flat I had, the landlord kept his mum in the freezer. This is an upgrade."

Vincent poured his ration into a mug and joined them at the table. The kebabs were laid out with a sort of sacrificial reverence: foil peeled back to expose fragrant spiced meat, a drift of onions and tomatoes forming a barrier against the rising tide of grease. The blood, by comparison, was an austere affair—no garnish, no ceremony, just the quiet thud of the mug against the table.

It was the sort of meal that demanded a toast, so Vincent raised his glass. "To absent friends," he said, "and to improbable survivors."

Mrs Barley clinked her mug of tea against his. "And to the bastards who didn't see it coming."

Ren took a swig of flat Coke and nodded. "And to kebabs that don't taste like regret until at least the next morning."

The air in the flat was thick with the residue of disaster, but also with something warmer—an inexpertly constructed but tenacious optimism. They ate in companionable silence, punctuated only by the crunch of gherkin and the slap of foil against table. Every so often, Ren would produce a new artefact from the food bag—chips, a tub of hummus, an orphaned slice of baklava—and offer it up to the group like a relic of rare power.

Zara's ghost, who had opted for a seat near the bookshelves, flickered in and out of focus with the uneven grace of an out-of-phase telepresence. She watched the meal with an air of anthropological curiosity, her eyes picking out details and storing them away for later commentary.

Ren, catching the ghost's attention, raised her tin can in salute. "Do you miss eating?" she asked, half-joking.

Zara gave the question its due consideration, then replied, "Only the chewing. The rest is just upkeep."

Mrs Barley, who'd heard this before, rolled her eyes. "She's not above a bit of spectral snacking. Last week I found three digestive biscuits missing and a trail of oat crumbs leading into the airing cupboard."

Vincent, finishing off the dregs of his blood, leaned back and let the warmth spread through him. "At least you don't have to worry about carbs," he said.

Zara's outline buzzed, amused. "Carbs are a living man's vice. I'm strictly on a diet of unfinished business."

Ren grinned. "Is that why you haunt us, or are you just bored?"

Zara didn't answer immediately. Her gaze swept the room—the stacks of books, the tangle of extension cords, the piles of paperwork on every available surface. "You lot generate enough loose ends to keep me busy for centuries. I'm an auditor, not a poltergeist."

Mrs Barley, now in her element, produced a battered pack

of playing cards from the sideboard and dealt a hand to each of them. "Let's see if any of you remember how to lose gracefully," she challenged. "Winner gets to pick the film tonight."

Vincent peered at his hand, saw three queens and two jokers, and suspected cheating, but decided to let it slide. "I always preferred the company to the winnings," he said. "Even when I lost."

Ren snorted. "You'll forgive us if we don't buy the noble loser act. I've seen you count cards."

Mrs Barley dealt with cold precision, her expression unreadable. "In my day, we played for cigarettes and government secrets. I miss the stakes."

They played three rounds before Vincent's bluffing gave out and Mrs Barley swept the table clean. She raised an eyebrow, unimpressed with her own victory. "We'll watch something with subtitles, then. Keep the brain sharp."

Vincent groaned, but Ren gave a little cheer. "I vote for zombies. Or witches. No more vampires, yeah?"

Mrs Barley pushed to her feet. "Witches it is," she said. "You fetch the remote. I'll get more tea."

Zara, who had hovered through the entire hand, lingered at the table as the living shuffled off. She tapped the surface, once, and left a faint outline of her fingertips on the varnish, as if to remind them she'd been there at all.

When the flat settled into its usual night silence, Vincent found himself alone, save for the echo of the ghost and the lingering aroma of kebab. He wandered up to his study, where a battered roll-top desk held the remnants of his real vocation: a locked drawer stuffed with prophecy fragments, unfinished manuscripts, and the occasional threatening letter from a rival author.

He took the key from its hiding spot (taped to the underside of a "Visit the British Library" mug), and unlocked the drawer. Inside, the fragments rustled, restless even in stasis. He thumbed through them, pausing at one—thin, crisp, the ink faded but legible. The text, scrawled in Carmine's characteristic hand, read:

The sequel always begins with blood.

As he watched, the footnote at the bottom glowed faintly— just for a second, as if trying to catch his attention—then blinked out. Vincent, more tired than curious, set the page back in its nest, locked the drawer, and shuffled back down to the living room.

He arranged himself once more in his blanket throne, adjusted the sling for maximum sympathy, and closed his eyes as the witches cackled on the telly.

Outside, the city's pulse continued: sirens, foxes, the rumble of the tube. In the flat, time folded in on itself, and for the first time in a long while, Vincent slept without dreaming.

On the desk, in the dark, the prophecy page shimmered, then lay still.

THE END (for now)

Keep reading the **Fang & Loathing Trilogy**—Vincent and friends cordially invite you to *The Stakeout Diaries.*

NOTE FROM THE AUTHOR

Hi,

Thanks so much for reading *Destiny Can Bite Me*!

It was a lot of fun to write. I truly hope it was an entertaining read.

If you enjoyed the book, I would be incredibly grateful if you'd be so kind as to leave a review.

Reviews really help authors for a number of reasons, not least, providing feedback on what readers like and improving visibility of the book on online retail sites.

Thanks in advance and I look forward to reading your thoughts.

Jon

ABOUT THE AUTHOR

Jon Smith is the bestselling author of more than 50 books for children, teens, and adults. His books have sold over half a million copies and have been published in seven languages.

In addition to writing books, Jon is an award-winning screenwriter and musical theatre lyricist and librettist with productions at the Birmingham Hippodrome, Belfast Waterfront, London's Park Theatre and PJPAC, Kuala Lumpur.

A father of four, he lives near Liverpool with his wife and their two school-age children.

When he grows up he'd like to be a librarian.

www.jonsmith.net

x.com/jonsmith_author

instagram.com/jonsmith_author

goodreads.com/jonsmith_author

amazon.com/author/jonsmith

facebook.com/authorjonsmith

MAILING LIST

Want to receive advance information about future publications?

Fancy exclusive access to freebies, special offers and bonus material?

Feel that your life isn't complete without Jon's monthly musings about writing, reading and publishing?

There's a solution! Sign up today to Jon's mailing list:

https://jonsmith.net/mailing-list

THE FANG & LOATHING TRILOGY

BAL
KON
media